HUNTRESS OF THE HALLOWED FOREST

THE THREE KINGDOMS
BOOK ONE

LILLY INKWOOD

One More Chapter
a division of HarperCollins*Publishers*
1 London Bridge Street
London SE1 9GF
www.harpercollins.co.uk

HarperCollins*Publishers*
Macken House, 39/40 Mayor Street Upper,
Dublin 1, D01 C9W8, Ireland

This paperback edition 2024
1
First published in Great Britain in ebook format
by HarperCollins*Publishers* 2024

A catalogue record of this book is available from the British Library

ISBN: 9780008672713

Printed and bound in the UK using 100% Renewable Electricity
by CPI Group (UK) Ltd

Lilly Inkwood always wanted to write books, ever since she penned (literally, with a pen) her dozen-page long 'novel' in fifth grade. It just took her much too long to realise that she loves fantasy, above all things. She also writes historical fiction as Patricia Adrian. Her novel *The Bletchley Women* is a *USA Today* Bestseller.

Lilly's interests also include history (especially women in history), skulking around social media for much longer than she should, and reading, particularly when she's on a tight deadline and should be writing instead. Originally from Eastern Europe and now living near the Black Forest in Germany, Lilly has always loved the old European folktales she grew up with.

X x.com/lilly_inkwood
⊙ instagram.com/lillyinkwood

ALSO BY LILLY INKWOOD

The Red Kingdom series

The Kingdom is a Golden Cage

Rise of the Fallen Court

This one's for my Mum

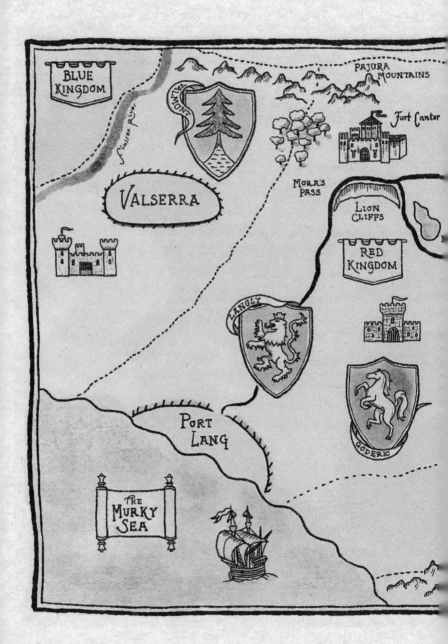

WHAT HAPPENED IN THE PREQUEL SERIES

Forty-six years before the events in this book, in the Year of the Red Maiden, Princess Blanche stages a revolution in the Red Kingdom against her brother, King Etienne, and crowns her nephew twice removed, Charles, as the new King.

She does this with the support of her Fallen Court, a handful of young women who were exiled with her at Mora's Tower. Among them are Mathilde de Champy, Amelie de Valmons, and Gisele d'Anselmois. Gisele is the daughter of King Etienne's right hand and the most powerful man in the Red Kingdom, until Blanche happens to them.

The coup is staged with the help of Robert – a mercenary captain – his company of paid soldiers, and a ragtag group of dissatisfied people who learn to work together: the Guildmasters; farmers of the Red Kingdom led by priestesses of the Mothers of the Forest; and the mages at the Golden Pavilion.

But before the mercenary company can come to the rescue, the mages begin weaving a spell that starts to tear down the chains around the Dark Mother, a terrible entity that had been sleeping for more than five centuries at the heart of the Opal Mountain.

By using her ghostwalking and mindwalking powers, Blanche enters an uneasy alliance with Sabya, the ancient goddess revered all across the Three Kingdoms, whose task had been to guard the Dark Mother for centuries. She needs to enlist her help in the final battle before Lafala – but this comes at a price.

In the aftermath of the battle, and toppling her own brother, Blanche carves out the Duchy of Langly from the Red Kingdom, which she demands as payment from the newly-crowned Charles, for Robert's services. Charles reluctantly agrees, and Blanche marries Robert, becoming the First Duchess of Langly. Their seat of power is Fort Cantor, built around Mora's Tower.

At the same time, the Fallen Court merges into a secret society, with a hand in the politics of two of the Three Kingdoms, with Blanche at its head as the Marchionessa.

But twelve years after their ascension to the duchy, Blanche must leave Robert and their children to go to the heart of the Opal Mountain and help Sabya guard the Dark Mother.

These events have been described in *Rise of the Fallen Court*.

* * *

Blanche and Robert have three children: Isabella (who later becomes the last Doyenne of the Golden Pavilion), and the twins, Kylian and Frederic. Before the inheritance matter can be settled between the twins, Robert vanishes. An embittered fight for inheritance follows. Kylian marries Gelda – a Priestess of the Mothers of the Forest who betrayed Blanche in the Year of the Red Maiden – and Frederic marries Magali, Gisele's daughter.

The duchy is disputed between the twins and bloody battles ensue. At first, the duchy goes to Frederic. Kylian, Gelda and their son, Hugo, are compelled to flee.

But Frederic is killed in the Green Kingdom and Kylian chases Magali from Fort Cantor. Magali hides at Castle Bencifert with her son, Maël. She falls in love with the widowed Seigneur Bencifert, and they have another son in secret, Philippe, whom they pass off as Isabella's child.

Ten years later, with the help of Seigneur Goderic (the duchy's warlord), Magali wins back Fort Cantor, and Frederic seemingly returns. But it is Maël who is forced to shapeshift into his father's form until he reaches majority so that he and his mother can keep a grip on the ducal seat.

At the age of eighteen, Hugo, now Princess Celine's lover, makes a last attempt to regain the duchy. He fails. In the aftermath, he's bound by Magali and Seigneur Bencifert in the form of a cat.

Two years before the events in this book, Hugo plots again with Princess Celine. King Mihiel wishes to marry Celine to Duke Maël de Langly, to strengthen the succession to the throne, since his only son, a boy of five, has a frail health. After Maël disappears without a trace, and with Hugo bound to the form of a cat for five years, Philippe becomes the new duke.

Celine and Philippe enter an arranged marriage, but as the two fall in love, they begin to untangle the web of lies around them. Philippe discovers that he's Magali's son – not Isabella's – and so has no real claim to the duchy. They also realise that Maël isn't dead, but that he has been bound to the shape of a mouse.

In a moment of remorse, Magali releases Maël from the shape they had forced on him. When he reappears, the duchy is on the brink of war. But Celine and Philippe, with the help of Isabella de Langly, banish Magali, Hugo and Maël from the Red Kingdom, binding their magical powers. The latter arrive in the Blue Kingdom, a bastion of the Fallen Court.

These events have been described in *The Kingdom Is a Golden Cage.*

TOUCH WITH SPLENDOUR, TOUCH WITH DEATH

BLANCHE

*I*t's been thirty-four years since my body became a prisoner at the heart of the Opal Mountain. It has been ten years, maybe, since my mind ceased to be a prisoner in the same cave.

My task might be to help a goddess keep an ancient, evil power bound, but my heart's duty is towards my family, as much as it ever was.

The First Duchess of Langly has been gone for a long time, but the Marchionessa of the Fallen Court is as present as ever.

And I'm watching over my grandchildren, using whatever Gifts I have at my disposal.

Tonight, I'm visiting the Blue Kingdom in my ghostly shape: an illusion of my body but with my awareness fully here. It's a reprieve from my time in the cave. I stand in a tall balcony overlooking the grand ballroom of Bluefort, at the

Harvest celebrations. But I'm not here to admire the splendid, lush dresses made of embroidered silks and rich velvets. Nor the strong shapes of the famed Knights of the Blue Kingdom, leading the ladies out onto the dance floor.

No.

I'm here to see to my 'ilk', as Sabya calls them. The grandchildren that were exiled two years ago from Langly – the duchy that rightly belonged to them by birth. They've been tossed aside by the unfortunate machinations of Princess Celine of the Red Kingdom and Maël's own mother, Magali.

It's not Maël who catches my eye, though. It's Hugo, my other grandchild, a lovely apparition in a green velvet doublet with golden embroidering, that matches his soft hair.

So fine, so polished, so deceptively sweet.

He weaves his way through the crush towards Delphine, the Heiress of the Blue Kingdom. There are two dress styles in the Blue Kingdom, representative of their regions. The people of the Mountains wear heavy velvet dresses with longs sleeves, and wide, rich skirts.

But Delphine has chosen to adopt the Lakes-style tonight: airy dresses that look barely more than a chemise, cinched at the waist, flaring at the hips, and revealing far too much above that. The Heiress wears a flimsy thing that exposes her back and barely covers her small breasts and shows the shape of her ribs at her sides.

Next to me, the ruler of the Blue Kingdom, Queen Valerie, scoffs.

Long has my grip on the Red Kingdom faded – for that I blame a frayed relationship with the Red Crown – but the one on the Blue Kingdom is strong. Not only is Valerie the Queen, but she's also the High Marshal of the Fallen Court. This is why I've arranged for my grandchildren to withdraw here. So I can protect them. So we can regroup.

That is, if my grandchildren don't do something monumentally stupid. And I wouldn't quite put anything past Hugo.

'I don't think Hugo has set his sights on your daughter, if it's any comfort,' I say to the Queen beside me.

'It's not,' Valerie says in her customary, tart style. She sighs. 'But there isn't a thing I could do about it. I don't like that dress, though.'

I know her reasons. I know why she wants Delphine to look past her Lakes heritage. I know what she's afraid of.

'I wager it's easier for her to move in that dress than for you to move in yours,' I say. The Queen wears about twenty feet of blue velvet, embroidered with silver thread, draped around her tall, stout shape.

Valerie chuckles, low and harsh. 'Needs must.'

I bristle at this. *Needs must.* This is something her sister, Magali, says too.

Magali, who has done so much harm to my duchy and to her own son, Maël, through her machinations two years ago. Hers and Hugo's. All three of them washed up on the shore of a mountain river in the Blue Kingdom, drenched and with their Gifts bound.

The Gifts are a rarity. Magical powers granted to so few in the Three Kingdoms, they're mostly a benefit of the grand aristocratic families. But there are ways to circumvent a sloppy bounding of the Gifts – as I discovered myself almost fifty years ago, when I made a king fall.

However, I made sure that Hugo and Magali bound their Gifts permanently. There are threats that must be put aside.

Not the same could be said about Maël. No, with Maël, I did the opposite.

At the side of the dance floor, Hugo catches hold of Delphine's hand, bows low, and gives the tips of her fingers a gentle kiss. The Heiress will have none of it, though. She throws a few words at Hugo, before turning away from him. He reaches out a hand to touch her shoulder, but she shrugs away as if his fingers burn her.

That is the thing with Delphine. She can shine as bright as the full moon on a cloudless night. Or she can be brittle, her mood as dark as the bottom of the cave lakes.

'See? Nothing to worry about,' I say.

Valerie cocks an eyebrow in disbelief.

And then, Maël approaches Delphine from her other side. Broad and with his dark curls in disarray, his jaw shadowed by a short beard, he looks the part of the ruffian. The duke-in-exile.

He gallantly catches Delphine's wrist as she stomps by him, pushing his goblet of wine into the hands of the man who stands closest to him – a knight who, by the look on his face, didn't expect to double as a cup-bearer tonight. The knight doesn't say anything, because Maël is Maël and nobody wants to rile him.

Because he's larger, stronger, and meaner than anyone else in this entire ballroom, with or without his Gifts.

I wish he could see that, too. If he could only pull himself together and stop sulking, he might understand the sheer extent of what he could do. Like making Delphine smile now, by pulling her into him, and sweeping her in the dance. Even if it's just to take a stab at Hugo.

'Sometimes, I wish they weren't cousins. That Maël wasn't my sister's son.' Valerie smooths the plaits in her dress. 'He's good for her.'

I snort. 'You might be the first mother to wish Maël on her own daughter.'

The songs ends and the dancers pause to bow to their partners and clap their hands. With a swift move, Delphine swirls away from Maël, and heads towards the wide-open doors of the terrace, suspended above the steep cliff underneath Bluefort. I catch a glimpse of the Merlusing Lake beyond, glittering a topaz-silver in the night.

There's a small crowd on the terrace, at the far end of the marble railings. But the sides are coated in shadows, and that's where Delphine is heading.

From across the ballroom, Hugo tracks her movements.

'He hasn't managed to make himself a king in the Red Kingdom, has he? He might aim to try the same here.' Fury is a deep scratch in Valerie's voice.

I wish I could say it isn't true, but knowing Hugo, I can't contradict her. Two years ago, that was what he'd been aiming for, in the end. To marry Princess Celine and make himself the next king. I say instead, 'She shouldn't be alone.' And I mean the terrace, not Delphine's prospects of marriage.

Valerie grimaces when Hugo sets himself in motion, casually moving through the crowd, as if he weren't following Delphine at all.

'He doesn't know when to give up, does he?' Valerie turns towards me.

'A family trait, I think.'

I did not give up on my grandchildren, either. I did not give up on the Fallen Court. I won't give up on trying to defend the Three Kingdoms, even more so when the threat of the Dark Mother breaking free of her amber prison is more real than ever. In spite of the efforts that Sabya and I are putting in.

The music resumes, a sedate song from the Mountains. The dancers arrange themselves in two lines, women interspersed with men, facing each other.

And then, it all happens so fast that it's almost unreal.

There's a cry from the terrace and then another. The crowd on the dance floor disperses. Hugo and Maël bound through a throng of sweeping fabrics, women trying to escape the incoming carnage.

It already smells like blood. It's in the air; it's in the way that knights and seigneurs draw swords. It's in the set of Maël's jaw. It's in the way Hugo draws out a concealed dagger.

It's instinct.

I throw my ghostly self from the gallery onto the terrace. Two women in wide green cloaks, their faces hooded, hold Delphine in a tight grip. One holds a knife to her throat. The group of armed men pause and halt just a few feet from them.

I feel the spark of magic before I can see it. 'Beware,' I call.

Pine trees grow on the side of the mountain. Their tips

reach beyond the marble railings, swish and twirl as if there's a great storm, though there isn't even a breeze. The trees sprout monstrous branches, closing like a cage around the women and Delphine. Not just women, I realise. The trees are no coincidence. Judging by their cloaks, the attackers are no scions of seigneurs. They must be Priestesses of the Mothers of the Forest.

'Make a single move, and she's dead,' says one of them, pressing the knife harder to Delphine' throat. There's blood dripping down the Heiress' dress, red gushing from the side of her ribs, pooling into the silver-blue silk.

'If you wanted her dead, she would be by now,' I say.

The cage. The knife. They're trying to take her, I realise.

They look up at me, at my ghostly silhouette. The moonlight makes me slightly transparent. Like someone carved from a dream.

There are downsides to being in this shape. No one can touch me, but neither can I touch anyone. I can hear and speak, but I'm no more substantial than air.

That can't be said about my grandchildren. I look to Maël. 'They're priestesses, not mages.'

He nods, understanding the quiet order. If a mage kills another mage, they will lose their Gift. But they are not mages – which means that the Gift is not within them, but they have learned to harness the magic of the land.

This makes them fair game for my grandchildren.

And Delphine.

Maël gives her a sign with his fingers. The very air around Delphine shifts and trembles.

There's no water around her. The lake is too far away. So she uses the incandescence of her own magic to roll the blood pooling in her dress into a tight ball, which she throws into the priestesses' eyes.

Delphine then swings and twirls, using the momentum to escape from her grip. The daggerless priestess launches herself at her, but Delphine is shifting: skin to sleek scales, the planes of her face broadening and sharpening. By the time the priestess wraps her arm around her, Delphine has sunk her sharp three-rowed teeth into her flesh.

The priestess yelps and lets go.

Delphine swings away, slipping to Maël feet.

Hugo's dagger flies. The blade digs into the eye of the priestess and the air tears with her howl of pain. Hugo bends, pulling Delphine up and into the surcoat he's shedding off.

Maël roars. The cage of pine branches uncoils and darts towards them, sharp javelins of wood aiming at his chest. Maël lifts his hands, flames bursting at the tips of his fingers.

He grins.

This is why… This is why Maël needed and deserved his Gift. Retrained with my help from shapeshifting into something else. The flames from the hundreds of candles in the ballroom behind us fly towards his outstretched hands, curling in great balls of fire.

And then, the balls fly, too, directly at the priestesses. There are screams, the crack of flames, the snap of fire as it engulfs them both, licking down the branches at their backs.

Delphine's gaze is riveted on the sight, her eyes grim. The shimmering stops around her and blood soaks Hugo's shirt.

He shouts for a healer, pressing his surcoat to the side of her ribs.

Valerie comes to my side. 'Get her to my chambers,' says the Queen. 'It's quieter.'

Safer, is what she means to say. Closer to the heart of the mountain. Closer to the cave lakes, where Delphine can draw strength from.

Maël says, 'That was incredibly stupid. Attacking her tonight, with everyone here.'

Valerie lifts her gaze to Maël. 'What *you* did was incredibly stupid. Charring them to pieces when we could have asked what they wanted.'

'I'm sorry,' he says. 'Next time I'll take that into consideration, when I try to avoid being impaled on pine branches.'

He's fire, I think.

Maël always went too quickly ablaze. Teaching him to channel his fire into shapeshifting has been Magali's idea. But that part of his Gift was bound by Philippe and Celine two years ago. Now that the shapeshifting days are over, Maël has yet to learn the extent of his own strength.

Valerie sighs – as much of a concession as he'll ever get from her. She touches her hand to his back, leading him to the charred remains of the priestesses. This is no usual fire that can burn through flesh so quickly, but everything about my grandson has been unusual.

Maël kneels, disgust written on his face. He flaps open the burnt remains of the cloaks and says, 'I appreciate the warning, Blanche.'

For telling him that he can destroy them, he means. For not having to hold back.

I shrug. It was good that I left the Opal Mountain tonight, in spite of Sabya's grumbling.

Maël fingers an amber medallion, unknotting it from the burnt leather strap twirled around one of the dead priestesses' necks. A dark tree is engraved on it.

Fir, it seems.

'What is this?' he says.

'I'll tell you what it is,' says Valerie. 'That is a declaration of war. From the Green Kingdom.'

Maël cocks his eyebrow at me.

The implications are staggering. For too long the Green Kingdom has hidden behind the magical shields that Sabya put in place five hundred years ago. For too long evil has been brewing there, unchecked. 'That's a marking of the Covenants of the Hallowed Forest,' I say, lowering my voice.

Valerie extends her palm, a silent request. She is so used to being obeyed that she rarely feels the need to voice her orders. Maël lifts his hand, but inches before dropping the medallion, he begins to twist it between his fingers, making it disappear and reappear.

A crease of sheer irritation touches the Queen's features.

No one can rile and irritate as Maël. One of his less magical gifts.

Finally, he drops the disc of amber in his aunt's hands. Valerie lifts the token, twisting it this way and that. 'Maël,' she says, 'can you light this up for me?'

My grandson lifts his hand, making fire spark and burn in

his palm. The light pierces right through the medallion, projecting the dark shape of a tree onto the opposite wall. Surrounded by the warm glow of amber, with the flickering light, it looks like the leaves are swaying.

It looks like the tree is alive.

Inwardly, I sigh. When I was young and untested and hadn't discovered even half of the things that I could do, Robert and I took an ill-advised walk into the grounds of a tournament. I had seen a juggler there, tossing around balls of fire, adding more and more to the pile, until the movements of his hands and the wide sweeps of the fireballs into the air became a blur. I kept watching and watching, waiting for them to drop.

But, of course, I never found out how that ended, because Robert and I were distracted.

That's how I feel tonight. Like that juggler with too many balls, and they're all about to drop.

I can't afford to be distracted from my many duties, and yet, it seems that I have to look in a different direction. And I certainly can't look away from this.

I tell Valerie, 'I agree. It's time pry into what's happening in the Hallowed Forest. To see what has been lurking there, what's been hiding from us for so many years.'

MAGE AMONG THE HUNTERS

MIHI

'Are you ready, Anne-Mihielle?' says Matthieu, leaning on the stone wall behind him. He looks like somebody's father with his broad face and trimmed moustache.

'I'm always ready.'

We've done this at least a dozen times, and it's still a thrill. Matthieu and I wait for the mage by the well in the centre of the village.

It's always a good thing for the others to see us taking them. Even if we're in a small village on the outskirts of Xante, the capital of the Green Kingdom, there always have to be witnesses to speak about the feared Mage-Hunters come to collect another mage.

Though the High Inquisitor calls them 'witches,' not 'mages,' when he hunts them down. And I know for a fact that what he does with them is entirely different from what I and the other Mage-Hunters have in mind.

I can still see the man's tormented face before the sword sliced down on his neck, at the last execution that had taken place in front of the Xante Temple. The whispers of fire as it took hold of his lifeless body, the stony smile of the High Inquisitor, at the foot of the pyre.

I would like nothing more in this world than to wipe that smile off his face.

Bugger him and the day someone all the way down in Romannhon decided that it would be a good idea to create an outpost of the Inquisitors up in the Green Kingdom, about a decade ago. Bugger the day the High Inquisitor set foot in Xante, and our King let him and his pack of scavengers in.

I blink to erase the High Inquisitor's fine features, the glint of those uncanny green-and-gold eyes, the way his thin smile curled up when we locked gazes above the pyre. I focus on the village around me – this is why I'm here, after all. To make sure that the donkey-arse doesn't lay his hands on yet another mage, to an outcome that we all know.

I shake my head, forcing a deep breath. The village we're in is typical of the Green Kingdom, I suppose. It's bordered by the forest on one side. There are three dozen houses made of stone or manure bricks, the rooftops made of bound rushes. There are plenty of rushes below, in the valley of the Green River, this slithering behemoth that runs into the Glittering Sea. There are rushes even in the smaller, quicker river that runs past the village, beyond the schoolhouse behind which Remy, another Mage-Hunter, is waiting in a small boat.

It's always good to have more than one escape plan.

This mage is pregnant, we have been told, and the complaint has been lodged by her own husband. She's a Water-Twirler, it seems. Our inquiries have shown that her family moved here from the Red Kingdom forty years ago, shortly after the Year of the Red Maiden.

Many mages here came from the Red Kingdom, originally, but many more have lately appeared in the Green Kingdom, with no mage ancestry. And most of them tell us that they received their Gifts after having a conversation with a priestess of the Mothers of the Forest.

But this particular mage we're hunting, her family comes from the Red Kingdom, just like mine. I push this thought aside quickly, like I usually do, just as I push the fragments of a broken song that burrows itself in my ear, from time to time.

'I don't think I'm ever ready for this,' says Matthieu, and I know what he means. Their terror. Their fear when they see us. It's better for us if everyone is still afraid.

Where the edges of the village melt into the forest, a young woman approaches with two buckets, strung on a pail across her shoulders. Her steps are laboured, and her belly is swollen.

Of course, a man who would report his own wife would send her in this state to fetch water.

She's not afraid yet, but she will be.

We're suspended in that moment in time, when something is bound to happen, and the actors of what is about to be unravelled are rushing towards each other, the collision unavoidable. I watch it unfurl – unable to stop it, unable to hurry it.

We slip behind the little thatched roof of the well. I make an inventory of my weapons. Rapier, daggers at my waist, in my boot, hidden inside my leather vest. All there, and within reach.

I look towards the valley of the Green River in the distance, checking that we are alone. The High Inquisitor's Paladins must have not yet had word of this woman.

Thank the Mothers of the Forest who have protected her, so far.

The woman approaches us with sure steps. We must look like two random travellers as we sit by the well, wrapped in our dark green cloaks. Nothing out of the ordinary.

Nothing like two people who have come here to carry her away from this village.

I turn my back to her, taking in a deep breath.

As I hear the sound of wood clanking on stone behind us, I nod to Matthieu.

We come up to the woman from both sides, blocking her escape.

She is so young, I notice. Even younger than my twenty-three years, with angrily red, swollen hands. I lay my fingers on her plain, homespun cloak. 'We are here for you.'

From the other side, Matthieu lifts his cloak, enough to show his sword with the owl-shaped pommel, the mark of the Mage-Hunters.

Or, in the language of the Green Kingdom, the *Magier-Jäger.*

Of which I am *Erste Jägerin.* First Huntress. High Huntress. Whichever.

A hopelessly high title for someone my age, who perhaps never deserved to rise so high, and likely would not have if I hadn't been blessed with a very particular Gift.

The Water-Twirler stiffens under my touch, completely frozen. She can't outrun us, she knows this. There's no escape from the fate that awaits her, and it breaks my heart, every single time, that we have to drag them from their homes, from their families.

That's if we don't drag entire families, instead.

'We mean you no harm,' says Matthieu in his gentle-father voice. 'Just come with us. We'll bring you somewhere safe.'

'Don't make a scene,' I tell her.

The truth is, it is good when they shout. When they struggle. When there are people, watching.

Whispering about us.

At the windows, in the dark threshold of the houses, faces have appeared. By the blacksmith's, where our horses are tied, a few men casually stand on the porch.

Bastards. Bastards.

Sometimes, there are those who come forward and struggle with us, who fight for them, and we have to fight back; and even if this gives birth to endless complications, it always warms my heart, to know that there would always be people who would fight for others.

But no one fights for this particular woman, who cradles her swollen belly as we drag her towards the horses, as I help her up onto my own mount. Just as I settle into the saddle, there's a high whistle and the clop of hooves from the patch of forest closest to the village.

I don't need more than the blink of an eye to realise that there are Paladins emerging from the trees and that they must be here for the woman, as well. I dig my heels into the belly of my mount. No time to make for the main road to Xante, so the school building it is, towards Remy and his boat.

'Delay them,' I hiss towards Matthieu.

What a debacle. What a complete heap of turd.

The High Inquisitor's Paladins, that's the last thing I wanted here.

We are, as of now, caught in a wild race for this woman's life. And with the Green King extending the High Inquisitor's authority and jurisdiction far beyond ours...

If the mage lands in their hands, it cannot possibly end well. For any of us.

Because I will not let her go without a fight, and the last thing I need to do is to pick a quarrel with the High Inquisitor.

I steer my horse between the buildings, seeking cover, veering away from my destination instead of veering towards it.

I think about what story to spin to the High Inquisitor in the aftermath, how to explain the fact that I'm running away from the Paladins, instead of listening to the King and 'collaborating' with them. There are enough witnesses who can see precisely what I'm doing. Every move, every step.

I race into the forest, leading us down one of the less trodden paths, and then track back through the trees, galloping at the edge of the village. The woman curls in front of me, sobbing. I don't want to consider if this is dangerous to the baby. Landing in the High Inquisitor's hands would be far more dangerous for both mother and child. 'Hold on tight,' I say through my teeth. 'Hold on very, very tight.'

I steer the horse uphill, towards the edges of the village, but far enough from the houses so that we won't be seen.

I say a silent prayer to the Mothers of the Forest that have been protecting the Water-Twirler so far, not to take their healing hands off her.

If the Paladins are here... The last thing I want is to have another dispute as to whom the prisoner belongs to. Or to hear another entreaty that we should give the prisoner over to them, after we are done.

It didn't end well the one time we gave in, and that was only because the King interfered and we couldn't find a single reason to refuse him.

That particular mage ended up on the executioner's block in front of the Xante Temple.

I weave through the trees, the line of houses just within my sight. The huffs of the horse and the sobs of the woman cover any sounds that might come from the valley, that could tell me how Matthieu is faring with the Paladins.

The mage holds fast to the saddle with all she can, her eyes darting wildly as we approach the river.

River.

'Can you build a water shield behind us, when we reach the banks?' I ask. It would hide Remy and his boat from sight, it would hide what I'm about to do.

She turns her wide eyes to me, shaking her head. 'No, I don't have that much control over my powers.'

'How so?' I ask. 'Hasn't your family taught you how to use the Gift?'

There are few who are gifted in the Green Kingdom. The Gift tends to disappear from the bloodlines after a few generations. And the most talented mages are selected to become Mage-Hunters. Like me. Like Matthieu. Like Remy.

In Xante, we don't have the privilege of a magic school, like the Golden Pavilion in the Red Kingdom. With so many people hating the mages, we have to make do – and lie in order to survive.

'I don't have it from my mother,' she says.

'How, then?' I ask.

'A priestess,' she says. 'Met her in the woods, while I was out collecting berries. She asked about me and my family.' She takes a deep breath. 'Next thing I knew, I could conjure water from the well, without lowering the pail.'

Behind us, there's the muffled clop of horses, a faint clink of armour.

Turd.

'What did she look like?'

'Fair-haired,' she says. 'Grey eyes.'

'It's not much to go by,' I say.

'Please,' she says. 'My child. I cursed the day that I met her. I never asked for this. I wish I'd never talked to her.'

'Can you remember anything?' I say. 'What was she wearing? Did she have a signet ring? Perhaps set with amber?' The seal of the Covenant of the Hallowed Forest.

She shakes her head. 'Not a ring. A medallion at her throat. Amber, and a fir tree engraved in it.'

By Sabya's Darkblades. Definitely one of the Priestesses of the Hallowed Forest, then.

But why would they do such a thing?

We've arrived at the edge of the village, and the questioning will have to wait. I bring my mount to a halt.

Beyond the edge of the forest, the streets are deserted. I wish I could do a little time leap, and jump us – horse, Water-Twirler and all – from the line of trees directly behind the school building onto the quay where the boat is waiting. Avoiding the Paladins chasing us.

Avoiding curious gazes, people who could report which way we'd gone.

Giving Remy enough time to run away with her.

But I can't pull another person with me in my time-hops. It's a lonely Gift, the likes of which have never been seen. I can stop time for everyone but myself by just using my own power. And I can make longer leaps back in time if I use another mage's Gift.

But that is a treacherous road, and even making a small jump back in time depletes considerable amounts of their power and causes them terrible pain. Leaves me reeling and confused and wishing I'd never done that. And, often, fate can't be changed.

I suppose there is always a price to pay.

I know all that because I tried with Ullar – my mentor, my fill-in father, the only man I answer to in this kingdom, who I've ever answered to. The man who trained me and made me everything that I am today, with the good and the bad. The man who took care of me to the best of his abilities, which had to be enough.

I could make use of my Gift, and then try to drag a time-frozen mare to the edge of the river, though I have no idea how I could manage to pull something that size through the time-freeze. Or, at least, I could try to carry the Water-Twirler away. But I don't want anyone to see the extent of what I can do. I whip my head back, and I notice two Paladins, downhill, right in my line of sight.

Too late, too late for a time-hop.

There is no need whatsoever for the High Inquisitor to suspect that I have a Gift, and what sort of Gift that is.

I can't even imagine the scandal. A Mage-Huntress with the Gift. And the *Erste Jägerin*, nonetheless. Considering that they have no idea what we really do with the mages we catch. Drag away. Rescue.

Even Ullar would have serious trouble in smoothing this over.

So, I have no choice but to spur the horse in a wild gallop towards the school building, the Twirler's body knocking against mine, a prayer to the Mothers muttered between my gritted teeth.

There are shouts coming from the woods, but I don't look back, making for the quay, where Remy awaits in the boat.

He throws back his hood, already stretching his hands towards the Water-Twirler I'm shoving towards him.

He grins. 'Why the rush?'

I wonder why I find him so handsome, when he shouldn't

be, really. His jaw is too square and his nose too narrow and long and he could use a haircut, and yet…

I haven't thought about any man in that way, not since I refused Claude. Not since I refused to become the future queen of the Green Kingdom.

My Mage-Hunters thought I was mad, and Ullar was endlessly disappointed with me. He said I could never make a better match. He was right, I'm sure, and I sometimes wonder, if I were to go back in time…

I'm not quite sure what I'd do, really.

And this not a good time to muse.

I help the Water-Twirler into the boat while she braces her belly with one hand. I tell Remy, 'Just take her to safety.'

Remy cocks his head, and I add, 'The Paladins are closing in on us, and I think the High Inquisitor might have a few questions for this mage, if they catch her.'

'Lucius's Flaming Finger,' says Remy.

'He can stick it up his own arse,' I reply.

The woman settles on the wooden bench, looking wearily from me to him.

River.

Water.

Water-Twirler.

Even though she said she doesn't have much control over her own powers…

'Gifted, not born,' I toss at Remy, and then turn to face her. 'Don't try anything stupid.' I put all the wrath I'm capable of in my eyes, because she doesn't want to find out what will happen if she harms Remy. I point towards him. 'That one is risking his life to get you out of here. Unless you want to have a little chat with the High Inquisitor, you'll stay put.'

'Where are you taking me?' she manages to say.

I throw Remy a glance. She needs to trust him, while he tries to sneak her to safety. 'There are plenty like you where you're going. They'll explain. The only thing you need to know now is that you need to trust us. That is, if you ever want to hold your baby and don't want to end up without a head. Or on a pyre. Or both.'

The Water-Twirler grips hard the edges of the bench. I know what she must be thinking.

'If you don't believe us, think how often you saw any mages executed by the Order of the Mage-Hunters.'

Which would be never.

She says nothing but looks as if she's about to throw up.

Good.

She needs to fear the Inquisitors more than she fears us.

It's only right.

I untie the boat quickly and give it a shove with my leg. Behind me, the clop of horses becomes louder and louder. 'Hurry.'

Remy mock-bows his head. 'Of course, *Erste Jägerin*.'

I'd smack him over his head, but he's too far away.

If I can't reach him, the Paladins won't either.

Good, good, good.

The only thing that I have to do now is to buy them some time.

I weave between the buildings, catching sight of the gleaming tip of a metal boot, laced through a stirrup. The fluttering edge of two dark blue cloaks. Two Paladins, then, just around the corner of the village school. If I saw them, then they must have seen me. I urge my horse – loudly – back towards the well, towards the heart of the village, as far from the river as possible.

'In the name of the High Inquisitor, stop right there,' one of them bellows, but I ignore them, zigzagging between the houses. Leading them away.

At the well, Matthieu leans on his mount, five armed Paladins surrounding him. He's saying something to them, I can't quite tell what. Probably buying time for me, as I am for Remy and the mage.

I don't have to pretend that I'm flushed and that my heart is pounding when I dismount, straight between Matthieu and the Paladins. They're heavily armoured knights, the fighting hands of the Order of the Inquisitors. I count the swords and spears and shields between them.

The odds don't favour us, if it came to a brawl.

I have beaten odds worse than that, but what would be the cost? I can't risk revealing myself, nor my abilities, to the High Inquisitor himself. I don't even want to think of the consequences.

'We lost her,' I lie to Matthieu, wild strands of hair beating me in the face under a whipping wind that has stirred out of nowhere. 'She's gone.'

'Is that so?' says one of the Paladins, a tall man on a red destrier.

A tall man in the dark blue cloak of the Inquisitors.

A tall man with honey-gold hair streaked with grey, carefully combed away from his face. A face with a long, straight nose, and hypnotic eyes, a sparkling green surrounding the dark pupils, the colour of amber towards the edges.

The High Inquisitor himself.

'Indeed,' I say, gritting my teeth.

He takes in my flushed face, my dishevelled dark hair, my torn leather breeches.

'Are the Mage-Hunters so out of shape,' he says, his voice clear like toiling bells, 'that a pregnant witch may outrun them? Are their horses so lame that they could not catch such a woman?'

Mage, not witch.

I lead my horse to stand as a shield between him and Matthieu. One blink of an eye, that's all I'd need to slit his throat.

But I'd rather not face the consequences.

If there is another way, another path.

It is the third time this year that he has interfered with our attempts to seize one of the mages.

'Did the pregnant witch also take your tongue, *Erste Jägerin?*' he says.

His Paladins chuckle.

'She had help,' I say.

Not a lie, exactly. She did get away. She did have help.

The High Inquisitor tilts his head towards one of his companions. 'See where she might have gone to.' The Paladin's horse breaks into a brisk trot.

'You do not trust my word?' I say.

'Are you offended?'

'Yes, I am.'

I am offended, but for entirely different reasons than those he might think of. The Inquisitors are a plague, and the Green King, instead of dealing with them, seems to give them more and more favour in Court. Too fearful to defy the Romannhon, I suppose.

Long enough have we been out of Romannhon's reach, clinging to our old traditions. Not covertly worshipping the Mothers of the Forest, but taking the best out of the two worlds, I always like to think. The ways of the Old Gods, Mars and Diana and Jupiter and Juno, and the ways of the Mothers, which, in fact, are more ancient than the so-called Old Gods of the Romannhon.

But it's hard to forget that five hundred years ago, the Three Kingdoms were provinces of the Romannhon Empire. The Blue and Red Kingdoms even clung to much of their language, though the Green Kingdom mostly kept to the dialects of the Waldemannen who lived here, long before the Romannhon came.

Yet now, we're isolated from the Blue and Red Kingdoms. We quarrel with them more often than they quarrel with each other, so as the Romannhon rise again, clutching for new territories, their threat is more real.

So when the High Priest of the Romannhon asked to establish the Order of the Inquisitors in Xante, the Green King agreed, unwilling to give them further reasons for aggression.

And now we're stuck with them.

The High Inquisitor is meant to teach us true faith, to the

Old Gods, with his endlessly inventive methods of torture that make my skin crawl to think of; with his merciless hunt of mages within our lands.

Mages whom, to point out again, he calls *witches*.

'Do you know what offends me, Anne-Mihielle?'

I grimace when I hear my name on his lips. It sounds sharp and cut on its ending.

It sounds as if it's a pale copy of my father's.

King Mihiel of the Red Kingdom.

Not that he has acted like a father, in any way, in the past fourteen years.

My hand goes to the owl-shaped hilt of my rapier. 'I do not.'

'It offends me that, even though we work towards the same purpose, you seem to antagonise me with every step.' A smile flits on the High Inquisitor's face, as if he isn't taking very seriously what he says, either. 'That we could aim for such extraordinary results, *Erste Jägerin*, and yet, you choose to oppose me. We do have the same goals in the end, don't we?'

I ponder.

It may appear so.

The Order of the Mage-Hunters has fought long and hard for it to seem so, concealed our purposes and our methods.

I ask, 'Do we now, truly?'

He tilts his head at this. Such fine gestures. Such a fine silk cloak floating behind him, of no use against rain, nor cold.

Such a pampered man with mean ambitions.

'I think you might be mistaken, High Inquisitor,' I add, even though my hair stands on end just by looking at those glimmering eyes of his, even though my every instinct screams that I should shut up. 'I think that a little while ago you came to interfere in a business that we have been doing perfectly well for centuries. I think that, on the whole, you are quite a hindrance.'

His face is alight with a trace of emotion, more than I have ever seen from him in all the years I have known him.

And we see more and more of each other lately, it seems.

'Bold words, *Erste Jägerin*, indeed. I think our results speak for themselves.'

Results?

Murderer, that's what he is.

The Paladins, whom he sent on the chase, descend the hill at a quick pace. The two who had been following me, joining us quite late. I didn't even spare a thought for them, if they might have retraced my steps, if they might have been sniffing after Remy's trail. I allow myself to breathe in relief, and to finally glance at Matthieu, his face pinched, listening, assessing.

I can tell he thinks I overstepped myself.

I can tell he thinks I shouldn't have provoked the High Inquisitor, but it is I who have had enough of his provocations.

'The witch is gone,' barks one of the Paladins.

'That's what I said.'

'A boat,' continues the man.

'I told you she had help.' I hop on my horse, signalling Matthieu he should do the same, trying not to show that my own heart is still racing in my chest, even though Remy and the pregnant mage might have just escaped this battlefield.

No more sparring with the High Inquisitor today. Time to put as much distance between us as possible.

We take the road back to Xante, hoping that the Paladins won't have the ridiculous idea we could travel together. I'm not sure how much of their company I could stand in a single day.

'I shall see you soon, I trust, *Erste Jägerin*,' the High Inquisitor shouts after me.

I don't bother to respond, not even with an obscene gesture, though I'm sorely tempted to.

THE OBSTINATE

BLANCHE

*A*fter fifty years of using my Gift of ghostwalking, I can almost always find a person, if I want to.

Maël, for instance, currently occupies his own quarters in Bluefort, the beating heart of the Blue Kingdom. My grandson is reclining in a scratched old armchair, his boots up on the table, while he sharpens his knives.

'Hello, grandmother,' he says, without even lifting his eyes. The silken whisper of blade against blade fills the chamber.

I step towards the narrow balcony that opens above the slopes the castle is built on. Bluefort is an assortment of solid towers and keeps, peppered across the plateaus, connected by a labyrinth of corridors dug in the solid rock of the mountain. The surface of the Merlusing Lake shimmers an impossible green-and-grey in the valley. 'Oh, you do love calling me that, don't you?'

If anyone saw us side by side, we wouldn't look more than a few years apart. Maël is growing an appalling beard now, covering nearly all his face. His lovely, wavy hair, so much like his grandfather's, has grown shaggy and unkempt. He's too much like his grandfather for his own good. But I tuck away any thoughts of Robert in a dark corner of my heart.

Even if my husband is still alive, he must look, what? All of his eighty years of age? When it comes to my own appearance, though...

I'm rather tall for a woman, with generous curves – even more so after I carried three children – dark red hair with a few silver streaks. I look about the same as the day I disappeared thirty-four years ago into the heart of the Opal Mountain, when I was thirty-seven years of age. I'd done the disappearing in order to prevent a complete and utter catastrophe from happening, which has, in turn, caused other catastrophes within my own family.

All peaking with this extraordinary specimen in front of me and what has happened to him.

'Do you prefer *Grand-mère* Blanche?'

I turn around and walk to the table, almost touching the engraved wooden box, which is set as far as possible from where Maël is sitting. The seal around its lock hasn't been broken. Which means that Maël hasn't accepted the contract yet and that perhaps he doesn't intend to. 'Ah, I see you haven't opened it yet,' I coo. 'It was sent to you only... How long has it been? Five days ago?'

Two weeks since the priestesses from the Green Kingdom tried to take Delphine. Since I saw Maël's shoulders straightening in anger and purpose, since that defeated look went away from his eyes for the first time in two years, even if it was for only a night.

He has been adrift, my grandson, ever since the Duchy of Langly was taken from him. Adrift, no matter how much he tries to hide it underneath the appearance of carelessness. I can't stand by and watch him wither anymore.

It's been a week since I decided what I needed to do about it, how to thread Maël's needs and his wellbeing around what has to be done about the threat coming from the Green Kingdom.

A week since I realised who I needed to speak to.

Five hundred years ago, our goddess Sabya lifted powerful magical shields around the Green Kingdom. Mostly to keep out of the Blue and Red Kingdoms the threat of Darg; the man she loved, the man who betrayed her in the last battle against the Dark Mother. But the shields mean that I cannot ghost-walk within its borders.

And the Fallen Court has only two members in the Green Kingdom. Reluctant members, to say the least.

No, I need someone else from my Fallen Court to go to Xante. Someone I can trust. Someone who can fulfil the contract.

'I like to save the best for last,' he says, peering at the engraved box.

'What in Sabya's Darkblades are you saving yourself for, then?'

'I like the touch with the new design,' he says, examining one of the sharp blades of his hunting knives.

I study the box, the engravings of Diana and her hounds gathered around her, sniffing for game. The bow slung around the goddess's shoulder. 'Yes, we had them custom made for the Fallen Court's hunting contracts.'

'All your contracts are hunting contracts.'

'Is this what the knives are for?'

'No.' Maël lets his massive legs drop to the ground. 'I'm really going hunting today. Boar, I think. Or bear. Something dangerous.' He shudders, but it's a shudder of pleasure. Underneath his shirt, his powerful muscles flex, readying for the challenge.

Yet, for all the posturing, his confidence is nowhere reflected in his eyes. He looks as defeated as he always has, ever since, two years ago, the stream washed him, Hugo and Magali up on the shores of the Blue Kingdom after they'd been banished.

'You could hunt for *her*, instead,' I chip in, my temper rising.

It's always this. Maël has cast himself in the role of the biggest disappointment in our family, and he's doing a terrific job at it. He's the best at what he does, and now, he intends to be the largest failure of them all. I wish he would set himself a different purpose.

If he can't, I'll set one for him.

A target, at least.

'Is the engraving perhaps tied to the Green Kingdom's High Inquisitor's last best-selling success? *The Witch-Axe*?' he says.

33

And yet, he's so clever. So, so clever. There's so little that escapes him.

'Of course it is,' I say. 'I think there's an entire chapter devoted to the goddess of hunt and her acolytes.'

A horror, that's what *The Witch-Axe* is. Leisurely describing methods of hunting down mages – whom the High Inquisitor calls witches – and testing them for their powers.

Entire chapters devoted to methods of interrogating suspected witches. Torture methods to wring the 'truth' out of them.

Of all the evils that have plagued the Three Kingdoms in the past decades, the High Inquisitor rates very, very highly among them.

'It's also a challenge,' I say.

'You're sending me on a hunt,' he says bluntly. 'To hunt a huntress.'

'Did the messenger give you the details of the mission?' I say.

The little manure-head grins. 'Yes, she did.'

'And do you accept the contract?'

He waves his hand towards the box. 'Does it look like I've opened it?'

'Why, Maël? Why won't you accept the challenge? Is any of what you do here – which is a staggering amount of nothing at all – better than doing what we ask of you?'

Potential. So much of it.

So much, wasted.

'You know why,' he says, and his black eyes darken even further.

Of course I do. From a young age, he has done his mother's bidding. And since he turned nineteen, to his current age of twenty-six, he's done everything in his power to antagonise everyone who might want to give him orders. For years, Magali had kept him as a pawn, forcing him to use his Gift to shift into his dead father's shape so that they could keep hold of the Duchy of Langly.

A duchy he has now lost.

'Magali can't hurt you anymore,' I say softly.

And how I regret that she ever could. That she ever did, while I hadn't yet learned to ghostwalk out of the Opal Mountain and protect my grandchildren. From their own mothers.

'It doesn't matter,' Maël snaps. 'I'm done with being a pawn. So off you go. You're wasting your time.'

I need to change tack. To remind him of who he cares about. 'Don't you want to find out who tried to take Delphine? And why?' She was bedridden for a week after she took that dagger to her ribs, piercing the lung underneath. She is still struggling to recover.

Maël frowns. 'You think that the target you gave me, the *Erste Jägerin*, did this?'

I wish I knew. I wish I could tell him what the Mage-Hunters do, but none of us know for sure. 'I think she could give us answers.'

She would be in a position to. Better than sending someone blindly into the Hallowed Forest. Not for the first time, I wish that my old friends, Mathilde and Gwenhael, would do a bit more to help with the business of the Fallen Court.

A shadow of something passes over Maël's face. 'So you don't know anything. You want to send me there based on a presumption.'

I don't have much more time for this. I can't leave Sabya to weave her Lightsongs on her own around the Dark Mother for long. I'm compelled to help. To do what I promised to do. But I will not sacrifice the welfare of my family, yet again. I have to find a way.

I still my thoughts. And then I say, 'Fine, then. I'll go and find someone who will accept the mission. I understand why you're afraid. They say that the *Erste Jägerin* of the Mage-Hunters is skilled in combat like no one else. That there's no match for her. Of course you don't want to accept the contract. Forget that I asked.'

I turn around, as if to leave, just a manoeuvre to let my words sink in. I could just vanish from these chambers, but that's not what I intend.

Not yet, at least.

'What. Did. You. Say?' Maël's voice sounds like an avalanche of boulders. Harsh and quaking with anger.

'And in order to complete the mission, of course, you'd have to go into the High Inquisitor's territory. Who would want to do that? Considering the way you've been honing your Gift, and how little control you have over it. I mean, I'm not blaming you, this sort of thing takes years. And who would want to fall into *his* hands? Oh no, surely staying here and hunting and mounting willing young women and drinking yourself into oblivion is much, much preferable to all that.'

Moments trickle by.

Silence, swelling.

Then, there's the shuffle of heavy boots on the stone floor.

A brush of hands.

The click of a lock being opened.

'I am *not* afraid of them.'

I swivel around to watch him.

Maël has braced his forearms on the table, the sleeves of his shirt rolled up. He's examining with a frown the contents of the box I sent him five days ago.

'I wouldn't blame you if you were afraid of both of them.'

'Did you hear me?' Irritation grates in his voice. 'I'm not afraid of them.'

'If you say so,' I mutter. 'She's also supposed to be very beautiful. Very wild and very beautiful.'

The *Erste Jägerin* of the Mage-Hunters. The granddaughter that Mathilde and Gwenhael sent to Xante for training, fourteen years ago.

The illegitimate Princess of the Red Kingdom.

And the only person I could think of that could provide adequate answers.

If Maël manages to bring her to me.

Because something is stirring, and we are not half as prepared as we should be, not in the Red Kingdom. So I decide to lay it on a bit thick, even for Maël.

'The last I heard,' I say, 'she rejected the heir of the Green Kingdom when he asked her to marry him.'

Maël reaches into the box.

He leans back into his armchair, thumping his boots back

on the table. Holding the mark of the Fallen Court between his fingers, he turns it on all sides, as if it's the first time he's seen one.

Then, he tosses it into the air. The silhouette of the maiden, set with rubies, glimmers in the cold light. 'What is her name, again? This woman I'm looking for.'

'Anne-Mihielle.'

'Anne-Mihielle. Quite a mouthful. Presumably named after her father?' He smirks and catches the mark in his fist. No matter what he says next, I know, I know I have his interest and something tight in my chest finally gives way.

It will be dangerous. It's a risky mission. But I can't watch my grandson for another day as he wastes away. He needs a purpose.

Maël tells me, 'I'll think about your contract.'

FEAST

MIHI

*I*t's custom for us to celebrate a successful mission at the Hunters' house, though, by the Mothers of the Forest, I have no idea what there might be to celebrate. That buggering High Inquisitor almost – almost – caught us this time, and if it wasn't for Remy's cunning and skill with a pair of oars, if it wasn't for that one stroke of luck, we wouldn't sit here, celebrating.

Oh, that High Inquisitor.

He makes more and more trouble every day.

If I'm shocked at anything, it's Ullar's inaction. My mentor, my fill-in father. The man – immortal? Ancient god? – who the Mage-Hunters truly answer to.

Officially, the Astrologist of the Court of Xante.

Who is conspicuously absent from the celebrations today.

Still, the Mage-Hunters feast.

A fiddler has been brought in and someone has the absolutely bollocks idea that we should dance, so we moved the table from our dining quarters all the way into the indoor training ring. Remy and Matthieu and I are pushing the chairs to the walls, while Hunters and Huntresses are pairing up for dances.

We're still in our uniforms – dark-green cloth breeches with beige tunics, brown vests on top. But the rapiers have been hung in the weapon wracks on the walls. Mine, also, though I'm never quite in the middle of the celebrations. Even if I'm the *Erste Jägerin* – First Huntress – there are still many hunters who see me as a foreigner.

No matter that my father, King Mihiel, banished me from the Red Court when I was only nine years of age. I still speak the language of the Green Kingdom with a peculiar rounding of vowels that makes some people say I don't belong here. If the First Huntress had been elected, I'm sure they wouldn't have chosen me, in spite of my powerful Gift.

But there was nothing they could do about it. I won the Hunters' Crucible, and every day since, for more than two years, I've done nothing else but trying to prove myself.

I still am, day by day. And sometimes I do wonder, what is the buggering point?

What am I doing here, really?

But where else would I go?

Remy plops a plain tin goblet in my hand and fills it with wine to the brim. 'That's a bit decadent, even according to your standards,' I say.

'This one's from the Arnauld lands in the Red Kingdom,' he says as if this is meant to be helpful.

'I don't like to think about the Red Kingdom much,' I say.

My own father banished me. And my half-sister, Celine, the person I thought was closer to me than anyone else in the world, didn't do a single thing. She hadn't even bothered to write to me, not until a few years ago. When it was too late, and the old wounds had closed and scarred. Badly.

There is no point whatsoever in reopening them.

I still take a hearty sip of the wine. There are days like today when it's all too much and not enough.

Remy sloshes the wine around in his own goblet. 'It *is* a bit dry for my taste.'

'You mean, it tastes like vinegar.'

'Perhaps our palates aren't fine enough, you troll.'

'She-troll, you mean,' I say. 'Trolless. Trolline.'

'Oh, everyone can tell you're a girl, don't worry.' He ruffles his light brown hair. I take in his features. The sparkling deep green eyes, the defined upper lip. Its arch looks like it had been drawn by an artist.

I wonder what it would feel like to kiss those lips of his. If I would feel anything, at all. I didn't feel much when Claude kissed me. It was pleasant enough, but not an experience that I ached to repeat over and over again.

In a corner of the room, one of our Huntresses is looking like she wants to eat another fellow Hunter's face. I wonder if Remy could make me feel like I'd want to do that, too.

Or if there's a sort of a problem with me. If I'm strung in such a way that I'll never feel like that for anyone.

My thoughts must be mirrored on my face, because Remy lays down his goblet and stares at me intently.

I look away. 'All of this music is giving me a headache,' I say. 'Or maybe it's the wine. I don't like it.'

These are both lies, because the music is nice, and even if I might not be enjoying myself, it's lovely to see that the other Hunters are. And, on second thought, I wouldn't mind if Remy asked me to dance, and he'd surely agree if I asked him, but somehow, just the simple gesture of asking would make me feel drained.

And the second lie I tell is the one about the wine, because it's good, it's so, so good, and I think that Remy knows. Still, I can't help but loathe this wine because of where it comes from, because it makes me think of a grandmother who, on the whole, never bothered much with me at all.

My own grandmother, Mathilde, had been involved with an Arnauld seigneur before she met my grandfather. Not that I heard that from her own mouth. I've barely seen my grandparents in the last fourteen years, even if they live in the Green Kingdom – in the Hallowed Forest, to be precise. I lived with them for a while after my father sent me away from Lafala, and then they sent me to Xante. They dropped me into Ullar's hands without much of an explanation.

Ullar, who proceeded to turn that girl who had been cast away by all her living relatives into a killing tool. A weapon. A huntress.

I suppose there's no way of knowing if I'm more than that.

Everyone can tell you're a girl, Remy has just said. I haven't felt like 'a girl' in a long time. But I long for something, yes. To be someone else, who can be lit up from the inside, who is made of sparks and light.

I'm wondering if Remy could help me find that part of myself, assuming it's even there. And right on cue, Remy candidly asks, 'Would you like to go somewhere quiet?'

I make a casual, bored gesture with my hand, slipping between revelling Mage-Hunters, and I don't need to look back to know that he's following me into the corridor, though casual is the last thing I feel when my stomach clenches.

How I can want.

And I don't even know precisely what. I want to feel, to be free, to come untethered from someone else's expectations. To find that incandescent, bright core of myself, that part that I can touch, and that can make me tell myself, *This, this, this makes it truly worth it.*

I have no explanation for the 'it' and the 'this' and the 'what'; all I know is that I want, and that is a thirst I can never quench.

But I'm still looking.

I stop in the half-dark corridor of the Hunters' House and turn around to face Remy. Hoping that I'll find there whatever keeps escaping my grip.

His eyes are set on me. When he moves closer, a whisper away from touching me, I can feel his scent drifting towards me. He smells like rain.

I lean on the door behind me, a bit unsure. I try to gauge how straightforward I should be, or how teasing. I do know how kissing goes – I practically grew up on the training grounds. And Ullar never bothered with chaperoning me too much.

If at all.

But Ullar shouldn't be on my mind, really, standing so close to Remy, so I settle for biting my lip and looking at him from underneath my lashes, and by the Mothers of the Forest, he takes the hint, and brushes aside a strand of my dark hair.

Black with reddish glints in the sunlight, so much like my mother's, and her mother's before her. One of the few things I have from Mathilde. I don't have much of my grandmother's height or strong frame. No one can describe me as 'tall.' And the height difference is even more so obvious when I reach up a hand to touch the side of Remy's neck. His skin feels hot and he closes his eyes briefly on a sharp inhale.

I don't think I'm beautiful. My nose is too long, and so is my face, but I have the most vivid dark eyes, I've been told. I have rounded thighs and hips, no matter how hard I train, and breasts that are neither small, nor large.

There's nothing extraordinary about me.

But I can tell that Remy finds me maybe a little pretty, at least in this moment.

'What are you thinking about?' he says.

Truly? Whether it would be a good idea or not to kiss him. But he wouldn't want to know that.

'Vintage wines and small bottles,' I say instead.

Thank Sabya that Remy spares me the trouble of making a decision about the kissing.

He leans in, closing the last bit of distance between us, his lips brushing mine, a tender touch that I answer with my own lips. My hands tangle through his soft hair and though I know I'm doing everything as I should, as I'm meant to, and even though he does every single thing right – from the hand that goes to my hip, angling me slightly towards him, to the soft, tentative way he brushes his lips against mine – all I can think about is that perhaps I shouldn't have invoked Sabya just now, considering her unfortunate love life.

And I'm not hungry for this to continue. I'm not hungry for this to go further than it is. I take in the nice sensations, the closeness, and I'm aware of every single bit of this, that isn't more in any way than the sum of its parts.

Maybe I should just accept that I'm simply not made for the carnal side of things. Just like some people have a weak far-sight, or they can't dance, I'm unable to feel the love-making and everything that leads to it as keenly as others do.

When Remy tentatively caresses my lips with his tongue, I don't open my mouth for him. Instead, I angle my head in such a way that my forehead now touches his, my hands falling to his shoulders.

This closeness feels nice, but I don't want more, I'm sure of it. What I'm not sure of is how I'm buggering going to back out of this situation, without offending Remy.

Or making him feel rejected. If there's a feeling I hate more than anything in the world, it's that. And I don't want to inflict it on him.

Remy drives his knuckles down my cheek and I'm about to tell him that I'm tired, when someone clears their throat.

Then coughs.

I look to the side. And there he is, our glorified Court

Astrologist standing in the middle of the corridor, a few paces away from us. Ullar is wearing his customary, leather breast-plate – I'm not sure how he can stand it all the time – and the short sword tied to his waist.

Honestly, if there's someone who is even poorer at this 'letting your hair down' business than I am, that would be him. I shouldn't wonder where I learned it from – or failed to learn how to loosen up a bit.

'Ullar,' I mutter, in a tone that tries to convey displeasure, when it's quite the opposite.

Relief floods through me. Even though he has a knack of appearing out of thin air in the most inappropriate of moments.

'Mihi. A word,' Ullar says, already darting to the door to his own study. Which is not far to my left.

He doesn't even bother to acknowledge Remy, whom he sidesteps with such a feline grace that you'd think that Remy was the ancient creature out of the two of them, as old as the Three Kingdoms.

'Goodnight,' I tell Remy, to make sure that he won't wait for me to finish with my mentor.

That there's nothing more to expect.

I step into Ullar's study without looking back. As always, the first thing I notice are the portraits on the walls. There are dozens of them, images of all the *Erster Jäger* and *Erste Jägerinnen*, some so old that I can't even make out their features anymore.

Ullar has guided the Mage-Hunters for centuries. Perhaps

even since the magical shields have been erected, the ones that separate us from the Blue and Red Kingdoms.

Underneath each painting, there's an inscription.

The years between which that hunter and huntress have served as the leader of the order is written in large script. Underneath, in much smaller fonts, their names are written, and the years between which the Hunters have lived.

On the walls, there are as many First Hunters as there are First Huntresses. I know what the people of the Red and Blue Kingdoms say. That the people of the Green Kingdom are backwards because we respect nature and we would rather build our houses around the ancient trees, instead of felling them. Because we do not encroach on the forest but allow it to make room for us.

But there's another truth – in the Green Kingdom, our women may learn any trade, may it be carpenter, or blacksmith, or warrior. Or Mage-Hunter.

As always when I'm in this chamber, my gaze also snags on the portrait that has been hung above all others, the top of the frame touching the high ceiling. It depicts a man with short cropped-hair and broad shoulders. A long nose that appears to have been broken at least once. All I can decipher from the plate are the years when he served as *Erster Jäger* – for about six decades, up until fifty years ago.

I can't read his name. I don't know who he was; still, he's my nemesis. I aspire to have Ullar hang my portrait as high as his when I'm gone.

'Don't shit where you eat,' Ullar says in a stern voice. 'Learn from centuries of experience.'

Straight into the theme, and into discussing Remy. But Ullar never beats around the bush. I can't help a wave of annoyance – that I should care so much about his displeasure. That it should make me flinch.

No matter how often I tell myself I'm not that nine-year-old who was tossed here by her relatives, that's how Ullar always makes me feel.

Not that girl anymore, I make myself think.

'And where might you have acquired that extensive experience?' I ask. 'I've never seen you with anyone.'

He allows the silence to stretch long and uncomfortable between us.

Ullar's past is wreathed in the shadows that he wields. He was a sort of god of war, I think, but in a different land. An immortal, in any case. He looks about forty years old or so. A god *forged in lightless places* – that's as much as he'd tell me. Unsurprising, considering that his Gift is the power to wield shadows.

He can also hold on to very long, very uncomfortable silences. And I don't have the patience for them. Nor does it ever help to try to hold out longer than he does.

'I wasn't about to,' I concede. 'Shit where I eat, I mean.'

It's useless to tell him that I don't think I'll be kissing Remy again very soon.

'Good,' he says, leaning a bit on the shelves behind him. The shelves where he holds very precious, very old scrolls with Lightsongs and spells that I had to learn from a very young age. 'Many a kingdom has been lost because people shat where they ate.'

Ullar isn't tall – perhaps merely a hand taller than me. He's lean and muscled, and his right cheek is heavily scarred, and so is his brow on that side. He never told me how he got those scars.

He can hold on to his secrets. And by Sabya's Darkblades, he can also lecture. 'Mistakes have been made, even if I'd warned the Hunter in question that he shouldn't tangle with his quarry. I lost myself a good *Erster Jäger*, then. The best.'

Mothers of the Forest, he likes to ramble. But I have a gleeful suspicion. 'Which one?' I say, waving my hand towards the portraits.

He points to the one set above everyone else. 'That one,' he says.

'Interesting.' A-ha. 'How the mighty fall.' And still, Ullar keeps his likeness high above all others.

My mentor gives me more of his stern, I'm-speaking-now glare.

I sigh, telling myself that I should just let the speech he is obviously about to give me wash over me. Refrain from interrupting. It would only prolong my torment.

'May I be frank with you, Mihi?'

'When aren't you?'

He crosses his arms. 'Excuse me?'

I seal my lips tight.

The shadows cast by the lit candles on his desk lengthen. 'I think you're wasting yourself, Mihi. You need a new purpose. A new mission.'

Cold dread pools in my stomach. 'I have my hands full as it is, thank you,' I say. 'The High Inquisitor is giving us so much trouble. Today was…' *a failure, nearly.* I settle for 'A close call.'

'We have the High Inquisitor well in hand.'

This is such a blatant misrepresentation of the situation, that it makes me wearier. While we seek to relocate the mages to a place where they might be safe – a string of small villages at the foot of the Green Mountains, where they can live in peace – the High Inquisitor aims for nothing less than obliterating them from existence in the name of the Romannhon, a city-state beyond the Alpen Mountains. And the Green King himself doesn't dare do anything about this. Who will rise to the defence of those poor mages, if the Mage-Hunters don't?

Ullar has clearly gone bonkers. Or he has a nefarious ulterior motive for saying such a thing. 'Well in hand? Ullar, the prick has executed three mages in the past four months. Nothing is in hand. We are losing our grip on him.'

'I think the *Jägers* are doing just fine.'

Yes. Completely bonkers. 'What are you getting at?'

'You can do so much more, Mihi. You wield so much power. This, all this here, is no more than a petty fight.'

'It doesn't seem petty to me. It's what I've been trained for, all my life.'

'Mihi, you're no more than a mage who struggles to survive in a kingdom that doesn't trust, and neither tolerates mages,' says Ullar. 'Look at the pains the Mage-Hunters take to hide their true purpose. You don't have to live this life. The world extends much farther than Xante. You *must be* much more than this.'

This again. My 'quest.' My higher purpose. The reason why

I'm learning all those Lightsongs and spells and why I'm oh-so-special. The responsibility that rests on my shoulders and all the drivel I've been fed since I became one of the Mage-Hunters.

The drivel that Ullar has been feeding me.

I'm not even *that* special, if I come to think of it. I'm, at best, a modest sword-fighter. My only ability is that I can literally freeze my opponent by stopping time.

I'm the greatest imposter in history, disguised as the head of the Mage-Hunters.

But there is much more to Ullar's sudden turn of conversation.

'Is this about me refusing Claude's offer of marriage?' I ask.

Ullar was endlessly disappointed that I chose not to be the next Green Queen. But he doesn't understand. Everything with Claude has always felt easy, and yet, not quite right. Besides, to the Green Court, I'll always been a foreigner. A princess from a not-quite-enemy kingdom.

I'm not a suitable match for the Heir. I'm, at the end of the day, an illegitimate child.

I don't want to live my life like this, fighting other people's rejection, every single day.

Ullar straightens to his full, unimpressive height. 'I think it's time we investigated more the doings of the Fallen Court. The tethers that keep the Dark Mother are growing weak. We have to be prepared for her.'

My blood goes cold. What a mountain of pish. Ramblings of a rumoured secret society. And the Dark Mother again. An evil entity who, according to anyone except Ullar, has been dead for centuries.

No, his suggestion is something else. What I dread so much, more than anything.

'I need you to go to Crane Harbour to investigate. And maybe even to Bluefort,' Ullar goes on.

He's sending me to the Blue Kingdom – to its largest port and then to the legendary citadel carved into the side of the mountain, where the nobility of the Blue Kingdom lives.

Lies, lies, lies.

For all intents and purposes, Ullar is sending me away. Ridding himself of me. And just like that, I'm a nine-year-old girl again, who has been tossed from one hand to another.

No. I'm not nine years old anymore. And if I couldn't fight for myself in the past, I will now. For the place that I so painstakingly found here.

Ullar says, 'I have good reason to believe that Blanche is alive.'

'What Blanche?' The pain of disappointment is so sharp, that I can barely think around it.

'What do you mean, "what Blanche?" How many Blanches of the Fallen Court do you know of, Anne-Mihielle?'

Ooh, if I'm Anne-Mihielle and not Mihi, he's seriously annoyed with me. So am I – annoyed with him, that is.

I say, 'Blanche. De. Langly?' as if I can't quite believe what I'm saying, either.

The woman has been dead for more than thirty years.

He nods. 'Yes, that Blanche.'

No, he can't be serious. He's sending me on a hunt for ghosts.

He goes on blithely. 'I have reason to believe that the Fallen Court is stirring. I want to know who they will throw their lot in with. What they have in store for us. The Dark Mother can be deceitful, Anne-Mihielle. We don't know if she has managed to draw them to her side.'

'Have you entirely lost your mind, old man?' I say this to gain time, more than anything. He can't send me away.

I won't allow him to.

His brows draw down in disbelief. 'Listen, Mihi. There are sayings that on the day of the Siege of Lafala, forty-six years ago, Blanche called out Sabya to fight with her, with her song. The Dark Mother and her minions are stirring. If Blanche can reach her... We need to speak to Sabya, before it's too late.'

He's completely lost his marbles. Or he doesn't know how to get rid of me faster, except to send me hunting for legends and a ghost.

'No.'

Finally, Ullar's mask of calm cracks. 'Pardon me, Mihi?'

'No.'

I will not give in. I'm not a little girl, frightened that the rug will be pulled from under her feet. Ullar has sharpened and darkened everything about me into something that fits neither here nor there, for a purpose he's now trying to pull me from. But I'll stand my ground.

'Before you bother,' I growl, 'no matter how often you ask, the answer will still be "no".'

Ullar crosses his arms, looking to the skies as if he's asking for divine patience. 'I should know better than this.'

I cross my arms, too, mirroring his stance.

'You need time to think,' he says. 'You're as stubborn as a mule. And you don't like change, of course. Why would you? But … it's selfish of me, Mihi, to keep you here. You're like a child to me.'

'Oh, don't.'

I don't want to hear this. Another woven story. My own has been altered to such a point by him that I can't see myself outside the sphere of his influence.

But I'm not a child anymore, to be told what to do. And I'm fighting hard that side of me that wants to please him, so he won't send me away.

Which is precisely what he's doing.

I storm out the door before he manages to shoehorn another word in, knowing that if he finds the right ones, he might just make me turn around to his way of seeing things.

BURDEN

CELINE

*I*t never ends.

Barely do I finish responding to a pile of messages – or take care of the ever-thorny matter of ensuring enough supplies for Fort Cantor – that more and more and more problems arise.

I smack down the quill on the surface of the desk and rub a sore spot on my finger. I'm in the steward's tower, taking care of business in my husband's absence.

Yet again.

My husband's absences are many and long. I suppose I should be grateful for the amount of work that I have to do. But never did I imagine two years ago, when Philippe and I took over the Duchy of Langly, that the work would never end.

And that the tasks would keep us apart for so long and interfere with us fulfilling our *other* duties as duke and duchess. The only one that matters, in my father's eyes. Two years, and my womb has yet to quicken. But how could it, since I've barely spent three nights with my husband since this spring?

I groan.

Isabella de Langly, my former teacher in the magical arts, turns from her place at the window. 'What is the matter, Celine?'

I bury my head between my hands. 'I'm so tired. Of everything.'

She takes a few hesitant steps towards me, and then turns back towards the window. I'm grateful for Isabella's help. She doesn't have much to do since the magic school, the Golden Pavilion, closed its doors seven years ago, and I'm grateful that she chooses to spend so much time at Fort Cantor. She's the daughter of the first Duke and Duchess of Langly, in the end, and there's much she helped me with when it came to matters of governance.

But there are moments like this when I need a soft touch, a good word to banish this gaping hole in my chest. I have all that I ever wished for: a husband I adore, the Duchy of Langly, and yet, I've never felt so empty. So utterly alone.

I cannot make friends among the other Dames in the kingdom. While Philippe is an excellent duke, the nobility still gripes about his humble origins. He's still the seigneur who has dirt under his fingers, because he's truly the hands-on sort of duke. He literally has his hands in the farming.

It's up to me to observe the propriety and to follow the rules. To tend to the decorum that always has to accompany the Duke and Duchess of Langly. Power in the Red Kingdom belongs to the landowners, the seigneurs. But the higher the seigneur – and only the King stands higher than a duke – the more strength they must display. Not brute force, but a certain degree of condescension, even. So, no close friends from me: I have to be the unapproachable one.

But how it hurts. By Sabya's Morningstar, how it hurts sometimes.

And there are times like now when I can't help myself. When I reach out with a cry for help, even knowing that no one will answer. 'I wish Philippe was here,' I say.

'Why did your husband have to go, please remind me?' says Isabella, carefully arranging the hem of her dress.

'Troop inspection, I think. It's always something.'

Especially with Maël, the duke we exiled, being so close to the Queen of the Blue Kingdom. If the rumours are to be believed. We could never underestimate that sort of threat.

He'll never be able to return, I tell myself. Not with the banishing spells we wrapped around him. For him, returning to the Red Kingdom is not a possibility.

My heart still pounds in my chest, the fears far from being soothed.

'My parents were also always terribly busy,' Isabella says. 'I think my mother regretted that she fashioned Langly in such a way. She said it was too much.'

'I thought it was your father, Robert the Lion, who made Langly what it was,' I say. Robert the Mercenary. The soldier who toppled a king, stole the Princess Blanche and forced her to marry him. So he could make himself a duke.

'That's what everybody thinks,' she says tartly.

'Well, busy or not, they still had time to make three children.' The words fly out before I can hold them back, all the decorum that the Duchess of Langly is supposed to maintain forgotten.

Isabella sighs.

'I'm sorry,' I say quickly. 'I should have never said that.' Especially since the first duke probably forced Blanche, over and over again, to guarantee his own succession. And after that, rumours say that it was he who killed her.

My skin crawls to think of everything that the poor woman has gone through. And Isabella is her *daughter*. No wonder she's become such a hard woman.

'They were truly married to each other. That's why they managed to have three children,' says Isabella, softer than I ever heard her. 'They weren't just married to their duty, like that husband of yours.'

My mind is grappling to make sense of all the incongruous pieces. And the hidden insult. I think.

But—

It never ends.

There's a hasty knock on the door and it blasts open. A messenger with dusty clothes marches through, wearing the red-and-silver of the livery of the Royal Palace's servants. 'A message for you, Duchess. From the King. Urgent.' The man hands me a rolled-up parchment and bows, stepping back. 'I was instructed to wait for the reply, Your Highness. The King says it's urgent.'

'Yes, you've said so.' Isabella dismisses him with a flick of her finger, the duke's daughter to her very bones.

My fingers are almost trembling when I rip off the seal. And I read and reread my father's few sentences a dozen times before their meaning finally sinks in.

And then, the feeling is completely gone from my hands.

'What's the matter?' says Isabella, leaning across the table.

He has been sickly. He has been doing poorly all his life. He has been so secluded, that even I barely saw him.

And now...

I swallow, tears clouding my eyes.

Isabella reaches out her hand to grip mine on top of the discarded piece of parchment.

There's a sharp knock on the already open door and on the threshold stands a man. Tall and lean. A great mop of dark hair on top of dark eyes on top of a cheeky grin. His arms are crossed, and while he scans my face, he takes a few steps into the chamber.

Worry is written across his features. 'Duchess, what's wrong?'

'What are you doing here?' hisses Isabella.

'I heard there was an urgent message,' he says, his eyes pinned on me. 'Duchess?'

'Go back to wherever you usually go and wait for your orders,' says Isabella.

'I will await *the duchess's* orders,' he says. 'Since I'm her captain of the guards.'

My captain of the guards, indeed. Fabien Goderic, the third son of the Duchy of Langly's Warlord. The ally I never counted upon, considering he used to be the foremost of Maël's partners in mischief.

But whenever I need help navigating a particular matter that requires a strong hand, as well as a dose of cunning, he is there.

I reflexively stretch the piece of parchment towards him. My father said it was a secret, but I extend my trust to a select few.

He's bound to hear soon enough, anyway.

His eyes quickly scan the contents of the message and the twinkle within them sobers. 'My condolences, Duchess.' He rolls the parchment and hands it back to me. 'What do you wish to do?'

I wonder if he's asking as my captain of the guards, or as someone who wishes to be my friend.

The Duchess of Langly has no friends, I remind myself.

Not even in times of mourning. Or in times of a dynastic crisis, like the one that is about to unfold.

My little seven-year-old brother, Petit-Mihiel, died two days ago. And the next in line to inherit the throne is—

I'd rather not think of that. According to the laws of inheritance in our kingdom – and to my father – next in line should be the eldest boy I'd have with Philippe.

But … two years, and no children for us. No hope of having one soon, either.

Not a word, not a single one, about my half-sister, Anne-

Mihielle. My father's illegitimate daughter, whom he would prefer erased from existence the way he erased her from palace life.

My hands tremble when I set them back down on the desk. 'I think my father was clear enough. We must leave for the Royal Palace immediately.'

'And the duke?' says Fabien, cocking an eyebrow.

'You must send word,' says Isabella, and I don't know if it's a piece of advice for me or a direct order for my captain of the guards.

I blink away the pain, the regrets. I try to keep my eyes focused on what must be done. And the path ahead us, that has changed so much. 'We leave today,' I say, trying – *trying* – to be the duchess. But I'll still need my allies. 'Send someone else to fetch Philippe. Both of you are coming with me to Lafala.'

* * *

I find my father, the King, in one of the receiving chambers that my mother used to love so much. The sofa embroidered with golden thread, with its gilded armrests, is the same as it always was.

So are the ceiling-high mirrors, the armchairs and low stools tastefully thrown about the room. The stunning view of the sea through the wide double doors to the terrace, the reddish shape of Lucius's Cliff to the right.

So much is the same, so much has changed.

Everything.

'Father,' I say, bowing my head.

His eyes are bright with unshed tears, I see. There are yellow spots on his swollen hands, and the skin on his cheeks has a waxy colour.

'I'd like to see him one last time,' I say, barely able to keep the tears away, clogging my voice.

My little brother. Petit-Mihiel.

'You can't,' he says, fiddling with a loose thread in the fabric of the sofa he sits on. 'I'm sorry. We had to— He rests, already, alongside your mother.'

There are no words. No words for this.

My sweet, quiet brother, who has already suffered so much.

Gone, forever.

I sink into one of the armchairs by the mirror. 'I didn't even manage to say goodbye.'

'It wasn't swift... But we hoped,' he says. 'We hoped until the very end.'

'How did he—'

'A fever,' he says. 'One of his fevers.'

Fevers and sickness have plagued my little brother ever since he was a baby, every one of them making it nearly impossible for him to breathe.

We hoped that he would improve, but I suppose that some part of me knew that my brother would never live to become king.

My father's gaze drifts across my stomach, concealed as it is by wide swaths of the velvet my dress is made of. My insides twist. For years, he'd been pushing me to marry the then Duke of Langly, Maël, and to set to the business of making children.

Because even if women may not inherit in our kingdom, their boys can. So my not-yet-conceived, not-yet-born child would wear a crown from the womb. If he ever comes.

I don't lie to myself about my purpose here, and the hasty summons. My father wishes for me to do one single thing.

I loathe that this is what I've been reduced to. I can do so much more than playing broodmare. Yet, I shrink under the weight of his gaze.

'Where is your husband?' he asks, and this is the voice of the King, not of the father who has just lost a child.

'In the Goderic lands, investigating fires in the sacred groves.' After Fabien sent someone to fetch him, Philippe sent word that there was a matter he had to attend to before he could join me. 'He'll be with us soon.'

'Soon,' my father grumbles. 'Why is your husband not with you now, Celine? Or why are you not with your husband?'

This.

Again, this.

'We have to—'

'Are you with child, Celine?'

He leans forward.

'I am not,' I say, softly.

'I beg your pardon.'

'I am not.'

'Then, why, could you please tell me, is your husband *not* with you? He barely is, I gather.' My father is thunder, rumbling. 'I indulged in your whim to marry that boy; I indulged your unwillingness to marry for such a long time, and now… You are twenty-five years of age, by Sabya's Darkblades. What is it? Is the young man not what you expected him to be?'

I face him fully. 'He is.' And how he is. In every single way possible, and even more.

'Then what seems to be the matter?'

I fold my hands in my lap, preparing to reply, but he cuts my words. 'Do you understand that it is now absolutely imperative that you produce an heir? And quickly. Do you realise nothing, absolutely nothing is more important now? Do you even know who is next in line to the throne?'

I do.

Oh, how I do know.

I can't stop thinking about this.

'Do you wonder why I had to bury your brother in such a haste?' My father reclines in his seat, his shoulders sagging. 'Because no one can know that your brother is no more. The kingdom cannot face the consequences. And think, just think whose fault it is.'

Tears cloud my eyes again at the unfairness of this attack. I want to tell him how much I want the same, how much I'd like to have a child with my husband.

I want to tell him how powerless I feel faced with all of this.

'I don't know what you think you have to do, Celine, what you think your duty is, but I tell you, nothing is more important than this. Family.'

Family.

Funny that he should be the one to speak about family.

'I think it might be time to call back Anne-Mihielle.' As I speak, the plan forms in my mind. 'I think she could help us.' She might be the solutions to our problems. If *she* marries, if *she* has a male heir … perhaps my father can be persuaded to find a way to legitimise her. To make her fully a part of the royal family.

Surprisingly, my father says nothing, just seems suddenly so much more tired. 'Leave her be. She has nothing to do with all of this.'

'She's my sister,' I say, growing angrier by the moment.

'No, she is not.'

I scoff. Sister, half-sister, who cares about semantics? Everyone at the Red Court knows that Anne-Mihielle is my father's child by another woman – Ainora of the Hallowed Forest. And that my own mother saw her banished from the Royal Palace as soon as Ainora died. My mother did even worse than that, though it wasn't until her death that I found out that she had intercepted every single one of the letters that I had written to Mihi.

So many wrongs, which I've tried to right in the past years.

'We don't know what sort of creature Anne-Mihielle has become,' my father says.

'What has she become, Father, other than what your actions made her?'

He didn't lift a single finger when my mother pried Mihi away from me and shipped her off to the Hallowed Forest, to live with her grandparents.

A sister, I think. If she were here, could I tell Mihi of my troubles with Philippe? Could she be the shoulder for me to lean on, the one to listen to my woes?

Never did I need a sister in my life as much as I need one now. And how I've tried in the past seven years, since my mother died, to ask for her forgiveness. We used to be so close.

Inseparable.

All these years later, and I still miss her.

But I can tell that discussing this with my father won't bring me any further. No, I must act, but without his permission. I stand on my feet, curtsey, and excuse myself from his presence.

I now have an inkling of what I must do.

* * *

I'm glad to find Isabella and Fabien waiting in my rooms. I'm occupying the princess's chambers in the western wing of the Royal Palace. Red and gold marble, a wide space with a massive bed at one end, with a bedpost engraved with mythological scenes, depicting Sabya, our revered goddess.

I know every single detail of these apartments so well. It almost feels like seeing an old friend.

Fabien is draped across the bed, booted feet dangling, his hands gathered under the back of his neck. He's staring at the canopy.

Isabella watches from a heavily embroidered sofa, even heavier disapproval stamped on her face.

'Why so gloomy, Duchess?' Fabien cocks his head to watch me.

'I'm glad that you've made yourself comfortable. Please, by all means.'

Fabien stretches his booted legs before him. I take him in, from the chainmail on top of his shirt, to his white cloak with the Langly insignia – the red lioness – crumpled beneath him.

Sheer and utter indolence.

'I assume the meeting didn't go well.' Isabella tucks her hands in the wide sleeves of her dress.

I sink into one of the armchairs in the sitting area. 'It was bound to go wrong,' I say, and Isabella gives me a tight nod.

Fabien rolls onto his side, supporting his head on his hand. 'What did the old codger want with you?'

I'm too ashamed of telling him the truth. 'It is not your prerogative to ask questions, Captain of the Langly Guards. It is to do as you are told.'

Fabien smirks and casually strolls to my side, plonking himself on the armrest of the chair next to me, his gaze roving over my face. I look towards the open terrace doors, the sea beyond.

'You truly shouldn't allow him to behave like that,' says Isabella, her voice firm. 'It undermines your authority.'

'Don't be such a bore, doyenne,' says Fabien. 'You know I'm a paragon of humility in public.'

'You should be so in every single situation. Even if no one can see you.'

Fabien rolls his eyes and gives me a secret wink. The tightness around my chest begins to recede. I feel bold enough to ask questions.

'Fabien,' I say, 'you used to know Maël well.'

'Are you about to hold that as proof against my character?' he says.

'Though I suppose one could look at the matter from that angle, no, that's not what I'm trying to say.'

I want to find out more about Maël's character, though there were plenty of opportunities when I was able to take his measure.

And I deeply disliked what I saw. 'What is he really like?'

Fabien hesitates, as if considering. 'I don't quite know how to say this. I think, more than anything, Maël wanted to be left alone.'

'I think that's the worst excuse I ever heard for poorly managing an entire duchy.' The sheer state of affairs when Philippe and I took over. 'If I only think about the amount of taxes that were levied in the territories—'

'Excuse me, but I think you're blaming the wrong person. Maël hardly worried a day about the taxes. He was happy to leave them as they were.'

'That's not an excuse.'

'If you want a culprit, you might look to Magali.' Fabien raises an eyebrow at Isabella. 'And don't you dare start defending her.'

'Of course you'd say it was Magali's fault,' says Isabella.

'You do know that even as the duke, he had to fight her on every account,' says Fabien.

Isabella scoffs. 'She only wanted what was best for the duchy.'

'For the duchy? Or for herself?' Fabien turns to me. 'Don't you listen to what she says. If Maël was my friend, Magali was hers.'

I lift my hands in the air. 'Fine, fine. But what about everything else? The orgies? The way he attacked maidens in Langly?' There's a knot in my gut just thinking about it.

Fabien raises both eyebrows. 'Is that what flames your imagination?'

I smack him on the shoulder. Hard. 'You have a filthy mind.'

'Ah,' he says, 'and here I was, thinking that this was a reflection upon your own mind.' He gets up on his feet and shuts the doors to the terrace. 'Maël never took something that wasn't being offered to him.' He hovers a few paces away from me. His face is serious, even cold. 'He didn't worry about the vilification of his own character, though.'

'Big words,' says Isabella.

'Let's go for petty words, then,' he replies. 'If the rumours suggested Maël was a man to be feared, he didn't contradict them. You know how much of being a duke is a show of strength.'

And I truly do. But when I saw Maël at the Royal Palace, he was every inch loud and boastful and irreverent. The rumours that were coursing about him seem perfectly in tune with the image I had of him.

But now, considering who stands next in line to the throne … the matter of Maël's character makes all the difference.

Not if I have something to say about it, though.

'I think we need to find my sister,' I say, lowering my voice.

Isabella's eyes widen. 'Anne-Mihielle?'

'What sister?' says Fabien.

'Not many people at Court remember her,' I say.

Fabien frowns. 'I vaguely remember a scandal. But I was so young.'

I nod. 'You would have been.' I was, too, and Fabien is about my own age. 'I was so powerless to do anything about it.' But not anymore.

Fabien nods as if he understands.

Perhaps he does. I take a deep breath and say what I've been bracing myself for. 'I need you to do something for me. I need your help. I need you to go to the Green Kingdom and find Anne-Mihielle. Find her and bring her back.'

* * *

After the letter has been written and handed over to Fabien, after he has gone on his way, with the promise of taking care of this, I am left alone in my chambers with a quiet Isabella.

Much quieter than usual.

'You don't agree with me,' I say into the silence.

'That you sent the court jester to find your sister, against your father's will? No, of course I don't agree with you. But I doubt that you could have asked anyone else. I'm going back and forth, trying to find a more suitable person, and I'm not sure that I can.'

Isabella's honesty is, as always, unforgiving.

And this is why I trust her so much.

'Will you tell Philippe about this?' she says.

I open my mouth to answer and then realise that I will, most likely, not. And it aches. It hurts so much to realise how much my husband and I have grown apart.

The unsaid stands between us, the rift quickly becoming a slippery ravine. Is this what my marriage has been reduced to – gaping holes?

ADRIFT

BLANCHE

A man who is moving is always harder to find, so I need more than a long time to finally stumble into Maël. I find my grandson drifting at sea, in a rowing boat.

I try to hover in a sitting position on the bench opposite him, but I believe the plank is sticking through half my thigh. Making sitting look believable when I ghostwalk is always harder than standing.

'This is no more than a raft,' I say, looking around.

Maël strokes his hand through the undulating waters, lulling us in slow motions. 'The ship had to dock in Lafala, and you know very well why I had to stay back.'

When Celine and Philippe exiled my grandson, they also wove a water curse around his person. Celine is a Water-Twirler, in the end, and she gave up a part of her power to bind the sea to her will – which was that the water should carry Maël away, should he ever try to return to the Red Kingdom.

Whatever that might mean, whatever the cost might be.

This is why he can't risk entering the port of Lafala, and he has to remain at sea.

He wouldn't be able to approach the capital, even if he wanted to.

So Maël is adrift, while the ship he has hired does its business in Lafala's port.

To his credit, Maël doesn't seem to be terribly bothered by it. He's been quick and efficient, so far. Under a false name, he hired a merchant ship, *L'Espoir*, a ship carrying precious iron ore to the Green Kingdom, to bring him to his destination.

But matters need to be expedited even more. New opportunities have arisen. And complications to come with them.

'Why are you here?' he asks. 'I don't appreciate being checked on. I'm not twelve. I said I'd do it, so I'll do it.'

'There has been a change of plans.' Lately, the ground beneath us feels precisely like this rocking boat.

'Why am I not surprised?' Maël sighs.

'I've given your contract to someone else in the Fallen Court.'

Maël narrows his eyes. 'Who?'

It's my turn to sigh. 'Fabien de Goderic. He carries a letter that might make our target more … amenable to our intents.' In any case, he can lure Anne-Mihielle faster away from the Green Kingdom and bring her somewhere I can reach her in my ghostwalking form.

'You can't give the contract to someone else,' says Maël. 'I accepted it.'

Of course I can. But no need to tell him that. I need to change tactics. 'I need you to turn back to Crane Harbour. Right now. Make yourself known, let everyone hear that you're alive and well. And I need you to start rallying the Blue Kingdom's seigneurs.'

'Why would I do that?'

I brace myself for what I'm about to tell him. 'Your very, very distant cousin, Petit-Mihiel, expired a few days ago. This makes you', I say, pointing my finger at his chest, 'the next in line to the throne of the Red Kingdom.'

A rare expression appears on Maël's face, which is complete and utter dazzlement. 'How is that even possible?'

'Through me,' I say. 'Mihiel's father was my nephew twice removed.' The King I helped put in place once my brother's reign ended. By my hand more than any other's. 'As my grandson, you are the closest living male relative to King Mihiel. And unless Celine produces a male heir before Mihiel expires, too, you are the next king.'

Maël's eyes widen in sheer terror. And then, he catches himself. 'No.'

'It's in your blood,' I say. 'You can't avoid this. And think of the consequences. If there is no one who would stand as the next in line... Do you even realise what would happen if Mihiel dies, and there is no heir at all?'

With the Dark Mother so close to awakening, we can't afford this kind of instability in the Red Kingdom. In fact, I need someone to rely on when the worst happens. Someone who would support me and the Fallen Court.

Though, even if Maël hates this and will hate *me* for it, perhaps this will finally give him a sense of purpose.

'You will be free to do as you please, as King,' I say.

Maël barks a bitter laugh. 'The King is less free than anyone else. Everyone's expectations…'

I know why he breaks off. Maël runs from responsibility, because he thinks he won't live up to the task.

How wrong he is.

Maël combs back his dark locks, now trimmed into submission. He has also shaved, I notice. This contract was good for him. But an even greater task stands before him.

'You do have another grandson,' says Maël.

I do. Hugo. But he isn't to be trusted, not after everything he has done. 'As far as anyone is concerned,' I say, 'especially within the Red Kingdom, Hugo has been dead for seven years.'

'What good is a king, then, if he can't set foot within his kingdom?' Maël points loosely at all the water around him, a reminder of the curse Celine wove around him.

He thinks that I haven't thought of this already.

He is wrong.

'You do know that Mihiel will probably persuade Celine to lift the curse, don't you? That he would rather have you as the heir, instead of risking another war?'

Surprise drifts across Maël's face, but he rallies himself quickly. He slaps his hands on his thighs. 'Right, well, that's a shame, because I won't do this. So. Find yourself another potential heir.'

As wild and unaccountable as he is, Maël sometimes manages to keep me in check.

But the game isn't over. It wasn't as if I was expecting full compliance today.

'Fine,' I say. 'I'll let you think about it.'

Maël rolls his eyes. 'Ask Fabien to board *L'Espoir*. And I'll speak to him and see what there is to be done about the contract.'

I'm preparing to refuse him when I realise that Fabien is his friend. That he hasn't seen him since he's been exiled. And that he might be pleased to see a kindred spirit. I don't like this at all, but... 'Fine. I'll send Fabien to *L'Espoir*. But take no risks. Stay in Greenport, if you must, but let Fabien carry out the mission. Don't put your life at stake unnecessarily. There are great things in store for you now.'

For a long time, Maël is quiet, sifting through things. Surely, he must see reason. In the end, he gives me a non-committal grunt, but I'm hard pressed for time, so I leave, taking this for as much of an approval as I'm about to receive.

THE VISITOR

MIHI

*M*y aim is off today.

I'm trying to strike the High Inquisitor right in the nose, plant a dagger between those disturbing and deeply disturbed eyes of his, but I keep missing.

It's all these bloody thoughts that I'm having.

I slink my boots off my desk and stalk to the opposite corner of my study, so I can retrieve my throwing knives.

One of the Mage-Huntresses, whose father is a carpenter, has carved for me a life-sized likeness of the High Inquisitor out of a thin sheet of wood.

The details of the crude copy are stunning: from the absurd circlet he always wears on his head, to that ridiculously thin cape that would never serve to keep the cold or the rain away.

Even in a rough, wooden shape, the High Inquisitor looks like someone pampered.

It makes me want to throw another knife at him.

I should be receiving audiences, truly, and I can hear the buzz of people gathering in the antechamber – coming to turn in more mages, or suspected mages – but I'm too distracted today.

So many people that we have to potentially protect from their fellow villagers and from the High Inquisitor, more than from anyone else.

But Ullar wants me gone from Xante.

The blade is heavy in my hand today. I put my feet up again.

Aim.

Throw.

Miss.

There's a racket in the antechamber and the door is tossed to the wall. A man marches in and my hand grips the remaining knife tighter. He's so tall that he seems to take up all the space between the door and my desk. He's huge, with dark, slightly curled hair that brushes the tip of his ears. He wears the most disconcerting outfit I've ever seen – sleeveless chainmail that shows his enormous arms, and vanguards to protect his forearms, with blades fitted on them.

A white cloak flutters behind him.

I check if, indeed, the blade is still in my hand, my other hand going to the hilt of my sword. I toss my feet down from my desk in a scramble.

He stops three paces away from my seat, placing a hand

across his chest and taking a deep bow. 'May Sabya's Light-song brighten your day, *Erste Jägerin*,' he says in the language of the Red Kingdom. This alone makes my hair bristle.

He pronounces my title with melodic inflections. The chivalrous, cultivated tones are in dissonance with the rugged appearance.

This man is a warrior, and he likes to flaunt it. And he has the cheekiest grin I've seen in a long, long time.

Oh.

Hello.

He's gorgeous.

He studies me from head to toe and I could swear that my skin feels tighter wherever his gaze brushes against it. I can't take my eyes off him, either. I'm gaping while my tongue seems to have forgotten that it has a different function – like speaking.

Instead, it's wondering what it would feel like to tangle with his.

But before I can articulate anything at all, Remy bursts through the open door. 'You can't be here, you have to wait for your turn,' he says, stalking toward the intruder.

I'm not sure what Remy intends to do.

Grab the stranger by the cloak and drag him outside?

I want to tell him, *Let the man say his bit, at least.* Then I can decide for myself if I want to throw him out or not.

But the big man is quick. He extends and arm and places his hand on top of Remy's head, pushing him back out the door.

As if Remy were no more than a disobedient child.

The man drawls, 'Oh, I think the *Erste Jägerin* will want to hear what I have to say.'

Remy turns on his heels, the clank of his boots receding through the antechamber, presumably towards the hallway. He shouts furiously for the others.

Possibly so they can drag the intruder away.

'I'm intrigued,' I say. 'Why would I want to hear what you have to say? And why is it so urgent, so that you have to skip the line?'

'I don't like to wait.' He grins and fiddles with a pouch hanging off his belt, opening the strings. He pulls out a rolled piece of parchment. A letter, it seems. 'And I don't think you'd want to, either.'

He tosses the parchment on my desk. The seal is red, a pouncing lioness. The Duchy of Langly, then. The Red Kingdom, indeed.

My heart starts pounding.

The man says simply, 'Your sister has a message for you.'

There's a whoosh in my ears, which makes it hard for me to hear what he's saying.

A message.

From my sister.

I stab the dagger into the surface of the desk and unfold the parchment.

'I am meant to join you on your journey back to the Red Kingdom. Think of me as a sort of an … escort,' he says.

Journey.

Red Kingdom.

I can't make out the words, the jumble in my head spins too much.

'And who might you be?' I say.

'Where are my manners?' The man makes a deep bow again just as four Mage-Hunters file into my receiving chambers. 'I'm Fabien de Goderic, Captain of the Duke and Duchess of Langly's guards.'

Langly. The Duchess.

Celine sent a Goderic to fetch me.

A buggering Goderic.

When Remy pushes to approach him, Fabien's smile turns feral. Matthieu is also among the Mage-Hunters who have come to the 'rescue,' and he takes one single look at me and wisely places a hand on Remy's elbow. 'Wait. Mihi?'

I wave them away with my free hand, the parchment with the message in the other. 'Leave us now, this isn't the time.'

I don't even bother to check if they're listening to my orders, if they've withdrawn as I asked. My ears aren't even listening to sounds of the door closing; I'm too distracted skimming through the message that, apparently, my sister has sent me.

And trusted no one but a Goderic to deliver it to me. Even this small detail speaks volumes, if it weren't for the content itself.

It is urgent, my sister says. That I should join her in Lafala. *The safety and the future of the Red Kingdom are at risk.*

I should come as soon as I can.

The man delivering the message is to be trusted and can serve as my guide.

Guide?

I don't need a buggering guide to return to the city where I was born and from where I was banished, and where I refuse to return, come what may.

I toss my feet on the desk again, one on top of the other.

Fabien stands in front of me, taking me in, from my smooth cloth breeches to the worn tips of my boots.

I've changed my mind. I don't want him here, and I don't want to know anything else.

I grab my knife, give him a look that I hope conveys just how I feel, and then turn around and toss the blade at the High Inquisitor's head.

It strikes him in the eye.

Fabien smirks.

'Please inform my sister that I'm not her lapdog to summon as she sees fit,' I say. 'Not now, and not in the future. I am currently extremely busy with affairs tied to the Mage-Hunters.'

I pluck the words one by one. My voice is steady, but my head is roaring. An emergency tied to the Red Kingdom. Why does my sister think that I can help, in any way? It's been fourteen years since I set foot in Lafala.

I don't know anyone there.

I'd be in no position to help.

I'm even less inclined to do so.

Fabien chuckles. 'I thought as much.'

'You don't know me,' I bark at him.

'Ah, but you see, I was hoping to become … better acquainted with you.'

'I think not,' I say, pointing him towards the door. 'Please convey to my sister that I'm afraid I can be of no service to her.'

'I understand if you need a few days to mull things through. I mean, I wouldn't do precisely as I'm told right away, either. Just out of principle.' He gives me a knowing smile.

'You don't understand. I won't come.'

Fabien shrugs. 'As you say. You can find me at The Phoenix Inn. I think I'll explore a bit what Xante has to offer, until you change your mind.' He turns around to leave, and the red lioness emblazoned on his white cloak shifts and dances. As if pouncing. 'If you want to have a quiet chat with me, I'll be available for dinner, if you have any questions about the Red Kingdom. I'm afraid I can't take any regarding the emergency. I'll have to allow your sister to explain that to you.'

I want to tell him a thousand things. How he can stick his inn and his invitation to dinner up his arse. How he can return to my sister right away and tell her that I can't be cast away and ignored for years and years, only to be remembered when I'm needed for something.

The only thing that comes out is, 'I will find you at the Phoenix Inn after I put all that I've told you into writing. Then, you can leave.'

He shrugs again, not even bothering to look at me. 'If you say so.'

He doesn't even try to be diplomatic.

Apparently, my sister sent me the most infuriating person that she could find.

Doesn't she know I don't react well to smugness? But then again, how would she know?

She hasn't seen me since I was nine.

Fabien turns on his heel and leaves without another word.

After he's gone, I dash towards the High Inquisitor's replica, pull out the knives and line up on the desk every single blade and dagger I have on my person. Toss them one after the other. Eye, neck, heart, belly.

Aim, hit.

Aim, hit.

At some point, Ullar drifts inside the receiving chambers, not even bothering to say hello. 'Your aim is better,' he says, throwing an appreciative look at the High Inquisitor. 'Who was that?'

I ponder whether I should say anything at all – out of spite – or whether I should be nice and try to gain his favour again. Maybe he'd change his mind about sending me away.

Sadly, the part of me that clings to him wins. Maybe rattled by the fact that the family who banished me has been in touch today.

'That, my friend, was Fabien de Goderic. Sent by my sister.' I push the parchment towards him and he rushes through its contents.

He might as well see it.

Not that I'm asking for his advice about what to do.

I know what I'll do, which is absolutely nothing.

'Interesting,' he says. 'An emergency in the Red Kingdom. Did he say what it was about?'

'No,' I concede reluctantly. 'He just said he was here to take me to Lafala. I mean, he expected me to leave everything, and go with him. The sheer arrogance.'

Did he expect that, though? He made the offer that my sister sent him with, and then he made it clear that he hadn't expected me to come.

Ullar taps at the piece of parchment. 'This could be important, Mihi. This could affect us, too. I think you should find out what it's about.'

'Last night, you said I should go to the Blue Kingdom.'

'Then do both. Find out what Celine wants, and then go on to Crane Harbour. It's just a small detour.'

I feel like smashing my own head against the table.

This, again.

By Sabya and Lucius and the Golden Mother and all the Mothers of the Forest. Does he not hear me? 'No.'

Ullar sighs, as if having to deal with a child in the middle of a tantrum. 'It would be good to at least find out what they want. Is he gone?'

'He'll be at the Phoenix Inn, he said. Until he gets bored of waiting, I suppose.'

'You don't know his marching orders,' he says.

'Nor do I care to.'

Ullar shifts on his feet. 'I see. I'll have to give you more time, then.'

Isn't that what Fabien had also said?

'I don't need time,' I yell, but having said his piece, Ullar is already walking out of the door. 'I just need to be left alone to handle my own buggering business.'

I throw the High Inquisitor's replica a murderous look.

Toss a few more knives at it. And then, and only then, do I start drafting the reply to my sister.

DANCE OF GIFTS

CELINE

I feel my husband approaching even before he steps into my chambers. I'm dawdling on the terrace that looks upon the restless surface of the sea, the waves breaking over the red spikes of Lucius's Cliff.

It's my Gift, stretching out towards the sea, sniffing it, drawing in circles around the undertow and other deadly currents, aching to dance with them. It's my Gift that has turned into something else since that day, two years ago, when I bound parts of it to keep Maël and Hugo in check. To bind their Gifts, and to bind water to keep them away from the Red Kingdom. *It will exact a price*, Isabella told me then.

And it was true. I can't control water as I once did. But the sea, its wild currents and its tides… Oh, the sea, it's something else entirely.

Philippe's Gift changed, too. There's something sharp and deadly in the places where there was once serenity and the bliss of growth. But my own Gift still recognises it, leaps and stirs in my blood whenever it feels his.

My husband is here, and my heart hammers in my chest. I suddenly find that I don't know what to do with my hands, except to rub them on the armrests of the chair I'm sitting on.

I shouldn't be so nervous. It's just my husband.

Just?

Things aren't easy with him.

I'm coiled as a spring when I hear the thud of his boots on the marble, the whoosh of his cloak, the clink of the metal in his belt. By the time he's appeared on the threshold, I've half risen from my chair, as if my body can't decide between doing what my impulses dictate – which is to spring into his arms – or putting a bit of distance between us.

I don't know how many more times my heart can take the disappointment of him coming close, only for him to pull away and leave. For days. Weeks.

I take him in, from the tips of his dusty boots to his creased breeches, the disarrayed shirt underneath the red velvet of his doublet.

I don't miss a single detail. His ruffled hair, loose ringlets that touch the tips of his ears – he's let his hair grow lately – the uncertain look in his green-brown eyes, how tired he is.

The way he abruptly stops, as if he had a purpose in coming here, and he forgot it the moment he saw me.

We take in each other for a long moment and I wonder

what it is like to look at me through his eyes. Does he see the hunger? Does he see the need I have for him?

Or did he make himself believe that, for me, he's only a means to an end?

'Celine?' he says, uncertain.

I can't say a single word, and I'm already on the verge of tears. I love him so much that it hurts. And I need him so much that I'm frozen, wondering how I didn't crumble completely in his absence.

He says, 'You asked me to come from Langly.' His voice. Mothers of the Forest, just hearing his voice, what it does to me. 'To meet you here urgently. There are some—'

'My brother is dead,' I tell him before I even realise what I'm saying. 'He died, he—'

Philippe is a storm. One moment, he's standing a few paces from me, and in the next, his arms are around my back, his head is touching mine, his heat is wrapped all around me.

It's too much. His scent, of something fresh that has broken out of the earth; his thick arms around me, making me feel a husk in comparison, my body something he could crush on a whim; the feel of his stubble, grazing my forehead.

Before I know it, tears are streaming down my face, and I'm hiccupping with sobs, trying to catch my breath. His rough hands are tangled in my hair, trying to soothe me.

I grasp at his doublet, clawing at it, trying to curl myself underneath his skin.

'I'm so sorry,' he breathes into my hair. 'I didn't know. You should have written. I'm so sorry.'

'You don't know, you don't know how it was here, how my father… He's been…' There's so much I want to tell him. About my sister. How my father expects us to produce the next king – but I can tell him none of that, because I know what he'll think.

That he's no more than a tool.

So I say nothing, but revel in his bodily presence instead. And cry until my eyes feel swollen and raw.

Until I catch a flash of movement behind him. A fluffed green cloak, fluttering with movement.

I wipe my tears with the back of my hand, and properly look.

A woman stands some distance behind my husband, half in the shadows that the Royal Palace casts. She's my age, perhaps.

Her hair the colour of wheat when it's ripe for harvesting, her eyes the colour of a summer sky. Surprise, and perhaps embarrassment are written on her face. 'I'm sorry, Your Grace,' she says. 'I didn't mean to intrude.'

Who is that? And what is she doing with Philippe?

My Philippe.

I hold on tighter to him.

But he's already half-turning towards her. 'Apologies, Gelda, my wife— I didn't expect—' His fingers tighten on my arm. 'Perhaps we can speak to the duchess later.'

She inclines her head and something sharp claws at my chest. I look to Philippe and I notice an emotion I can't define on his face.

She withdraws on silent steps from the room.

I hadn't even realised she was here when Philippe arrived.

I narrow my eyes. 'What was that woman doing in my chambers?'

He kisses my temple, breathing into my hair, 'I'll tell you later. It has to do with what we found in the Goderic lands.'

The name – Gelda – jingles in my head with familiarity, a connection I can't yet make.

I pull back a little, my fists knotting Philippe's doublet. 'Who is she?'

'A priestess of the Mothers of the Forest. She came down from Valmons, to look at what we found in the woods, and—' He stops himself. 'Honestly, I don't think we should speak about this now.'

Indeed.

I slip my hand underneath the velvet doublet, feeling the scorching skin of his chest through the thin shirt. 'Did I tell you I missed you?' I say.

He nuzzles the top of my head. 'You know what, I don't think you did.'

I turn my head, catching his lips with mine. I long for his closeness, yearn for it to fill me up to the brim, to banish the emptiness I always carry within. Now, more than ever. I brush my mouth against his, nipping and teasing. I burrow myself closer to him, while myriad emotions explode in the depths of my belly. Joy and relief, and so much heat that I think I must be burning bright with it.

I should probably tell him about Maël, and how he stands to inherit the kingdom now, but I can't bring myself to. Sometimes, I can tell that when Philippe looks at me, he can't stop thinking about the way he betrayed his own mother and step-brother, helping me take the duchy away from them, so we could rule instead.

No, I don't want to bring Maël between us tonight.

I tighten my arms around Philippe's neck, pulling him down, pulling him closer to me.

Too long, it's been too long, and I can't have enough. I lower one of my hands, just enough to wrap it around his arm, and drag him towards the bed.

Philippe stiffens. 'Celine. I don't think—'

I whirl around. His features look pinched and I can feel the blow of rejection even before it falls. 'What?'

He shifts on his feet. 'I'm … tired. Could we just sleep?'

I open and close my mouth, unsure what to say.

But this isn't the first time he's done this, is it?

I wrap my arms tight around myself, wondering what it is that I'm doing wrong, what makes him reject me. He squeezes my shoulders briefly and deposits another soft kiss on the top of my head. 'Let's just sleep for now, shall we?'

Later, we lie side by side in bed, my mind jarring and rattled. For a long while, sleep evades me, while odd thoughts jumble through my head. A name, for instance, that I couldn't pin down earlier. Gelda was the name of Hugo's mother. The woman has been missing for years. What an unusual name, though. I wonder, somewhat disjointedly, if the Gelda Philippe brought with him has children of her own.

Unlike me.

* * *

In the morning, while we break our fast in the sitting corner in my chambers, Philippe tells me about his findings in the Goderic county.

Fires in the woods. Burn marks on the tree trunks. Large imprints of paws in the bush, the ground underneath hardened to clay.

'The people are blaming mages,' he says. 'Fire-Blazers. Though I think I can count on my fingers the number of Fire-Blazers that remain in the kingdom.'

Mages are not looked kindly upon. Not since the Year of the Red Maiden. But it started even before that, centuries ago, when the mages gathered power and lands into their hands. Most of them became seigneurs. There are few among the aristocratic families that don't have Gifts – like the Goderics.

So much unrest. And what happens if my father dies, and the crown goes to Maël, indeed? And even if Philippe and I had a boy, and my father died while he was still a small child, would Maël challenge his right to rule? Would some of the seigneurs stand by him?

Fires in the cities, fires in the groves.

'The tracks lead north, to Valmons,' says Philippe, oblivious to my thoughts. 'I'll have to speak to your father. You know how Seigneur Valmons loathes us. He'd never allow me or Count Goderic to look into the matter ourselves. But maybe your father can prevail on him. I don't think he'd challenge the king.'

Who knows? Seigneur Valmons is a prickly old bear. If it

came to it, he would stand on Maël's side, I am sure. Even if just to vex my husband.

I brace myself for what I'm about to ask. 'What about that woman? Gelda?'

'Ah, Gelda,' he says. 'She has been a tremendous help. We met her when—'

There's a knock at the door, sharp and impatient. 'Yes?' says my husband, visibly annoyed.

One of my father's liveried servants enters. 'Your Grace. His Majesty is awaiting you.'

I could not expect that Philippe would arrive and my father wouldn't know about it. That he wouldn't want to see him at once.

* * *

We find ourselves in the same receiving chamber where I argued with my father a few days before. Well, he argued, and I listened.

By the look on his face, things aren't about to take a better turn. 'Philippe,' he says dryly, 'what has been keeping you from your wife's side?'

Philippe's face takes the same pinched expression as last night. 'The duchy's business,' he replies, just as dryly.

'Business?' says my father, brushing a hand through his pointed beard. 'What business is more important than—'

Lucius's Flaming Finger, not this. I can't imagine anything more humiliating than my father discussing what happens in the ducal bed with my husband.

'There are fires in the Goderic groves,' I say quickly. 'Strange marks. Tracks leading to Valmons.'

Philippe takes the cue. 'I wanted to ask for assistance, to ask if there's someone you could send to Valmons—'

'I honestly couldn't give a rat's arse about Valmons,' says my father. 'Did Celine inform you about her brother?'

'Of course, Your Majesty. My sincere condolences. Perhaps I should have started with that.'

My father stands up with a groan, paces in front of the mirrors, his hands laced behind his back. 'Perhaps.'

An eerie sort of silence descends upon us. A silence that speaks of nothing good.

'You do know who is now set to inherit the kingdom, don't you?' says my father.

Philippe frowns. 'I suppose that would be Maël.'

My husband takes on that eerie, distant expression he always does whenever he thinks about his half-brother. He's good, Philippe. He hates himself for what he had to do, even if, two years ago, it was the only way we could have avoided bloodshed. A clash between his own supporters and Maël's on the battlefield.

I sometimes think that's the reason why he pulls away from me so often. Because he can't look at me without thinking of what he did to his own brother, at my instigation. They used to be close when they were children. Until life – and their mother, Magali – sent them on completely different paths.

'Indeed, he is.' My father stops in front of a window. 'What do you have to say about that?'

Philippe says, not even looking at me, 'Perhaps it is time to remove the binding spells around him. Perhaps he should be allowed to return to the kingdom.'

I feel the stab of betrayal deep in my chest.

'Perhaps' is all my father says.

'It's something I have been advocating for a long time.' Of course he has. The regrets are eating away at him. But how could I allow it, when it would endanger the foundations of the life we have built for ourselves in Langly?

'Certainly. That is a possibility.' My father's tone suggests the opposite. 'On the other hand, you and your wife could do your *duty*, and we'd have no need for further unrest.'

Philippe's fingers curl on his knees, his spine stiffening. He could be made of stone. And I want to sink into the ground.

Doesn't my father see that he's making everything worse? How could Philippe want me? Want to be intimate with me *at my father's behest*?

My father doesn't understand my husband.

And I'm desperate. I don't know which way to turn anymore. I don't know how to fix this.

'Yes?' says my father, looking at Philippe.

'I have nothing further to say on the matter,' says my husband, looking neither at him, nor me.

I could burst into tears.

My father curls his lip. 'If you think that the matter is settled by not thinking of it—'

Philippe rises abruptly to his feet. 'We are speaking of my unborn child here. A living, breathing being. Not a pawn you can use for your own purposes. And with this, I've said all I care to on the matter.' He slings a hand across his chest and takes a low bow. 'If you will excuse me, Your Majesty.'

My husband doesn't even wait for a reply before stalking away from the room. Which leaves me, as always, alone.

So alone. And with no clue what to do about it. How to rescue this.

THE FORGIVEN, THE FORGOTTEN

BLANCHE

The Mage-Hunters and the Mothers of the Hallowed Forest aren't the only things that I ignored when it came to the Green Kingdom.

There are other ties that I preferred to look away from. Other ties that I should stop trying to avoid.

For the sake of my grandchildren, at least. Even if it hurts to dig so deeply into old wounds.

I visit one of the said grandchildren in his splendid suite of apartments in Bluefort. Smaller than Maël's, Hugo's chambers are decorated more handsomely. Hand-woven carpets everywhere depicting magnificent battles of the Blue Kingdom's knights or aquatic scenes depicting the people of the Lakes.

The pieces of furniture are intricately carved, many resting on gold-gilded feet. I can imagine that most of them are handouts from Delphine, the Heiress of the Blue Kingdom. Interesting how she wants Hugo to be comfortable.

My grandson stands in front of a wide table. His back is turned to me, but I can almost feel the tension that squares his shoulders. He's wearing plain, beige cloth breeches today, and a shirt with rolled sleeves.

A far cry from his usual elegant attires. 'Hugo?'

His entire body jolts as if I speared him with lightning. There's a loud splash and a crack and before I know what's happening, burnt clay shards are flying through the room.

I throw myself in front of him, more from instinct than anything else. Nothing can touch me when I'm ghostwalking. I'm not much of a shield.

'By Sabya's Darkblades,' he mutters, turning to look where I stood, just moments ago.

'Are you hurt?' I ask. Water drips down from the table, and shards are scattered everywhere. A large piece of rock is plopped in the middle of the remnants of what seems to have been a burnt clay bowl.

'Grandmother,' Hugo says, flinching. He brushes water off his breeches, avoiding my gaze. 'To what do I owe the pleasure? Come to check if I'm up to something nefarious?'

'I'm sorry to have startled you.'

He throws me a quick, side-gaze. 'You did startle me.' He clears his throat. 'I dropped the stone when I heard you. Were you behind me?'

'Yes,' I say, frowning at the piece of rock. 'Is that iron ore?'

'It is.'

He crosses his arms, and I notice a few scratches on his skin. 'Are you here to spy on me? Can't you entrust that to your minions? Aren't you far too busy to stoop to this?'

Spying, indeed. He shouldn't gripe that I have him closely watched. Two years ago, he conspired with Magali and brought the Duchy of Langly to the brink of war. Their actions saw them exiled from the Red Kingdom, alongside Maël.

But, unlike Maël, I took away Magali's and Hugo's Gifts permanently, once they were ensconced in Bluefort. I could never forget who Hugo's mother is, and what she did.

Gelda came to me nearly fifty years ago, when I staged the coup against my brother, the King, and pretended to help. She also pretended to be a priestess – while I suspect that in fact she's a genuine Mother of the Forest. She must be centuries old, perhaps, but her looks are that of someone in their twenties.

After I disappeared into the heart of the Opal Mountain, and Robert vanished, Gelda seduced Kylian and started a round of wars in Langly that saw my twin boys pitted against one another.

And while Hugo assures me that he hasn't been in touch with his mother in years, I'm always weary.

Up to a point.

He's still my grandson, blood of my blood, even if he comes from two such wretched parents.

And I need to extend him a bit of trust. I also need him for something I have in mind. 'I was hoping you could help me,' I say.

He cocks an eyebrow. 'Is that so?'

'Your slyness and discretion will come in handy.'

There's no mistaking his expression of interest. 'Pray, do tell.'

I steel myself for what I have to say. 'I'm not sure that you're aware, but long after your grandfather Robert vanished, there were … clues that he had certain ties to the Green Kingdom. Ties he'd hidden from me.'

The words almost choke me. This is what I didn't want to brood upon. This is what I must investigate.

Robert always kept secrets from me, that much was clear. Even after we decided to marry. But on that point, I was weak. For his sake, I never pried, and I overlooked a few hints that he hadn't been entirely honest with me. And if there had been something that had bothered me, after three children and endless work to make a duchy rise, I stopped thinking of it.

Robert was my rock, my heart, my everything. So bright in my eyes that he blinded me to all his faults. The secrets he still kept in shadowed corners.

Hugo's expression is wistful. 'What kind of ties?'

'That is for you to determine,' I say. I can hardly look him in the eye. 'Valerie will pass on whatever information we have so far. There are leads that point to a stay of his in Crane Harbour, not long before he vanished, twenty-seven years ago.'

Vanished, or dead? I never knew. And the fool that I am, I can't help but hope that, lies or no lies, secrets or no secrets, someone might discover him somewhere alive. Though he must be an old man, by now.

That is, if he still lives. What could have driven him away from Langly, when our children needed him so much? Why did he leave them, all alone, allowing them to become embroiled in embittered fights for succession?

The answers must lie in the past, I'm afraid.

Hugo drums his fingers on the table. 'Crane Harbour. Would this mean that I'd have more ... freedom to move? You do realise that's imperative. If you want me to complete the task.'

I sigh. I've grappled with this. I'm reluctant to have Hugo out of my – and the Fallen Court's – sights, but I suppose I need to test his allegiances. Lengthen the chain and see where he'll go. What he'll do.

He can't return to the Red Kingdom, in any case, because of the water curse Celine placed on him.

'Of course,' I say. 'Whatever you need. As long as you stay in the Blue Kingdom.'

Not to mention that Valerie would be relieved to separate him and Delphine, for a while.

Hugo grins. There's a certain air about him sometimes, sophisticated and sleek, that reminds me so much of Kylian, my son, that it's almost painful to look at him.

I don't know what came of Kylian, in the end. I don't know where he is.

'My, my,' says Hugo. 'Is this a contract, Grandmother?'

'It is. I'll have a mark of the Fallen Court sent to you.'

Hugo's smile turns even brighter. 'In that case, I'm pleased to accept.'

I nod. Perhaps all he needs to righten his ways is a bit of trust.

Or perhaps I'm on the verge of making a huge, huge mistake.

THE LOST

MIHI

*W*e're having an unusually quiet breakfast at the Hunters' House when Matthieu bursts into the dining hall. 'They have Remy.'

'What?' I'm up on my feet in the blink of an eye. 'Who?'

'The High Inquisitor.' All the blood is drained from Matthieu's face.

My legs are unsteady.

The High Inquisitor.

Has Remy.

I don't even have to think about what I need to do.

I don't have to ask.

The Hunters follow me when I dart out of the hall and make directly for the armoury. We pick swords and daggers, don our leather armours, the tailored chainmail.

The Mage-Hunters are not knights – I prefer to see us as

highly mobile, well-trained troops, excellent for missions that rely on speed and efficiency. Preferably in tight spaces.

But we are not made for the battlefield. We are nothing against the heavily armoured Paladins.

Unless we are in close quarters.

Unless we can use our Gifts, which I prefer we didn't, because it would give away our game to the High Inquisitor and turn us into targets for him.

We file out of the back door, which leads into the winding streets. The Hunters' House is built on a steep hill. The path to the Inquisitors' House zigzags around the hill, then coils at the bottom, past the Xante Market, the quays of the Green River, the nine Bridges of Darg.

And twelve armed Mage-Hunters and Huntresses, winding on the narrow streets, are drawing attention. People stop to stare, but I barely notice.

My heart is drumming while I brace for a fight. My thoughts twist and turn, rushing to the same conclusion, over and over again: that this is my fault. It's because of the way I spoke to the High Inquisitor when we took that Water-Twirler. The two Paladins who were following me must have seen Remy in the boat. I should have been careful; I should have been less provocative, and it's too late. Now, *this* is happening.

And not even to me.

Matthieu walks beside me. 'Maybe we should wait for Ullar,' he whispers.

'I'm not waiting a single moment.' All I can think about are the gruesome methods that the High Inquisitor uses to 'test' a person, to see if they're a mage or not, as listed in his book, *The Witch-Axe*. They range from making them hold a glowing iron, to making them walk on hot coals.

Not Remy, not Remy, I won't let him to do this to Remy.

I can't spare an eye for the buildings that stand on the terraced cliffs of Xante. Nor for the temperamental, lush gardens, the gnarling trees and rich bushes, most of them half concealing the entrances of the stone houses.

I can only breathe hard as we hurry downhill, towards the Temple that is still being renovated at the Romannhon's orders, which the High Inquisitor brought to the Green Kingdom. The flawless white stone of the Temple looks bald and cold and jarring compared to the lush gardens of Xante. And in the Temple's courtyard, my gaze stops on the red-brick, two-storey building of the Inquisitors' House.

A bloody red thorn in our ribs.

'What's the plan?' asks Matthieu.

'We go in. And ask to see Remy.'

'That's it?'

I have thought about it. I did. But this might be nothing more than a test. Nothing more than the High Inquisitor pushing, to see if we would push back.

And that's precisely what we'll do, while also trying to find out if there are any grounds for them to detain Remy.

The Inquisitors have no authority over us. Though who knows what truths they might have wrenched out of Remy already.

'Do we engage?' asks Matthieu. 'If things aren't to our liking?'

Engage in battle, he means. But in broad daylight, in everyone's sight... What if one of us slips up, or is cornered into using their Gift? 'I think not, but we'll see.'

Matthieu nods. 'That's what I was also thinking.'

My chest feels too tight at the enormity of what has happened. How can the High Inquisitor dare to touch us?

Does he think that there will be no consequences?

In every single one of our interactions over the years, he has struck me as someone bold but calculated.

No, if he made such a move, he must have thought of the consequences. And decided they were worth the risk.

'How sure are you that they have Remy?' I whisper to Matthieu.

Six Mage-Hunters are following us, another four are darting in and out of gardens, up and down rooftops, scouting the premises. I suppose it would be an unusual sight – green-cloaked hunters climbing into trees in townspeople's gardens – but the Xantians are used to this.

A privilege of the Mage-Hunters – every door is open to them, every patch of garden – as old as the order itself.

'His landlady told me,' says Matthieu. 'The Paladins were waiting for him, snatched him as soon as he left his rented rooms.'

'Lucius's Flaming Finger.' While some of us choose to live at the Hunters' House, others choose to keep their own lodgings.

For obvious reasons.

That have to do with privacy.

The Temple's courtyard is now but a few dozen paces from

us. There's the sound of wood being sawn, the thud of heavy stones. The shouts of those who work on the building site. The Inquisitors are paying handsomely those who are helping repair the Temple, but even so, many of the local people were reluctant to take up work there. They were afraid to anger the Mothers of the Forest, and with a good reason. But now, even the Mothers are silent.

When Veliara Tannecy-Valmons was the High Priestess of the Hallowed Forest Covenant, things were different. But Veliara vanished a few years after the Order of the Inquisitors was established in the Green Kingdom, and the new High Priestess, Gelda, doesn't put up as much resistance to the High Inquisitor.

Hardly anyone does.

We stop at the entrance in the Temple's Courtyard, nine Mage-Hunters fanning around me. Two will stay behind, in a tree, or on a rooftop, just in case something goes awry.

To give them enough time to escape and sound the alarm.

I keep my orders short. 'Don't engage,' I say. 'Don't let them provoke you.'

We're lightly armoured. And, in the end, this is the Inquisitors' House. There are fifty or sixty Paladins, in all, or so my sources have told me. A force that wouldn't be hard to wipe out entirely from our kingdom, if our King was thus inclined.

But he would rather not incur Romannhon's wrath or draw too much of its attention. At least, that's what Claude told me. And he should know, as the Heir.

My sources also told me that the Inquisitors' House has dungeons that expand on three levels underground, stretching underneath the enclosed training grounds. The latter are surrounded by walls almost as tall as the Temple itself. I often wondered what it was about the Paladins' training that the High Inquisitor so desperately sought to keep hidden.

I suppose we're about to find out.

I step towards the courtyard with a confidence I don't feel.

The building site goes completely quiet, and the four Paladins guarding the House come up to meet us. They're heavily armoured – not in full gear, but they have enough steel on them to be hard to put down.

If it comes to blows.

I make my voice soft when I say, 'We would like to speak to the High Inquisitor.'

'He's not here,' says one of the Paladins. His face is hidden inside his half-helm, but his words have a chanted quality to them.

The Paladins aren't of the Green Kingdom. They don't visit drinking establishments, though women have been asked to visit the Inquisitors' House in the High Inquisitor's absence.

Those women are very, very reluctant to speak about what they saw there.

'We'll wait, then,' I say.

'I don't think so,' says the Paladin. He mutters something to his companions in the language of Romannhon.

I plant my legs widely, cross my arms. 'I'd like to see how you'll try to convince me otherwise.'

On the building site, work has ceased, and everyone is watching us.

'You have no right to be here,' the Paladin says.

'I do, according to the Hunters' Privileges.'

His face scrunches. Probably in disbelief. I doubt he's acquainted with the Hunters' Privileges, which say that we can step into anyone's private property, be it merchant or manufacturer or king, as long as we do so in the service of our duty.

And it's my duty to protect my fellow Hunters.

The door to the Inquisitors' House opens, and the High Inquisitor himself comes to join us, at a leisurely pace. His soft, dark blue cape has been pulled on top of a crumpled, white shirt.

Crumpled, *stained* white shirt. A few specks of blood stand out on the High Inquisitor's chest. There's no flicker of surprise on his face as he takes us in.

He was expecting us.

'I'm sorry for the interruption,' I say, pointing at his clothing. 'We don't want to keep you for long. Please return what belongs to us, and we'll be on our way.'

His smile is sharp. 'Ah, but then, I would be left without an occupation.'

I clench my fist so hard that if it weren't for my leather gloves, I'm sure my nails would have left marks in my own skin. 'You have no right to detain one of us. I'm afraid you are overstepping yourself. I'm afraid there will be consequences.'

He taps one of the Paladins on the shoulder and whispers an order. The Paladin returns to the house, his steps heavy.

'Oh, but I do. Since the moment your friend was careless enough to interfere with one of our operations, I have just the right.' His clothes might be crumpled, but his hair has carefully been combed to the back, his features arranged in cold amusement.

Nothing seems to ruffle this man.

I have never hated him more than I do now, and that says something, since I've hated him ever since the first time I laid eyes on him.

'You have no idea what you're doing by taking Remy,' I say.

'You have no idea what you're doing by refusing to work with me. By continuing to oppose me.' He narrows those odd eyes, green with a ring of gold. 'So stubborn. Such a lack of vision.'

Other things will be lacking if he goes on to provoke me. We might not be able to defeat all his Paladins, but I might not even need do.

I only need to land a good blow. I wonder how well he can wield a sword.

I wonder about that a lot, lately.

The Paladin drifts back from the house and hands the High Inquisitor a scroll. He wastes no time in shoving it under my nose. I read quickly.

Interference in the High Inquisitor's affairs... Right to inquire further into the matter... Permission to proceed as appropriate.

And underneath, with a flourish, the King's personal seal and his signature.

Bugger me with Lucius's Flaming Finger, this is the worst thing that could happen to us. This puts us under the authority of the Order of the Inquisitors, under their scrutiny. I wonder if our King knew what he was doing. And if Ullar had caught wind of this in advance.

The Mage-Hunters close ranks around me, fanned out in a half-circle, the ones to the edges so close to the Paladins that they almost touch.

I snarl, 'Where have you taken him?'

The High Inquisitor snaps the scroll shut, then glares behind my shoulder. 'That is, as this document says, none of your business. For now.'

I turn to look at what the High Inquisitor is staring at so intently. Relief is a palpable thing, a wave unclenching my stomach. Ullar is approaching.

Good.

Not that I was waiting for him to save me, but...

If knives are about to be flashed, which they are, it would save me a lot of explanations afterwards as to the 'how's and 'why's.

The Court Astrologist drifts to my side, laying a steadying hand on my arm. 'Is there a problem?'

'I don't know,' says the High Inquisitor, tilting his chin at me. 'Is there? We are only doing what we are entitled to do.'

I snort.

Entitled to do.

Ullar pulls at my arm. A silent question.

'They have Remy,' I whisper.

'I know,' he says. He snatches his eyes to mine, something dark and deep floating through them. A warning. 'That is why I'm here.'

'Then—' I say.

'We should go.'

'What?'

I think my own hearing is playing games with me. I think I'm utterly and completely wrong.

But the other Mage-Hunters stiffen, so they must be as shocked as I am. As incapable to make head or tail of what Ullar has just said, of what he's urging us to do.

'We must go,' says Ullar in his I-was-once-a-god-of-war voice. An order that has to be accepted without any question.

I follow.

Not because I'm weak, not because I don't want to call him out on his decision. Certainly not because I agree with him.

But there's something in the way his fingers dig into my shoulder that tells me there are things that he can't say here, not with the buggering High Inquisitor and his Paladins watching.

The Mage-Hunters follow us, too, without a single look behind.

I know the High Inquisitor has won today, and he knows it as well. I don't want to see that in his face.

As soon as we're out of that courtyard, I stop, pulling Ullar to a halt beside me. 'Is this a joke? Are we meant to leave Remy there, with him?'

'We don't know if Remy is in there,' says Ullar. 'And yes, today, we leave him. We can't make a single move without risking the King's wrath.'

If I had a copper for every single time Ullar has said this.

'Then we talk to the King.'

Ullar flashes a look at the Mage-Hunters gathered around us. 'I will. But you know how he is. Give me time. Until tomorrow.' His eyes say more than he can tell me.

Stand aside.

Don't interfere.

But I am past that. 'And if he refuses?'

'You're the *Erste Jägerin*,' he says. 'You're the only one who can fix this. Stand up for your people.'

I don't understand. 'If it's up to me, then why did you come here to stop me? That's what I wanted to do. To stand up for my Mage-Hunters.'

'There are steps to be taken,' Ullar says. 'If you want a piece of advice, I'd refrain from any rushed course of action. Wait until tomorrow.'

Rage flashes behind my eyes, white like a glowing iron, searing my skull.

'Until tomorrow? I'm meant to stand down until tomorrow?'

'You will, if you know what's good for you. And for Remy.' But he lays a hand on my shoulder and squeezes it as he says the words, in a gesture of support.

And dismissal.

After he leaves, the rest of the Mage-Hunters gather around me. In their faces, I see hope. Expectation.

I look back to the Inquisitors' House, wondering if the High Inquisitor is watching from a high window.

Laughing at our impotence.

This is enough to set my teeth completely on edge.

And I can't bear to watch, knowing that Remy might be inside, and—

'Let's go,' I say. 'We meet for breakfast tomorrow and decide what there is to do.'

* * *

My Mage-Hunters head for the Hunters' House and I realise that I can't bear the weight of disappointing them, not just now. I have nothing to say. No plan. No words of encouragement.

So I head in the opposite direction, not quite sure where I'm going, except away from them.

If there wasn't proof enough already that I'm inadequate to be the *Erste Jägerin*, I'm currently failing Remy, utterly and completely.

Stand up for your people, said Ullar. The same Ullar who wants me to go to the Blue Kingdom and leave the Mage-Hunters.

Not only that, but my sister wants me in the Red Kingdom, as well.

Everyone, everywhere seems to want me away from here. And then, I think, *My sister.*

I have a purpose now, at least.

A message to deliver.

The hall of the Phoenix Inn is stuffy and crowded and teeming with too-loud, too-drunk people. But as sure as an arrow, my gaze goes directly to Fabien. He would be hard to miss, with his bare arms in the middle of autumn, and that white, crinkled cloak.

He sits at a long table with a merchant, a few sailors – Xante is also a port on the Green River – and a few travellers whose business I'm not entirely sure of.

The Phoenix Inn is one of the pricier, more sought-after inns in Xante, with its open terrace that looks to the largest of Darg's Bridges, a construction that dates from the times when the Green Kingdom was just a province in the Romannhon Empire.

Nonetheless.

It's still too hot, and smells like onions, too many armpits and cheap liqueur. I can't wait to leave, even though I have nowhere to go to. Nowhere I want to be. Nowhere I can escape the fact that they are doing something to Remy and that there's nothing I can do about it, short of storming the Inquisitors' House with the entire Order of Mage-Hunters, which might not be a good idea, on the whole.

But coming here was also a bad idea. I'm preparing to leave when Fabien sees me, and is up from his bench, stalking towards me with a speed that I wouldn't have thought possible, considering that his movements look so lazy. I walk towards a side door that leads to the more private dining chambers.

In the common hall, there are too many people watching.

'You came,' he says, slipping after me into the narrow

corridor. His gaze brushes my dishevelled hair, and then takes stock of all the weapons I'm carrying. He seems to approve, not that his approval is something I need.

Nor is the fact that, apparently, he was waiting for me. Maybe he suspected I'd come?

This sets me on edge. I don't like people making assumptions about me.

I rummage in my leather sack and extract the message I wrote in haste the day before. 'There you go,' I say, pressing it into Fabien's hands.

He's so surprised that he instantly accepts it. 'What is this?'

'I did what I said I would. The message to my sister. I'm not coming. Now, off you go, on your way. *Bon voyage.*'

He crosses his arms, drawing himself up to his full height.

By Sabya, he is enormous. Taking up the entire threshold, blocking my way back to the inn's common hall.

'Don't you dare,' I say. I may be much smaller and probably a much less skilled fighter than he is, but in the blink of an eye, I can have a blade at his throat, with the help of my Gift.

I am always the best fighter in a room, no matter the room. No matter who is in it. Through my Gift, I can freeze anyone's movement, slice anywhere I want before they've even drawn their swords, or their daggers.

This thought alone prevents me from being afraid of anyone. Ever.

I may need to draw power from someone else for even small hops back in time, but I never need anything else for making time stand still.

Fabien narrows his eyes. 'I thought you wanted to go that

way.' He tilts his chin towards the heavy door at the end of the corridor, the one that leads outside.

And which is also a precaution for the guests who want more discretion.

'Right,' I say. 'I just don't appreciate you bristling at me. Goodbye, then.'

I am heading towards the aforementioned door when he says, more a growl than words, 'I don't appreciate you being rude to me.'

This stops me in my tracks. 'I'm not coming with you. And I see no reason whatsoever to be nice to you.'

'I see no reason whatsoever for you to disrespect me.'

I have much important matters on my mind. Like how the blasted High Inquisitor has Remy. Like why Ullar is so keen to be rid of me. In the past few days, the ground underneath me has become slippery and I feel that I'm teetering and about to fall very badly.

But Fabien is right. I don't know what it is about him that sets me on edge, makes me feel a bit agitated, a bit overheated.

He adds, 'You know, just like you, I don't take kindly to being ordered around.'

I give him a small appreciative nod because somehow ... he understands.

And I like him, perhaps a little bit, for that. Even if he's my sister's minion and I want nothing to do with her, or anyone from Langly, as a matter of fact.

'I wasn't ordered to be here.' He tucks the message at his waist, slipping it through his sword belt. 'I was asked if I wanted to come. I was given a choice. And I thought that you would be worth my time.'

I snort. 'Sorry to disappoint you.'

'Did you disappoint me?' he says and takes a casual step towards me.

Not towards me, I realise, but to lean on one of the doors to the private dining chambers.

And in spite of myself, I ask, 'Why did you think I was worth your time?'

He shrugs. 'You're the *Erste Jägerin* of the Mage-Hunters. I've never met a woman warrior.'

'Odd, don't you think? You honour Sabya above all in the Red Kingdom and she was a warrior herself, before she was Queen. And yet, in Lafala, women have less freedom than anywhere else. They're barred from so many professions. And somehow, your lot call *us* "backwards".'

'Ah, the vagaries of history.' He pushes open the door behind me. 'Many a war would have been avoided if women had been allowed to inherit just like the men, in the Red Kingdom.'

I crane my neck beyond him, to peer inside the dining chamber, and notice that it's empty.

This is an invitation, then.

'Don't make the mistake, though, of confusing my beliefs with the ones that are common in the Red Kingdom. You don't know me. You don't know what I think, or what I had to face.'

'So, is that why you're here, then?' I hiss. 'Many knights

have come from the Red and Blue Kingdoms, to face me in a fighting ring. I never accept.'

I don't have anything to prove to them. And I know I'd win, anyway.

'I'm not a knight,' he drawls. 'And that wasn't what I had in mind.' He gives an appreciative look at my ruffled shirt and then down to my tight cloth breeches, before lifting his gaze to search for something on my face.

My heart flutters with annoyance.

'You came all the way here. Can I treat you to some wine, at least?' He pushes into the room without waiting for me to reply.

The sheer arrogance.

I want to turn on my heel and leave, but I have nowhere to be, except alone somewhere, with my thoughts. So I follow him.

He tugs at the cord intended to alert the staff to our presence. A young man drifts into the chamber while we're settling across from each other at a small table.

'I'll have red wine,' I say, glancing at my broken nails. I'm still not sure what I'm doing here.

Fabien proceeds to order an assortment of ale and white wine, and enough cheese and fruit to feed four.

'Are we waiting for more guests?' I say.

He braces his arms on the table, the muscles snaking under his skin.

I wonder what he eats, exactly, to make him look like that.

'No, I just don't want us to be bothered later.'

'I'm not sure what you think this is.'

'Believe me,' he says carelessly, 'I have learned to forego any kind of expectations entirely. Especially of myself. It makes things so much easier.'

I snort. 'If only it was so easy. Consider yourself lucky.'

'No, it wasn't easy. But I persisted.'

He stares at me in that way again, as if he's soaking up every grimace I make, every gesture. 'Right,' I say, still wondering why I haven't left. 'What's this Red Kingdom emergency about?'

'If I told you, would you come?'

'Maybe,' I tease.

'What makes you think that I know?'

I stretch my legs, crossing them under the table. So this is how it's going to be. 'I have no reason to think that you don't.'

'Maybe I'm not trustworthy enough.'

'Saying that won't make me change my mind.'

'Would anything I say make you change your mind?'

'What is it to you?' I ask. He grins, all white teeth and arrogance, and I can't take my eyes off his mouth.

I shouldn't be here. I truly shouldn't.

'I'm here on a mission,' he says. 'I don't like to fail.'

'I thought you didn't have expectations.'

He gestures widely with his hands and I'm entranced by the way the muscles in his arms move. The fine dusting of dark hair. Something heavy settles deep in my belly. I shift to dislodge it, but it's still there.

'I'm a man of great contradictions,' he says.

The inn boy bursts into the room. He lays the feast that

Fabien ordered down in front of us. I help myself to some cheese.

I didn't even realise I was hungry.

This day has been … something. And I have yet to think of a way to help Remy. But I'm not even sure where the Inquisitors are keeping him.

Give me time, Ullar said.

Complete nonsense.

Tomorrow. If by tomorrow, at noon, there hasn't been a sign of him…

I'm not even sure what I'll do.

'What's wrong?' says Fabien, when we're alone again.

'Why would something be wrong?'

'You started stuffing cheese into your mouth as though you want to bite someone's head off.'

I chuckle. 'That's about right.' I'm half leaning over the table. We're much closer than we should be. The flaps of my leather vest have fallen wide open, and Fabien's gaze falls to my shirt.

My neck and face grow hot. I'm not shy. But there's something in the way he looks at me that's unsettling. 'If you were a knight, or chivalrous in any way, you'd pass that plate of cheese.'

He wraps his arm around it. 'Why would I do that? It's mine.' His eyes drift to my face. 'And I'm not a knight, either. I think I mentioned that already.'

'Who are you, then?'

'Someone very dishonourable, I assure you. You wouldn't want to keep my company.'

Fragments of what I know about the Red Kingdom and its denizens start falling into place. 'You were a part of the old duke's court, weren't you?'

He flicks an eyebrow. 'Old?'

'You know what I mean. The infamous Maël.' I pick a grape and rip it with my teeth. 'What would he make of you being such a good, faithful helper to my sister?'

'I believe Maël would be clever enough to realise that we all have to look after ourselves, first and foremost.'

'Do you write to him?'

'On the whole, we don't spend an awful amount of time mooning about each other.'

'So you *weren't* friends?'

He smirks. 'What's with this sudden interest in Maël de Langly? Would you care for me to arrange a meeting?'

I give him a thunderous glare. Ullar has been pushing me to go to the Blue Kingdom. I suppose this would give me the opportunity to meet Maël himself. I have to admit I'm intrigued about him, the infamous lion, robbed of his duchy, cursed to never again set foot in the Red Kingdom.

But no more curious than I am about every person I've heard spoken of so often that I feel I halfway know them. No more than I would be to meet Queen Valerie of the Blue Kingdom, or Count Goderic, or the new duke, Philippe of Langly.

Well, being honest, maybe I'm a bit more curious about Maël. He sounds positively dissolute and evil. It makes me wonder.

But I suppose I *could* meet Goderic and Philippe. I'm literally being handed the opportunity to do so.

I don't know anymore.

'Yes?' he says, expectantly.

'I just wanted to know where your loyalties lie.'

'You think your sister hasn't already made sure that they lie with her?'

I rip a piece of bread and drift back into my seat. 'I'm not sure,' I say. 'I don't know what sort of person she is.'

Fabien leans forward, closing a bit the distance that I've put between us. 'Would you like to know?'

I know what he'll say. That I have to come with him, if I want to find out.

'I can't leave now. There's plenty of trouble here.'

'The High Inquisitor, I suppose?' he says, flashing me a grin again. 'I saw that little token of your adoration in your receiving chambers. Though I'm not sure how wise it is, on the whole, to have it on display there, for everyone to see.'

A cold shiver crosses my spine. 'I'm not afraid of him.' As I say this, I know it's not entirely true. What I saw today, how much he dares to do, believing he can get away with it... The fact that he just might.

Remy, I think.

I have to find a way to get Remy out, without involving the entire order of the Mage-Hunters, and then I think, *I don't need to*. It would only take one to sneak by the guards, unseen.

One who would be able to whisk him out.

Bloody Ullar and his talking in riddles. I finally see what he meant to achieve by telling me that I have to stand up for my people.

I could do this on my own.

He also said, *Wait until tomorrow.*

'If you say so.' Fabien's voice jolts me back to the room. 'Were you dreaming about the High Inquisitor?'

'In a way,' I concede.

He snorts. 'You have odd tastes.'

'You don't want to know.' I rise to leave. I've dallied long enough and I won't find what I'm seeking here. I need to think. I need to plan. 'Goodbye, then,' I say.

It was nice meeting him, I suppose.

He says, 'She's nothing like you, you know.'

My sister, I think. He's talking about my sister.

I stop in the doorway, listening, hoping he won't notice how hungry I am for these details, knowing that he probably does.

'For years, she did nothing but host receptions at the Royal Palace – but she was never at the centre of them. The world almost forgot about her existence. In the end, she wasn't even half as important as her brother, the heir. Just a stubborn little thing who refused to marry. And then, she did.'

'Philippe,' I say.

'Yes, a man who everyone overlooked, as well. I think they were well matched, in that way. Everyone overlooked them.' His gaze grows steely.

'You know him well,' I say, a question as much as a state-ment. The new Duke of Langly must have seen something in this man, in order to employ him.

Or Fabien must have persuaded him that he can be trusted. Somehow.

I'm not sure that I would have trusted him, being in my

sister's position. A suspicion gnaws at me, which is that the man in front of me is hiding something.

Fabien says, 'Of course I do. I know everyone.'

I wonder what my sister saw in a man she'd barely met, to make up her mind to marry him so quickly. Within days, as the rumours go.

'But I won't bore you any longer, since you're clearly not interested.' Fabien says this with a grin. As if he knows the opposite is true. 'Have a lovely evening, *Erste Jägerin*.'

I drift out of the room, closing the door behind me, not quite sure what to make of anything he said.

HEIR TO THE KINGDOM

BLANCHE

*U*nsurprisingly, Mihiel's mind is shaped like the Royal Palace, and it looks just as busy as a day when foreign diplomats are visiting.

Many of them.

I use my other Gift, the one of mindwalking, to stumble through the tangle of chambers and inner gardens of his memories, trying to find him. This is the first of my Gifts I ever knew about. The first that I trained at the Golden Pavilion, under the careful guidance of the woman who served as doyenne at the time. I grew up as an odd, lonely child who suffered from much too vivid dreams, and it took years to realise that those dreams weren't my own.

That they were, in fact, other people's memories, which I could visit when I was sleeping.

And each of our minds is shaped differently. I drift

through King Mihiel's until I'm in the Curia Chambers. A faithful copy of the real chambers at the Royal Palace. I peer at the surface of the sea, at the hypnotising swish of waves, Lucius's Cliff glittering red in the distance.

When I was a girl, my brother used to stand on the throne at the end of the redwood table. Threatening and coaxing to use my Gift for his own purposes, to keep hold of a disintegrating reign. He made me spy on other people's memories for him.

And then, I made him pay. And sat for a while on that throne myself. Rose there with Robert's help. *What had been his purpose in all of it?* I wonder with a pang. Can I still trust everything my husband has ever done for me?

Mihiel's voice cleaves through my memories. 'Is this you, Blanche?'

He must have felt the disturbance in his mind. My own feelings filling these chambers.

I turn around to face him.

'Marchionessa?' says Mihiel, his voice commanding.

He does not look well, I realise. He is thin and swollen in all the wrong places.

He is sick.

'We need to speak,' I say, realising how urgent this is.

'Why was I expecting this?' He paces around the table to take his seat on the throne.

A move to establish where power lies in this room, no doubt.

Fine.

Let him.

'To what do I owe the pleasure of this visit?' he says.

'I know about your son. I'm sorry. You have my deepest condolences. I know what it is to lose a child.'

Mihiel flinches but manages to almost hide that behind a severe look. He must wonder how I know.

But my daughter Isabella tells me everything. And she is privy to all of Celine's secrets.

'Are you sorry, Marchionessa? Truly? If anything, I suppose this serves the interests of the Fallen Court more than anything.'

Not a good time to bring up Maël, then. Unfortunately, I have to. 'There is only one thing the Fallen Court is interested in, and you know what that is. Finding a way to defeat the Dark Mother. To ensure she does not escape, that she does not catch the Red Kingdom in her clutches again.'

'Excuse me if my own experiences encourage me to doubt that.'

'I was hoping we could work together,' I say. 'Like we did in the past. It is now more important than ever. The Dark Mother is stirring, Mihiel. We don't have much time. We never know when she might try to break the chains around her. We can't afford another bloody civil war. We'd be dead even before she breaks through the amber.'

'Of course you'd say that.'

I walk up to him. 'Just as you have kin that you want to protect, I have mine, as well.'

'Do you, Marchionessa? Don't you think your own kin is much better off, and safer, in the Blue Kingdom? I think the current state of affairs benefits everyone.'

So full of himself, always. So suspicious. But suspicion is something I have battled all my life, and it's not the impediment it once was. 'No, I think not. I think once the Dark Mother awakens, she'll want all of the Three Kingdoms. Red, Blue, Green, even beyond. You don't know her. What she wants. What she can do.'

And as a Necromancer, there's virtually no limit to her power. She has stolen plenty of it from mages five centuries ago. Used dark magic older than her, knowledge that I hope is now long forgotten, to bind other Gifts to hers. To make her so strong.

Almost unbeatable.

Almost. Until Sabya.

'Let's not beat around the bush, Blanche. You're not here to express your deep condolences. What do you want?'

I square my shoulders, stand tall. 'You need to lift the curses and the binding spells around Maël. You need him here, Mihiel. As your heir. You need to help him establish himself. We don't have much time.'

What's written on Mihiel's face is pure, undiluted hate. 'Ah, there it is. My son's body has not even gone cold and here you are, grabbing for power. I have another child, Marchionessa.'

'And you, my old friend, are sick. There is no more time for Celine to produce another heir. What will happen to the kingdom if you expire tomorrow? Is this the legacy you want to leave behind? War?'

'Maël has nothing to do with my own legacy. I offered him guidance.'

'You offered him a wife, and Celine wanted no part of it.'

'Oh, I don't think he wanted her, either. So, what *does* he want, Blanche?'

I don't answer because I don't think even Maël knows what he wants. He's still searching. Finding out who he is, if he's not the Duke of Langly.

Mihiel rubs his pointed beard. There's exhaustion in his eyes. 'He looks so much like him, doesn't he? Everyone feared Robert. We all knew what he was capable of. But Maël is too busy being angry at everyone to do the right thing. Robert had...'

Secrets, I think. And a difficult childhood out of which he had to claw himself. I know these things about my husband, and it hurts that there's so much more he still kept hidden from me. The turn of the conversation has made us both cranky and weary, I notice.

'You're not really opposed to Maël taking the throne, are you?' I say.

Mihiel sighs. The Fallen Court's dealings with the Red Court have always been so difficult. First with Mihiel's father, Charles, then with him. He inherited the weariness towards us.

'I only want what's best for the Red Kingdom,' I add.

Mihiel throws me an assessing glance. 'So do I. But I don't think we're thinking of the same thing.'

There is nothing left to say today, and we both know it, so I leave.

This is a game we've been playing for a long time, and now we both have to wait for the next round.

THE PRISONER

MIHI

I get out of my bed before dawn. I hardly slept. The hours of the night passed in a crazed succession, while I was, in turn, raging with myself for having done nothing to help Remy, worrying myself to tears about what the High Inquisitor might be doing to him. I'm determined – if Remy isn't returned to us by noon, I'll tear the Inquisitors' House down.

Make that by breakfast.

I dress in a hurry, rage and anticipation throbbing in my blood, making my fingers tremble while I sift through my weapons, choosing what I'll need today.

I settle for two daggers and a rapier, which I hone and oil and clean, over and over again, in my study. The wooden likeness of the High Inquisitor seems to taunt me, and on a whim, I decide to prepare my throwing knives, as well.

I wonder if Ullar could gain anything from the King.

It cannot be that the High Inquisitor can seize one of our own.

He has no power over us, he is overstepping himself, and if we don't push back now…

In fact, we should stab back, probably.

I want this to hurt so much that he shivers with dread every single time he throws a single glance in our direction.

I think about Claude.

If the King won't help us, perhaps Claude might. Perhaps it might be wiser to ask Claude to intercede for us, even before the King has the chance to refuse us.

I feel oily and smudged on the inside to think of using Claude like this, the remnants of affection he might still have for me. But there's nothing I will stop at for my Mage-Hunters, and that buggering High Inquisitor doesn't even know what he's started.

I toss the knives towards the wooden likeness of the High Inquisitor, aiming for his face. I will destroy him; I will annihilate him, but it's not enough, not enough, so I step up to the likeness and extract my daggers one by one, clattering them to the ground. No, a knife, that's too clean. I will instead tear him to pieces.

I grip the shoulders of the likeness and I don't care that rough splinters pierce the skin of my fingers as I grab it and hurl it across the chamber, where it crashes against the wall, not even denting the stone.

Not enough, it's not enough. I grab it again and smash the wooden High Inquisitor against the desk again and again and again. Splinters are flying about the room, and there's the hammering, and crack of wood against wood.

The head flies loose and crashes into the stack of books behind my chair, and my desk scratches and dents. Pieces of him break off and land with hollow thuds, until there's nothing but bits of wood remaining from his likeness, smeared by my blood.

The silence that ensues makes my ears ring and it's still not enough as I lean over the messy pile that remains of him. I spit on it.

'*Erste Jägerin?*'

I swirl around. In the antechamber, Matthieu is standing with a tall, bulky man, with leather vanguards on top of his bare arms.

Fabien.

'What are you doing here, at this hour?' I snap.

I'm certainly not in the mood for this.

'I suppose he's just doing his work, *Erste Jägerin*,' says Fabien, looking to my fellow Mage-Hunter. 'Aren't you, Matthieu?'

'Since when are you two so friendly with each other?'

I take a seat, sling my feet on the scratched desk. I pick up a random sword and the oiling cloth.

'There has been a problem with the message you asked me to deliver to your sister.' Fabien steps forward slowly, as if gauging my reactions.

'I don't have time for this.'

Matthieu gives Fabien a pat on the back, and withdraws, leaving this absurdly dressed man, who is here absurdly early, to crunch his specked boots on the remnants of the High Inquisitor's face, strewn on the threadbare carpet.

He gives a low, vicious whistle. 'Now this was a thorough job.'

'Not yet,' I say. I haven't even started. 'But it will be.'

Complications will arise, I know. The King doesn't want the Romannhon's attention.

They used to be an Empire, the Romannhon, but they crumbled under their own weight, a long, long time ago. The result of a fire that started in the Three Kingdoms, with Sabya, who pushed them back from our lands. Then other provinces overthrew them as well.

And when it was all over, the Romannhon were confined for many years to little more than the borders of their city. But fifty years ago, the High Priests of Mars rose again to tremendous power, calling the people to arms. They swallowed Genvive and Milena, powerful trading cities. They swallowed the entire peninsula around them. And now, not only do they command their own forces, but also bands of knights throughout many kingdoms, ready to go to war in the name of the true faith of Mars – the Paladins.

This is why we must proceed with care. With the Green Kingdom being directly to the south of the Red and Blue Kingdoms, and thus much closer to the Romannhon, we've been acting like a shield for them. The Green King fears too much interference from them in our affairs.

But when the High Inquisitor took Remy, he took it all a step too far.

As for 'working together'...

I'd spit again on the wood splinters, if Fabien weren't standing in the way. A dagger strapped to his right leg catches my eye and I look up from his thick thighs, straining against dark grey cloth, my gaze skimming the laces holding his breeches together, then higher up to his wrinkled shirt and the broad chest, hidden underneath.

That unfamiliar heat stirs within me again. I can't tell if the man is making me uncomfortable or if it's something else.

'Can I help?' he says. His lips are twisted in a smile. His dark eyes glitter with amusement.

He's buggering amused. 'What do you mean?'

He points at the oiling cloth and the sword I'm holding. 'You stopped. I thought you forgot what you were supposed to do.' My mouth opens at that, and I look down. I *did* stop. He goes on to say, 'You're supposed to rub. Up and down. Squeezing.'

I am this close to throwing the cloth – and the blade – at his face. 'Did you come in here to advise on rubbing?'

'Well, no, but I could do that, if that's what you'd like.' He drops his voice.

'Certainly not at this hour.' A wave of heat creeps into my belly.

He's unbelievable.

And I have no idea whatsoever how my sister stomachs him. She's rather prudish, I heard.

Fabien brushes a few splinters off the chair across me and sits down. It creaks under his weight. 'What incited this outburst of … feeling?' he says, picking up a bit of the High Inquisitor's wooden cloak and turning it around in his hands.

'Who said I'm feeling anything?'

'You seem restless today. The same as you were yesterday. Something happened. Did you change your mind about leaving with me?'

I roll my eyes. 'I'm not going anywhere with you.' I set down the sword, lean my elbows on the table. 'And why are you here? Why aren't you delivering the message to my sister, messenger boy?'

His grin turns a shade of vicious. 'I told you; I never do anything that I don't want to do. Not anymore.'

'What a coincidence. Neither do I.'

'And as I mentioned, there has been an incident with the message.'

My eyebrows jut up. 'An incident?' I exhale deeply through my nose, as if I could breathe flames through it. 'What. Sort. Of. Incident?'

'Your letter had an unfortunate collision with fire.' He shrugs. 'I will need a replacement for said message.'

What was my sister even thinking when she sent *him* to me? 'I don't appreciate being toyed with,' I say. 'Get out.'

Fabien relaxes into his chair, crossing his long legs at the ankles. 'I can't go to your sister empty-handed.'

'You will.' The absence of any message would be just the same as the message I had penned yesterday.

His gaze roves over my face, in that infuriating way of his. 'You truly want me to go? Today? Empty-handed?'

My answer is swallowed by the hard clank of boots, coming from the antechamber.

Matthieu comes in, followed by three more Mage-Hunters. '*Erste Jägerin*, they're here.'

I take in the stiffness in Matthieu's limbs, his wide eyes.

I jump to my feet before even asking, 'Who?'

Oh, but I hear them, the clank of metal on stone, even before they've rounded the corner. I slip one dagger in the sheath at my hip and one into my boot, just as the High Inquisitor and five of his Paladins push aside the Mage-Hunters, planting themselves in the middle of the antechamber.

They are dragging someone with them.

They toss their charge in the middle of the room, where he kneels, his crumpled shirt streaked with blood, its back soaked and brown and crusted.

I'm walking towards him before I even realise what I'm doing, before I even realise it's Remy.

Two long cuts crest his bruised face, an eye is swollen shut, and his thumbs are crushed in what I know is a particularly grim sort of torture.

If I could breathe right now, I would scream my lungs out.

A moment passes by. Two.

None of the Paladins moves, none of the Mage-Hunters. Remy rocks backs and forth, hugging himself, as if it could erase any of the horrors he has been through.

A day.

They've barely had him a day.

Rage is a living thing within me when I think of what they've done to him, of what they do to the mages they catch.

Not that I hadn't seen the signs.

'It surely stinks like turd in here,' says Fabien in a grumbling voice.

The High Inquisitor lifts his head, a look of surprise on his face before he quickly brushes it aside and replaces it with his mask of coolness. 'Look who the tide dragged in.'

I kneel in front of Remy.

His entire face is streaked with dried blood and tears. 'Can you get up?' My voice is trembling.

I am trembling.

My gaze locks with the High Inquisitor. He raises his eyebrows, as if challenging me to make my next move.

I'll kill him for this.

He crossed the last line that kept me within the boundaries of decency.

I don't care when, I don't care how, but he *will* die by my hand.

Remy nods, slowly, and I extend my fingers towards him, when I realise that it might not be enough to help him up, but I'm not sure where I can grab him, so that it won't hurt.

Hot tears fill my eyes.

'If I were you, I'd ask someone else to do that.' The High Inquisitor's voice is low. As if he's about to whisper a secret.

Fabien shuffles behind me.

'What?' I bite out.

'Take her,' says the High Inquisitor, and before I can make a single move, two Paladins are upon me, restraining my moves.

'What do you think you're doing?' I say, just as the Mage-Hunters draw whatever weapons they have upon them. 'You don't want to do that. Not here,' I say to the High Inquisitor. Only a few of us might be in the room, but there are far more in the dormitories above, bound to be awakened by the racket.

'Oh, but I think it's your Mage-Hunters who don't want to do that. Attacking the Order of the Inquisitors, I mean.' The High Inquisitor pushes his cloak aside, visibly irritated. Whatever he's about to do, it sets him on edge.

But he hasn't seen what being on edge means.

He hasn't seen me.

I take in the two Paladins holding me by my wrists. Their iron-gloved hands are like manacles. A simple time-hop and I'd be out of their clutches as quick as lightning, but there's a risk: showing the High Inquisitor what I am.

What they would call a 'witch'.

Precisely the sort of person they're hunting.

I nod to Matthieu. 'Get Ullar. Now.'

'Don't move,' says the High Inquisitor. 'I think you'll want to hear this.'

'Let me go,' I say. 'You have no idea what you're doing.'

'Put your steel down,' says the High Inquisitor to my Mage-Hunters. 'Your friend Remy told me something very interesting during the time we spent together. Did you know that your *Erste Jägerin* is a witch?' He takes them all in, and my heart starts pounding, pounding, pounding. I know I'm beginning to lose.

I may have already lost, if I didn't—

'A lie,' I say. 'Extracted under torture.'

'Then you'll have no objection to coming with me, Anne-

Mihielle, to prove your innocence. Will you? Even the King has agreed to this.'

The King has agreed to this.

Before I can even take in the magnitude of what is happening, the High Inquisitor nods. One of the heavily armoured Paladins sweeps my feet from underneath me. I land hard on my knees, just as he presses his boot of steel into my back.

Pain is so immediate and sharp that I can't stifle a cry. And yet.

'Let her go,' says Matthieu, who definitely hasn't gone to fetch Ullar. 'You are in our House, High Inquisitor. More of us will come. You can't get out of this alive.'

In front of me, Remy has resumed his rocking, breathing quiet words. 'I'm sorry, I'm sorry, I'm sorry, he knew, he knew, he knew.'

'I do think I can get out of this alive,' says the High Inquisitor. 'The rest of my Paladins have surrounded this building. And as I've said, I've already alerted the King that the Mage-Hunters are harbouring a witch. What do you think will happen to the Order, once your King hears that you were all conspiring?'

No one can hear about this.

We can't risk the entire Order of the Mage-Hunters. And the lives of the people we help.

Not even I am so valuable.

No one is.

Time seems to stand still for a moment, while so many fates hang in the balance.

Everything I've ever worked for, my entire life.

I snap my eyes to Matthieu's. 'Stand down. All of you. Right now.'

Uncertainty drifts across their faces. Followed by anger.

'Stand down,' I shout. 'I command you to. I'll go with him.'

The High Inquisitor shakes his head. 'You might think this gives me pleasure, Anne-Mihielle, but I do *not* want to be here any more than you do. I just wish you'd listened to me, that you agreed to cooperate when I asked you to.'

'Bugger you,' I say. 'Tell them to let me go. I'm coming with you.'

'Not until your men stand back,' says the High Inquisitor.

I shout my order again. 'Put down your weapons.'

Reluctantly, they do. Something breathes in relief inside of me, just as something else constricts to the point of pain. That Paladin digs his steel boot harder into my back – a warning.

I can't risk making a move inside the Hunters' House. I can't risk the High Inquisitor believing that the Mage-Hunters know what I am. I can't risk revealing to the world that what we seem to do is just a charade, so we can do our work in the shadows.

I can't risk people thinking that the Mage-Hunters knew there was a mage among them.

I can't risk exposing the entire order, even if it means that, today, I have to give up the fight.

Or move it somewhere else, far from the Hunters' House.

'Good,' says the High Inquisitor. 'Now, get her out of here.'

Two of the Paladins snatch at my wrists, pulling me up and then forward, towards the open door. The others lead the way, leaving the chamber ahead of us. I'm almost in the corridor, just behind the High Inquisitor, when everything happens at once.

There's the drag of heavy furniture on the stone floors, and I snap my head back to see Fabien, half-forgotten, dragging my heavy desk towards the door. The man does have the strength of a lion.

'Get your dirty hands off her,' he says in a rumbling voice. 'Now.'

Mothers of the Forest, he's clutching a small crossbow. I have no idea where he had it hidden. It's not mine, that's for sure.

The notched bolt is pointed at the High Inquisitor.

'Didn't you hear, Mage-Hunter?' says one of the Paladins restraining me. 'She told you to stand down.'

'I'm. Not. A Mage-Hunter,' says Fabien, as if stating an obvious fact to a child. He swishes his cloak with his free hand, the Lioness of Langly rippling. 'Your leader knows that.'

The High Inquisitor gives Fabien a pointed stare, then turns to his Paladins. 'Ignore him. Let's go.'

But my head is still angled towards Fabien, even though it hurts to do so, and I catch the quick look he gives me, roving between the two Paladins restraining me. He squeezes his eyes shut – a signal – and then he fires the first bolt, changing his aim at the very last moment.

It catches the Paladin to my left in his thigh, and he crumples in pain and surprise.

I shout again, 'Stand down, Mage-Hunters,' before I do a time-hop, without even thinking.

The moment freezes within my grasp, while I free myself

from the second Paladin's clutches. His hand is like a solid chain around my wrist, so I reach for the dagger at my waist, prying his steel gauntlets off with the blade, careful so that it doesn't slip and I don't stab myself in the process.

I'm standing just inches from the High Inquisitor now, his eyes on me, that odd colour, green with a circle of amber. Even though he can't see, and he won't remember this.

I could kill him now and end it.

I could kill him now and start a huge debacle that will involve the entire Green Kingdom, the Romannhon and the Mage-Hunters.

Lucius's Flaming Finger.

I can't do this. Not today, not here.

I shouldn't have even tried to escape.

But there's no going back, not anymore. I can't excuse my way out of this fight.

I curse between my teeth just as time begins to flow again. The Paladin wiggles the hand that was encircled around my wrist moments ago.

The High Inquisitor's expression shifts to something vicious. I slam the door in his face. A bolt whooshes by my ear, digging into the wood.

Fabien had been aiming for the High Inquisitor. Had I been slower by just an instant— But I can't afford the complications that would come with his death. 'Leave him,' I mumble. 'Not here.' I jump behind the desk, trying to push.

Mothers of the Forest, it's heavy.

Fabien stares at the shut door, sheer disbelief on his face.

'Help me,' I say, and he leaps next to me, incredibly swift for someone of his size.

Together, we ram the desk into the door, and he brandishes his crossbow to break the window behind me. I pick up one of the unsheathed swords from the desk.

'That was fast,' he says, just as I clamber out into the courtyard.

It's not a long way down, since my study is on the ground floor.

There are shouts and thuds in the antechamber, and the now-sealed door quakes and quakes.

'What was that?' says Fabien, assessing me. 'What did you do?'

'Later,' I say. 'To the stables. We need horses.'

I'm running, but my mind stops to wonder whether he's ready to come with me or not, why he would do such a thing, what possessed him to even interfere.

Later, later, later.

There's no time for that now.

'We'll need saddled horses,' he says, pulling at my sleeve, turning me from my path. 'I wager they came with some.'

I follow him as we round the building and reach the front yard of the Hunters' House.

There's a carriage, painted dark blue, and five horses gathered around it.

Three Paladins are guarding them.

Fabien nudges me with his elbow, pointing at the Paladin to the far left, clearly signalling me to take him out, while he unsheathes his longsword, getting ready.

But they must have been warned, must have been waiting for us.

For me.

They try to dart past Fabien, but he is upon two of them instantly, deflecting and landing blows almost simultaneously.

I draw the third one aside, slashing and parrying. But there's only so much I can do without proper armour in front of a killing beast that came here ready for battle. It's clear to me when I parry one of the blows that I can't sidestep and my shoulder aches with the effort.

I shouldn't take unnecessary risks, I know this. Not after the little display I gave inside, which undoubtedly confirmed the High Inquisitor's suspicions about my Gift. But it's either this or face death. And I cannot risk Fabien's life, too. It's not his fault he was caught in this stupid cross-fight.

He dodges one of the Paladin's blows, trying to land another one, and earning a slice on his bare arm for the effort.

When I look up again at my own opponent, all I can see is the naked gleam of the blade, coming down upon me.

Enough.

I stop time, slide my hand quickly to the exposed bit of skin on the underside of the man's jaw. I send a small ripple of power, just to make sure that, should I happen to kill him by accident, it won't cost me my own Gift.

No shiver of power answers to my ripple, so I strike the side of the Paladin's helmet with my sword, hoping it will be enough to knock him out. I look to the horses, already deciding which to untie, and then finally spare Fabien a full look.

He's frozen mid-motion, his longsword held with both of his hands, his upper body tilted forward, ready to give a blow to the Paladin to his left. His features are contorted in cold violence, an odd focus making his eyes shine.

I shudder. That's a mountain of strength, all intent upon destruction. He's beautiful, in the way that a deadly weapon is. Those flexed muscles, the power uncoiling in his body. With the untamed beauty comes a warning not to come too close.

And yet, when I think of it, he does this for me, all for me, to protect me. He had no business interfering, and yet, here he is, lifting his sword, blood trickling down his own arm, the price that defending me has already exacted.

I swerve by him, brushing his shoulder lightly, a touch he'll never remember. I'm already upon the other Paladin, the one who is aiming for Fabien's exposed underside.

I sweep the Paladin's feet from under him to ensure that the blow he was preparing for Fabien will never fall.

I allow time to flow again, gripping the horses' reins. Behind me, the two Paladins I struck fall to the ground with dull thuds. Fabien lands the blow he had been preparing for when I froze time, and looks frantically around, as if he can't piece together what has happened.

'Later,' I tell him, motioning him towards the horse.

He hops into the saddle while I mount mine and we dart in the direction of the city gates. We gallop down the still-quiet streets. I take the lead. The wind snaps at my braid, which is falling loose.

'Where to?' he says.

'Southern Gate,' I reply.

'And then?'

I twist my head to watch him, half keeping an eye on the road ahead. What he has done for me today … very few have done before.

I'm not used to being rescued.

My heart is pounding in my chest, and we are still far from safety.

'I'll tell you,' I say, 'when we're out of the city. You can decide then if you want to come with me or not.'

He laughs, low and loud. His dark locks are bouncing about his head and he seems oddly amused, even though we just had a brush with death. 'And here I was, hoping that *you* would finally agree to come with me.'

BROOD

BLANCHE

I should go to Bluefort, to check on Hugo's progress on the contract I gave him, but Sabya is already at my throat because I spend so much time using my Gifts to roam outside of the cave, instead of doing what I was meant to do when I stepped into the heart of the Opal Mountain.

When I left my children and my duchy.

For thirty-four years, I have helped keep the Dark Mother contained in her boulder of amber. This is the price I had to pay for Sabya's help during the battle against my brother.

'She's about to be set free, anyway,' I say. There's only so much we can do with Lightsongs. 'We'd better use the time we have to prepare the Three Kingdoms for her coming.'

Sabya, the ancient goddess that the Three Kingdoms revere, mumbles something in her ancient tongue. She thinks I don't understand, but I can catch most of it by now, after all these years. She grumbles about my flitting to the outside world and enjoying it too bloody much.

Inside the boulder, the Dark Mother swirls, a creature made of shadows. I can never make out her shape or her face, just a glimpse, here and there. The glint of honey-coloured hair close to the surface.

There isn't much in the cave – a throne on which Sabya sits when she rests, a bed of furs in the corner where my physical body sleeps, almost frozen in time, and the boulder. The torches glow eerily, play games with the shadows.

It's where I was trapped until about a decade ago, when I learned to wield my Gifts to contact the outside world, my Fallen Court. When I was able to start looking after my grandchildren, however I could.

It wasn't much.

But if I hadn't honoured my promise, the Dark Mother would have been released, and would have probably wiped us all out. Including me and my children.

'You haven't left yet,' says Sabya, moving her weight from one foot to the other. Her golden armour clinks. 'What a surprise. Usually, if I say something, you ignore it.'

'Liar,' I mutter under my breath.

Sabya stretches. Her long, dark braid swishes from side to side. Sometimes, she barely moves for weeks in a row. She has been doing this, singing Lightsongs to keep the Dark Mother tethered, for centuries. I wonder if she feels it was worth it.

'What was she like?' I say, my ghostwalking self moving closer to the amber.

What I know for sure is that, in the beginning, the Dark

Mother used to be a Mother of the Forest. The land gifted her with tremendous power and she gifted the land back with her care.

Sabya puffs her cheeks and her deep brown eyes fill with sadness. 'At first, people thought she was a blessing. She used her powers to overthrow the Romannhon from the Walde-mannen territories – what are now called the Three King-doms. She was pretty. So delicate, so pretty, and she used that to her best advantage.'

There's a bitterness to her tone when she says this. Sabya is also delicately built – much shorter than me, with a long, narrow face – yet no one would mistake her for anything but a warrior.

And yet, according to the legends, she loved. She loved very, very much. She loved the man who rescued her from death, the man who taught her how to fight. Darg, a powerful god that had taken to living in the woods. And what she achieved, it was mostly done with him – until he betrayed Sabya for the Dark Mother, on the last battlefield.

I only have to think of Robert and how I can no longer trust a single word he says to me, and I realise how much that must have hurt Sabya.

'Did you truly love him?' I say, already steeling myself for a verbal set-down from the goddess.

I have never dared ask before.

'I needed him so much sometimes that I felt I couldn't breathe if he wouldn't touch me. If he didn't look at me. We spent years in the woods, Mindwalker. Years, just me and him. And I didn't want for anything else. For anyone. I thought…'

Her eyes are fire. 'And what he did, in the end... You have no idea what he's done. I promised him a dagger through the heart, if I ever found him again. And I will deliver it. Make no mistake.'

There's so much pain in her voice, that it nearly breaks.

I will deliver it? I thought that she already had. All the stories say that she killed Darg, in the end, but I can't interrupt to ask.

Sabya shudders, her armour clinking with the movement. 'But you were asking about the Dark Mother. Once the Romannhon were out of the way, there was no one left to oppose her. Lucius tried, but everyone was frightened of her.'

I frown. 'Lucius? The Enlightened one? The King of Kings?'

She snorts. 'He couldn't even hold a candle to her. Do you know what she could do?'

I shake my head. This is what I was asking. I don't know what's truth, and what's legend.

'She was foremost a Necromancer. She revived creatures that roamed our lands so many years ago, that it's impossible for me to understand. Those giant lizards with wings. She found nests and nests of them, preserved, close to the Opal Mountains. She called them Nightdragons. And then, she used them to bite off the heads of the ones who displeased her.' Sabya's voice never waivers. 'And it was very easy to displease her, at the end. Because she was so powerful, she'd gotten it into her head that it was her divine right to rule. And so she did.'

Sabya rubs at her face. I'm shocked and sickened by what

I'm hearing. 'I heard the Nightdragons couldn't be defeated,' I say.

'No, not with usual weapons. But I was gifted the Morningstar, and … there was a pulsing core of power in that weapon. And I used it to bring down Nightdragon after Nightdragon.'

'But now, it has vanished,' I say.

Sabya shrugs. 'I wouldn't know. That is something you might want to make a contract of, Marchionessa. We might need that weapon, at the end. It might come in handy.'

I make a mental note to do so. 'And then? Once the Nightdragons were taken care of?'

Sabya begins to tick points off her fingers. 'She had used ancient spells to bind other mages' Gifts to her, so she could use them. To tremendous pain for the mages, of course.' She ticks off another finger. 'She crossed other mages with animals, creating what we called half-creatures. Among them, the Flussen.'

The people of the Lakes.

The Mervolk, who can transform – and must transform regularly – into their half-fish shapes, or they die. The Flussen are now limited to a few underwater villages in the Blue Kingdom.

'How can one even cross a person with an animal?'

'She needed mages with a special Gift, called Heart-Flower. I don't want to even start telling you what she did to them.'

'Do you truly think she'd try to gain power for herself again?'

Sabya snorts. 'As true as I know myself. I told you, she

considered it her divine right to rule. To show the way to the Waldemannen. And trust me, that is precisely what she'll set herself to do, once she's free.'

Unless we find a way, I think.

Unless we find a way to kill her.

But how can you kill someone who is permanently attuned to the land, who never ceases to draw strength from it?

HALLOWED FOREST

MIHI

'Will you tell me now where we're going?' says Fabien in a bit more than a whisper.

I take in the sounds around me, birds chirping, rustles in the crowns of the trees above us. Brittle light shining in swishing mosaics of shadows on the ground. We have been in the forest for hours, having veered from the roads the first moment I saw a patch of woods.

Maybe we're finally lucky on this blasted day and the Paladins didn't send pigeons with messages across the kingdom to sound the alarm, to send people hunting for us, looking for us at every crossroads and on every path. Maybe we gained a bit of time, but soon we'll be the most sought-after people in the Green Kingdom. I wish them good luck finding us, though.

Finding someone in the Hallowed Forest is as good as searching for a particular straw in a haystack.

Not a needle. Needles are metallic and can prick, but a straw can disguise its own essence with the hay's. The stalk and the blade of grass, that's what the forest and I are.

When I first came to the Green Kingdom, I spent months and months roving the Hallowed Forest with my grandmother and Gwenhael, before I was placed in the hands of a man – a god – I barely knew. But while I was here, I learned to look and listen and blend in, how to move without overturning even a leaf.

And then, much later, Ullar taught me how to use the Hidden Paths, to move swiftly over great distances. I'm relying on this to shake our pursuers off.

All sorts of beasts roam the Hallowed Forest. Aurochs, packs of small, particularly vicious wolves, grey bears... The list can go on and on and on.

That's the one place where not even the High Inquisitor would dare look for us.

I hope.

'Princess?' says Fabien, leaning forward on his horse. 'Did you think about my suggestion?'

His suggestion.

What he wants.

To whisk me away from here.

I take in the slightly harsh corner of his jaw, the stubble that peppers it. The almost-smiling tilt of his lips. Under my skin, I'm all thrumming blood, swirling thoughts.

Today has been a nightmare. Whenever I blink, I see

Remy's bloodied face before my eyes, his haunted look. The disbelief on my Mage-Hunters' faces when I told them to stand down. It happened so fast, too fast, and thank the Mothers of the Forest for that. If it hadn't, if one of them had lifted their sword to defend me…

'I'm not a princess,' I say. My voice is clogged with the tears I won't allow myself to cry. I might have managed to escape, but what I left behind…

I dread to think of it.

The Mage-Hunters will have to deny that they ever knew about my Gift.

They'll have to at least pretend that they're doing all they can to find me and deliver me to the Inquisitors.

'Enough,' says Fabien, and pulls his mount to a halt. He sits in the saddle like nothing could ever knock him off a horse. 'I need to know where you're taking me. You can't expect me to follow you blindly into the forest. I barely know you.'

A lick of fire swoops through my blood. 'And yet, you expected the same of me, when you arrived in Xante.'

Fabien is unimpressed. 'I wasn't trying to lead you into the dead of woods. I merely wanted you to come with me to Greenport.'

'Fine, then.' I lift my hands, pointing to the trees all around us. 'Welcome to the Hallowed Forest. The last bastion of the Golden Covenant of the Mothers. This is where they withdrew when the High Inquisitor was sent here by the Romannhon to preach the faith of Mars. The Forest is the domain of the Covenant.'

At least it has been since Gelda took over as High Priestess.

Before that, the entire Green Kingdom belonged to the Mothers.

Fabien narrows his eyes at me. 'I wasn't looking for a history lesson. Tell me where we are.'

I don't know how to explain.

If the Green Kingdom were a living thing, the woods would be its heart and all its blood vessels. They spread throughout the kingdom, from the edges of the Glittering Sea to the Mothers' Mountains, drawing a protective ring around Xante.

There are two ways to move within the Kingdom: on the roads, and within the woods, but the latter is reserved for the Mothers of the Forest and a few other inhabitants who had no choice but to brave the Forest. In the end, it's the perfect hiding place, if you don't value your life too much. Or, if said life is literally forfeited outside of the woods. I'm thinking of the people who hide here: criminals, adulterers, maybe the odd Necromancer.

One I'm extremely familiar with.

'I still have a boat in Greenport,' he says. 'Waiting for us. Where else would you go, Princess?'

'I'm not a princess,' I explode.

'Really? If you're not a princess of the Red Kingdom, what are you, then? You're not *Erste Jägerin* anymore, that much is clear.' He lifts his left shoulder and rolls it, grimacing.

'Stop twisting the knife in my wound,' I nearly scream.

I have lost my home, my position, my everything. I'm in danger of even losing my life. And there's only one place where I can think of scurrying with the tail between my legs.

He spurs his mount, drawing in line with me. 'Not thinking about it doesn't help, Princess. Not looking the ugly truth in the face. As soon as you're done with it, you can move forward. You can look to whatever else there is.'

His words hit the mark harder than he could ever know.

Everything I ever worked for. Everything I was ever good at. My place, which I'd worked so, so hard to carve, so that I might never find myself adrift.

Gone, all gone in a moment.

And I am left alone, with nowhere to go.

I take the unshed tears and twist them into anger. I can't fall apart and cry. I need to... I need to find a safe place. Though I'm not sure there is one for me.

However, he has no right to lecture me. 'What would *you* know about losing everything?'

Fabien gives me a bitter laugh. 'Would it matter how I know? Stop feeling sorry for yourself and move forward.'

And to my endless chagrin, the arrogant bastard actually nudges my mount to start moving at a leisurely pace.

I let out a string of curses. Who does he buggering think he is?

'That's right. Move forward,' he says.

I turn around to glare at him, and then I notice the blood trickling down his arm. I remember how he rolled his shoulder, moments ago. I hiss under my breath. 'You're hurt.'

'It's nothing,' he says.

I bring my mount to a halt, scout the surroundings. There's a fallen log, not far away from us. There's a creek just beyond it. 'We should stop.'

'Why?'

'To water the horses.'

Foolish big man and his foolish pride. He acts like nothing can touch him.

I've lost enough on this day. I don't need to deal with his stubborn pride on top of it all.

I jump down from the saddle, lead my mare towards the creek. By the time he has joined me, I've tied my horse and I'm rummaging through the saddlebag. There's not much in there – the Paladin, whose mount this was, didn't expect to be gone for long today – but there *is* a pair of breeches.

They seem clean. They'll have to do.

I snatch the reins of Fabien's horse from his hands. 'Sit down,' I say.

He is hurt. He is hurt and he didn't say a thing. After what he's done for me.

Saving my life and all that.

I suppose I could be nicer to him. I could try, at least. It's not his fault that I lost everything.

I lead his horse to the water. 'We're going to see my grand-parents,' I say.

By Sabya's Darkblades, how much it costs me to admit that.

It's one of the places I'd sworn never to return to after I'd been cast away. And now I'm bound to go back as a failure.

Fabien finally sits down on the log, stretching his legs ahead of him. 'Mathilde de Champy, is that right? And Gwen-hael of the Tower.'

I snap my head towards him. 'You've heard about them?'

He snorts. 'I'm sure you don't know this, but they're some-thing of legends in the Red Kingdom. Part of the Tale of the Red Maiden and all that.'

I wonder if the stories say why they had to hide in the Hallowed Forest. They're neither criminals, not adulterers. They want to have nothing to do with the priestesses.

So that leaves precisely one reason why they had to hide.

I don't like it when outsiders see my grandfather. But so many years have passed, and maybe Fabien won't realise what he is. Maybe he'll assume that the … changes in him are due to old age.

It's not as if I have much of a choice, at this point.

'Where do they live?' he says.

'In the part of the woods close to Fiburg.'

He seems to ponder. 'We'll need days to get there.'

'I know shortcuts through the forest,' I tell him. *Magical shortcuts*, is what I don't say. If I sing the right Lightsongs under my breath, he won't even know how I'm opening the secret pathways for us. 'We'll be there by nightfall.'

'Did I mention that I have a boat waiting for us in Greenport?'

I rip the Paladin's breeches in two.

'I'll take that for my answer,' he says.

I dip one half of the breeches into the water, then stalk back towards him, stopping at the last moment, before laying a hand on his arm. This is the first time we've ever touched. Fabien tilts his head towards me, staring at my skin on his. My much smaller hand with broken nails, on his dust-coated, dried-and-fresh-blood-covered arm.

We're far from perfect. A bit broken, a bit battered, a bit weary of it all.

In some inexplicable way, it fits. I feel it to the marrow.

I flap my mouth open and closed before I say, 'Show me. Your wounds.'

I want to see more than the blow he received today on my behalf. This is also about what he said, not long ago, about moving forward. That knowledge came from *something*.

He looks up, and then I see myself reflected in his eyes. It takes my breath away. The Mihi who stares back at me is as bright as the sun and as dark as the deepest night. She's made up of contradictions that shouldn't exist. She's a bit brave and a bit frightened, falling apart and keeping it all together. And at her core, there's something stubborn and resilient.

It seems as if the ground tilts underneath me, but hasn't the rug already been pulled from underneath my feet today? Fabien feels that, somehow, and lays a steadying hand on my waist. He reaches out with his other hand towards the flask at his hip.

'Here,' he says. 'I think we've been riding hard, for longer than we realised.'

I lower my eyes and gratefully accept the flask. I can't look anymore at the way he sees me. It's overwhelming. It's too much.

Once I pass him the flask back, I push aside the cloak while he's busy drinking, and examine the gash on his shoulder. His eyes fly open, and he tries to bat me away.

'Tsk,' I reprimand. 'Don't be such a child.'

I touch the moistened breeches to his skin, careful to avoid the gash, cleaning its fringes of dried blood. I try not to think too much of the sheer girth of his arms, the hard, unyielding flesh underneath.

Mothers of the Forest.

I'm losing my mind.

'I won't be able to sew it shut now,' I say. 'I don't have the tools.'

Fabien doesn't say anything, doesn't even move, but I feel the weight of his stare.

To direct my thoughts on a different course, I begin chanting a healing Lightsong. It won't close the wound, but it makes its edges come closer, staunching the bleeding. Helps it crust over enough for him to be able to ride.

When I'm done, I pull the cloak back over it.

'You're a Light-Cantor?' says Fabien, his thick eyebrows scrunching.

Of course, he'd know plenty about the Gifts – he comes from the stock of Red Kingdom high nobility. He is also my sister's Captain of the Guards. This is something I need to remind myself of.

I clear my throat. 'Not exactly. But Ullar always said that I had a bit of a Cantor side to my Gift.' Spell-Sunderer, that's what I also am. But spells are forbidden in the Red Kingdom, and this is ground that doesn't need to be trodden right now.

'Like Sabya. And Blanche of Langly,' he says.

I whip my head up. Ullar had mentioned Blanche a few days ago, too. And he'd always had a somewhat unhealthy obsession with Sabya, I suppose.

Well, look at this. I left Xante, after all, just as he asked me to. I wonder what he's making of what happened to me.

Fabien's voice is low, like trying to soothe a startled horse. 'Ullar is the Court Astrologist, yes?'

I chuckle. 'Among other things.'

'And the … other side to your Gift? You can move very fast, can you not?'

'Or time slows for me,' I say teasingly.

'Time-Hopper?'

That, exactly. The question is cutting a bit too close to the bone. There isn't much that escapes his notice. And I'm a bit frightened by what he sees.

I take a step back, tilting away, but he stops me with a hand on my waist. The move is controlled, but powerful. Someone who knows what he wants. He makes me want to look at him when he says, 'What are you running away from, really?'

'I'm not running,' I say dryly. 'I was trying very hard to stay put. The High Inquisitor had other ideas today.'

He pulls me into the heat of his body, between his open thighs. I feel like I want to sink my teeth into something. He smells like steel and leather and something wild. My hands move of their own accord to his shoulders, the touch light, but steadying.

My eyes take in his face, the hint of stubble, the hard line of his jaw. I'd like to trace it with my fingers.

I'd like to trace it with my tongue.

Frightening, all of this. I'm not thinking clearly.

I should.

'Why did you interfere for me today?' I ask.

If he hadn't, maybe I wouldn't be here. I would have slipped out of the Paladin's grip somewhere on the way to the Inquisitors' House. Or in the House itself.

But what's done is done. I wonder if I could have done anything differently, in a way that wouldn't have landed me here. I wonder, if I turned back time and changed my course of action, where I would be right now.

'I don't back away from fights. And I made a promise,' he says. 'To keep you safe.'

To my sister? That's sobering.

I try to pull away, but his grip on me tightens in a way that knocks the breath out of my chest. His eyes trace the lines of my face and stop on my lips.

Mothers. Of. The. Forest.

I can't help the way I tilt forward, my lips brushing against his. The touch is tentative. He pulls me closer, my chest flush to his. My hands fly up, spread on the burning skin of his neck.

And Fabien, he begins devouring me. Our lips slide against each other, and it's a fight in itself. Who can be hungrier. Who can take more. A brush of tongue, and his mouth opens for me. But his other hand lifts to my nape, angling my head for him. This is deeper, harder, more desperate than anything I've ever experienced. Like we're trying to crawl under each other's skin.

Soft, teasing brushes of tongues. Deep, hungry ones. Heat spreads through my limbs, pools deep in my belly. The back of my knees feel weak. My hands fly into his hair, pulling. His hand drifts lower, squeezing my behind. I arch into him, rubbing my aching breasts to his chest.

This is madness. This isn't like anything I've ever experienced.

It's terrifying in its intensity, in what I'm ready to allow him to do. What I want him to.

I can't lose my grip on myself like this. I can't, I won't, not when everything has fallen apart today.

I have no control of anything anymore, except perhaps myself, and I claw hard to get it back. I push against him, suddenly breaking the kiss.

I turn around, unable to look at him. Because I'm tempted to pick up where I broke off, and I can't, if I want to keep a grip on my sanity.

So I head the other way, and move to untether the horses. 'We should go. The hour is growing late.'

Fabien says nothing.

We ride for a long, long time before I can look at him again.

KINDRED

BLANCHE

Since I sent Hugo on his quest, he's nowhere to be found. Nowhere in Bluefort.

None of our contacts in Crane Harbour has seen or heard from him in days.

I gave him a contract, I try to tell myself, but even I know it's surely more than that.

There is one person who might know of his whereabouts, though. I find Delphine in one of the caves deep within the mountain upon which Bluefort is built.

It's a vast chamber made of polished blue stone, with icicles of rock hanging down from its ceilings. An underground lake is at its centre, its waters opal-blue, shimmering with the light of the Blueflames ensconced in torches on the walls.

Delphine stands at the edge, her thin frame lost in a wide, pale silk robe. I take in her features, from the small, pinched nose, to the clear blue eyes with deep shadows underneath them. The blonde curls drawn in a tight knot on the top of her head. Delphine has to come here from time to time, because of who she is. She needs the water as much as she needs air.

But on this day, Magali accompanies her – she sits on a boulder, not far from the water.

Aren't they fast friends.

I narrow my eyes at her hateful sight. 'Delphine. *Magali.*'

'Marchionessa,' say both of them, bowing their heads.

I don't believe the demure sign of respect from Magali for a single instant. From the moment she married my son Frederic, and Gelda married Kylian, there has been nothing but trouble in Langly. Fights for succession, ending with different results for my twins. And even after Frederic died, Magali used Maël in any way conceivable to wrench the duchy back for herself.

It ended two years ago, with Magali's exile from the Red Kingdom. And after that, I made sure that her powers were bound permanently, along with Hugo's, so they could stop causing mischief. I'd be naïve, though, not to be weary. I still have to tolerate her. Because she's Maël's mother. Queen Valerie's sister.

Ah, the royal families and their terrible habits of creating complicated blood connections between each other.

I, for one, married a complete outsider. But look how well that has turned out. He brought the shadows of his own past into our marriage.

I shiver that thought away, and tell Delphine, 'You shouldn't be here alone. Not after what happened at the Harvest Ball.' When those priestesses tried to take her.

The Blue Kingdom's Heiress toys with the cord of her robe. 'I'm not alone,' she mumbles. 'Aunt Magali is here, as you can see.' Her fingers tremble slightly. She needs to go into the water, and fast.

I won't keep her from it, then. 'Do you know where Hugo is?'

Delphine's mouth twists with displeasure. 'Why are you asking me? Am I Hugo's keeper?'

'What are you to him, then?'

Delphine rolls her eyes. 'You sound just like my mother.'

'Is that an insult?' I say. 'I think Queen Valerie is quite splendid.'

Delphine gives me a half-smile. 'She is. But she's also very nosy.'

No, she's just worried, I think. The Queen has enough to fret about when it comes to Delphine, as it is.

'Be that as it may,' I say. 'Hugo has vanished.' As soon as I gave him a bit more freedom. I never learn.

'Delphine,' says Magali quietly. 'I think we should tell her.'

'Tell. Me. What?' Lucius's Flaming Finger. I should have known Magali's presence was a sign of trouble.

Delphine takes a deep breath. 'Hugo was contacted by one of his parents, a few months ago. In person. Since Kylian has probably been dead for years, we assume it's Gelda.'

'Gelda? Impossible,' I say. When Magali won the last round of battles with her sister-in-law, she wove a complicated curse around her, confining Gelda to the borders of the Green Kingdom. 'There's no way Gelda could have been here *in person*. She couldn't have come to Bluefort.'

Magali looks away.

I'm chilled to the marrow. Because I suspect something is amiss. Gelda contacting her son – considering the dubious agendas she always had, and her penchant for treachery…

Have I lost Hugo again to her machinations? Has he been betraying me? After I tried to give him another chance to redeem himself?

'I…' Magali clears her throat. Fidgets with the silver chain at her neck.

'Yes? What did you know, Magali?' Rage is a wave, rising, making my ghostly self pulse.

'The curse I placed on Gelda was tied to my Gift,' Magali says. 'When you took my Gift away, the curse dissipated.'

It's been two years since Gelda has been able to move freely, to pull strings.

And I knew nothing of it.

Two years. Two years since Gelda's exile from the Red Kingdom ended.

'And you didn't think to mention this to me before now?' I shout.

Even Magali is at a loss for words. 'I'm… I'm sorry. I… I didn't even think of it. Until Hugo mentioned the meetings.'

Meetings. Plural.

And considering that Gelda can bestow Gifts, as a Mother of the Forest… I can't even begin to contemplate what she has done. How she might have been turning her son against me.

What a fool I am. But Sabya always said that my weakness for my kin would be my downfall.

'Is that all you have to say, Magali? If you'd told us, maybe Isabella could have done something. Woven another spell, to ensure that the backstabber never returns. Are you out of your mind?'

'It was—'

'It was stupid, that's what it was.'

'Come, Blanche,' says Delphine. 'Aunt Magali didn't do this on purpose. I'm sure it was just a slip. She was upset.'

I throw her a savage look. She has no idea what her 'Aunt Magali' is capable of. What she did to her own son, so that she could hold on to power.

'I didn't even think she'd realise that she could return,' says Magali weakly.

I lean in. 'Then you made the terrible mistake of underestimating Gelda. Something I'll never do again.'

Where do I start? Where do I even begin tracking her? Trying to find out what she's been up to? What strings she's been pulling?

Hugo. I need to find Hugo. That's where I begin. 'When did you last hear from my grandson?'

Delphine shakes her head. 'The last time I saw him he was leaving Bluefort. Going to Crane Harbour. Like you asked him to.'

Oh, I might have just received much more than I bargained for. The complications never end, do they? It's nigh on impossible to find a man in Crane Harbour. It's the largest, most luxurious port on the Glittering Sea. The most decadent, as well. The pleasure houses, the theatres, the travelling circuses, the drinking palaces, the dining rooms... The possibilities would be endless.

But I suppose I must start somewhere. I'll ask the Crane Harbour branch of the Fallen Court to keep an eye out for him.

Mothers of the Forest. What a mistake I've made.

Delphine unfastens her robe and lets it drop at her bare feet. She smiles as she plunges into the underground lake, barely making a splash.

There's a shimmering underneath the translucent waters of the lake, a play of light and shadows, glowing blue. After a few moments, a tail, wide and fanned, breaks the water's surface. It's all the colours of the rainbow at once, glittering in the faint light, melting into each other.

It's Delphine's nature to seek the water, since she's half Mervolk. But I wonder what Hugo's true nature is.

What he seeks, what he can't live without.

MIHI

Night is falling by the time my grandparents' house comes into view. It's deep in the wolves' pack territories, hours' ride away from the village of Friburg. It's unassuming, the home they built for themselves.

A two-storeyed building made of timber, with a slanted

roof. The edges of the building are hidden within a close-set group of trees, and a small brook runs behind the house.

A fire burns in the enclosed courtyard, and a silhouette is crouched in front of it. My grandfather? Something tells me it's not him.

I stiffen in the saddle. Someone is watching us. Fabien has drawn so close that he can stretch his hand to nudge me in the elbow. He points to our left. On a steep slope, a few dozen paces from us, there's someone, hidden in the shadows. Rather tall. A lean, strong arm lifts a hunting javelin.

'*Grand-Maman*?' I call, my voice weak.

'Who goes there?' cries my grandmother in a cold voice.

Anger surges through my blood, hot and all-consuming. I didn't expect much of a welcome in coming here, but I had at least expected not to be turned away.

A dark pit of despair opens in my chest. I was right to fight tooth and nail for my position with the Mage-Hunters. There's nothing whatsoever for me outside of Xante.

I'm nothing.

Someone who isn't welcome anywhere.

There's the creak of a bow being strung, a quiet threat, and I could scream in rage. Is it too much to expect of one's grand-parents not to want to murder their only grandchild? I know Mathilde is protective of my grandfather, but I'm blood of their blood.

Doesn't this matter to them, at all?

I should have known. I haven't seen them in years, and while I'm aware they can't travel anywhere, nor did they ever summon me to come see them.

There's a soft pad of steps, and I recognise my grandfather approaching by his eerily quiet gait. Magic and decades of living in the forest do this to a person. Maybe even his past propensity as a poacher.

As always, three greyhounds are following him. Inseparable.

Unbidden tears clog my throat.

My grandfather is a few paces from us when he stops, as if struck by lightning. 'Mihi?' he says. 'Is that you?'

'Yes,' I say, steeling myself.

In a few swift, jerky moves, he's at my side, gripping the reins of my horse. Milky blue eyes take me in greedily. I notice all the ways in which he's unchanged. The lack of lines on his face. The blueish pallor of his skin, the edges of his old wound at this temple, that disappears under his hairline. His soft, light hair.

One of the greyhounds sniffs my boot and whimpers.

Gwenhael's mouth twists. 'How blessed am I in my old age, to lay my eyes on such a sight.' His voice is trembling. Is something wrong with him?

Then, he lifts his hand and grasps mine softly. I feel every callus. How cold his skin is.

'My heart. Oh, my heart,' he says. 'Mathilde, come see our Mihi. Look how much she's grown.'

I let his hand go and dismount. I'm teetering again, unsure what to make of this. Gwenahel pats my cheek. 'You're as beautiful as your mother, aren't you? But stronger. You're made of something else. I can see it in your eyes.'

And then, my grandmother is standing shoulder to

shoulder with him. Her once-dark hair is almost entirely silver, pulled tightly into a braid that falls down her back. She still stands tall and strong, but there are so many lines around her eyes. Around the severe tilt of her mouth. 'You brought someone with you,' she says, glaring at Fabien coldly.

I know why she's so protective of my grandfather. Of their secret.

My grandfather died in the battle of Lafala, forty-six years ago, but Mathilde had been granted a Gift as a Necromancer, and her magic has been keeping Gwenhael – somewhat –alive ever since.

Necromancers are killed on sight, anywhere in the Three Kingdoms, so the two of them have stayed *out* of sight, in the Hallowed Forest. I shudder to think what the High Inquisitor would make of my grandfather, should he ever find him.

No wonder Mathilde is weary of strangers.

'This is Fabien de Goderic,' I say.

In the corner of my eye, I see that the silhouette by the fire is approaching, too.

They have guests?

How unusual.

My grandfather bows. 'Gwenhael of the Hallowed Forest. And this is my wife, Mathilde.'

'I know you by another name,' says Fabien, tossing a coin in the air and catching it again. It glimmers red in the firelight. I'm mesmerised by that glint as Fabien tosses it over and over again. 'Gwenhael, Captain of Mora's Tower. Pillar of the Court.'

What Court? The Red Court?

Mathilde stiffens for a moment, her eyes tracing the movement of the coin, too.

There's a shift in my grandfather's eyes. 'I have been called that in the past.'

And then, the man who was sitting near the fire comes towards us. He's lean and much too well dressed for this forest. Velvet doublet and cloth breeches. He has carefully combed honey-blonde hair.

I can't quite put my finger on who he reminds me of. In any case, my dislike of him is instant. Even more so when he says, 'Fabien de Goderic, eh?' He smirks at my companion, ignoring me completely. Such arrogance. 'Imagine my surprise to see *you* here.'

The man fingers a silver medallion, hanging on a thick chain. The pendant depicts a cloaked woman, her silhouette set in rubies.

Fabien narrows his eyes in a way that conveys to me that he dislikes the man, too. 'Well, well, well. Someone loosened the leash and the little dog started yapping.'

The man snorts and then looks to me. His smile has a put-upon quality, matching the extremely low, exaggeratedly courteous bow he gives me. '*Erste Jägerin*, what a tremendous pleasure. Hugo de Langly, at your service.'

Not the Erste Jägerin anymore, I almost say. And then I realise with a jolt who is standing in front of me. Hugo de Langly? Here?

As in Hugo, my sister's former lover? Who has been dead for seven years, or assumed so, at least?

But none of the people present – who clearly know him –

contest his identity.

This day is more and more bewildering. I think not even in my dream I could have conceived such twists of fate.

Gwenhael takes my arm. It's as if he can't stop trying to convince himself that I'm real. 'What brings the two of you here, foxling?' he says.

I smile at the old pet name. He used to have dozens for me.

But I'll have to burst this seemingly quiet bubble. 'The High Inquisitor tried to … apprehend me. Fabien helped me escape Xante.'

Both my grandparents tense.

'Are you hurt?' says Gwenhael.

Scared. Unsure. Exhausted. But I escaped relatively unscathed.

I shake my head. 'The Order of Inquisitors will try to hunt us down,' I say, looking at my grandmother, gauging her reaction. 'They know about my Gift. I thought that I should tell you. Before you accept to take us in.'

Cold dread gathers in my chest. This is one of the reasons I didn't dare to come back here: I was afraid to be turned away. Why not save myself the disappointment? After all, what Ullar taught me was much to the same effect: that I can never rely on anyone but myself.

Mathilde purses her lips. 'How little you must think of me, Mihi. That you believe I wouldn't do anything to keep you safe. You can stay here for as long as you like.'

What is this feeling, making my head spin slightly? I wasn't expecting it.

'Well, at least until I can persuade her to come with me,' says Fabien.

I roll my eyes. 'Not this, again.'

'My, my.' Hugo's eyes dart between Fabien and me. 'Aren't the two of you quite cosy?'

Mathilde scoffs. And Gwenahel pulls me towards the house. 'You must be tired. How about a little something to eat?'

* * *

By the fire, we tell the others, in short, about our day. Fabien even gives them an account of the purpose of his mission – to fetch me back to the Red Kingdom.

Mathilde and Gwenahel exchange a look.

'What?' I say.

'That might not be so bad, badgerling,' says my grandfather. 'Why not go to Lafala? I'm sure Celine would be happy to shelter you. And the Order of the Inquisitors has no reach there.'

Not like here, is what he doesn't say.

But I can't help wondering if they're not trying to send me back just to get me on my way.

Yet I only just arrived. Now I'm meant to go to the Red Kingdom, and hope that I'll be better received? I braved my fear of being rejected to come here. I don't need to face it again so soon.

Hugo taps Fabien on his shoulder. The wounded one.

Fabien flinches, and I wonder if Hugo's gesture was on purpose. 'Let's gather some firewood, eh? *Fabien?*'

My companion bats him away, but he stands. I eye the pile of wood at the side of the house. It doesn't seem as if we'll need more soon.

They skirt the edge of the clearing, bending down to pick sticks, obviously speaking to each other. And bristling. With their puffed chests, they look like two roosters about to establish the pecking order in the hen house.

Gwenhael asks something that sounds suspiciously like, 'How much do you know about the Fallen Court?'

'Has Hugo been hiding in the Hallowed Forest, too?' I ask.

My sister has been sending letters these past seven years – as if she could fix what was broken just like that. How naïve she must be to believe it. However, one of her first letters deplored the way that the man she loved vanished completely. Without a trace.

This man here at my grandparents' house matches exactly her descriptions of him. Would she have been so keen to marry Philippe if she'd known Hugo was alive? And, more importantly, would her head of guards tell Celine that he saw Hugo, when he returns to Langly?

None of my business, I tell myself.

Mathilde says, 'No. Hugo has been staying in Bluefort.'

The Blue Kingdom, then. Where Ullar wanted to send me.

'Your mother was so eager to go to Lafala when Queen Amelie invited her,' says Gwenhael, somewhat disjointedly.

Mathilde nods. 'She loathed it here. In the woods.'

This sounds like another not-so-subtle attempt to send me to the Red Kingdom. 'I'm nothing like my mother,' I say curtly. 'She might have loved the pageantry. I was *Erste Jägerin*. There would be no place for me at the Red Court.'

The bitter truth escapes before I can hold it back. Ullar and this kingdom have shaped me into something different. I know enough about the Red Kingdom to realise that a princess would be expected to be quiet and demure. To become a wife as soon as she comes of age, and gift her husband with the much-coveted heirs.

I'm terribly unsuited for such a life.

There is nothing for me in Lafala.

'And yet, wolfling, this isn't the life that we want for you,' says Gwenhael. 'To be a fugitive for the rest of your days. Someone like you isn't meant to hide.'

I understand what he doesn't say. That they were compelled to flee, with my grandfather being un-dead and all.

But I had to run, too, didn't I? A ring of steel tightens around my chest, makes it hard for me to breathe. I get to my feet. 'I'm tired. I think I want to go to bed.'

My grandmother nods and leads me towards a small chamber on the ground level. 'Hugo can share the guest bedroom with Fabien. It will do them good,' she says.

She points at the bed made of planks, a few thick coverlets on top of it. 'I'll go into the village tomorrow and buy more pillows and blankets and whatever a young girl needs. Hugo shouldn't be with us for much longer.'

I nod. Silence stretches between us. My grandmother inhales sharply. 'You still have your entire life ahead of you,

Mihi. I hope that you can see this. Don't throw it away too soon. All the possibilities.'

* * *

I twist and turn in my bedding for a long time, unable to sleep. What a buggering day. Everything that I ever dreaded, has come to happen within a few hours. I don't know who I am if I'm not a Mage-Hunter. That's all I ever learned to do.

I want to burrow myself in a hole in the ground. And yet, how can I stay in the Hallowed Forest? What if I draw the Order of the Inquisitors here? I'd never be able to forgive myself if something happened to my grandparents.

The low hum of voices drifts through the cracked window. My grandparents withdraw to their chamber, but Fabien and Hugo are still speaking around the fire. I can't be alone with my circling thoughts for another moment, so I draw a cloak over my sleeping shift, and stalk outside, towards the warmth.

Hugo is sitting on a small bench, his ankle crossed over his knee. Fabien is on the ground, his back leaning against a boulder, his hands laced at his nape. He gives me a small, almost-reluctant smile.

'How splendid,' says Hugo. 'I'm honoured. I was hoping, indeed, that I could become better acquainted with you, Princess.'

Fabien smacks him over the thigh. 'Stop it. She doesn't like to be called that.'

I cock an eyebrow. Rich, coming from the man who's called me precisely that all day.

'In any case, how fortunate that you're here,' Hugo continues. 'My friend and I were discussing the particularities of the Court of Xante and the Mage-Hunters.'

Fabien's blank expression makes me wonder if that was, indeed, the case.

'I find the figure of your Court Astrologist particularly interesting,' says Hugo.

'This one likes the sound of his own voice, doesn't he?' I say, looking at Fabien.

'You have no idea,' he says.

'Is it true that the Court Astrologist – Ullar, right? – also trains the Mage-Hunters?' Hugo forges on.

'He has no idea whatsoever when to shut up.' Fabien draws a hand over his face. He looks as tired as I feel.

I may not be as alone as I think. He helped me today. And my grandparents have been more forthcoming than I'd have ever thought.

'Ullar's also quite old, isn't he? What is his magic, I wonder?' continues Hugo. 'What is his Gift? A terribly powerful one, I'd wager.'

I'm not about to tell him *that*.

Surprisingly, Fabien says, 'Shadows. He can wield shadows.'

'How do you even know?' I say.

Fabien's smile is a bit rueful. 'He came to visit me at the inn on the day I delivered Celine's letter to you.'

I can imagine what sort of 'visit' that was, if Ullar displayed his Gift.

'He wanted to make sure that I was who I said I was,' Fabien says.

I'm speechless. I would have never imagined that Ullar cared so much. Especially after I'd shown him the letter, and he'd already encouraged me to go.

'Fascinating,' says Hugo. 'And quite rare. Don't the stories say that was the Gift that Darg could wield, as well?'

I never gave this much consideration. And Hugo is annoying me with his questions. 'What is your point?' I say.

He smiles at me. A Court-like unctuous smile. As polished as the rest of him. 'I'm ever in awe of you, and what you've achieved. Forgive me if I blabber in your presence. I've wanted to meet you for such a long time. There aren't many mages of the Red Kingdom who became Mage-Hunters, are there? Have any of them become *Erster Jäger*? Or *Erste Jägerin*?'

'One,' I say. 'Only one.'

He whose portrait hung above all others in Ullar's study. But that mage kept his position – even as an outsider – for more than sixty years. I only managed to hang on to mine for two, before Xante spat me out.

'What was his name?' says Hugo, examining his nails. 'Do you happen to know that?'

'No,' I say. I don't care for Hugo's prying. It sets me on edge.

'That's about enough,' says Fabien, smacking Hugo on the thigh again. 'Leave her be. She's had a turd day. You can hound her some other time.'

Hugo pulls at the lapels of his green velvet doublet and rises elegantly to his feet. He gives me another of his courteous bows. 'Of course. I wish you good night, *Erste Jägerin*.' His gaze flits between me and Fabien. 'Or should I say, "Enjoy your evening"?' He turns and walks up towards the house before I can answer.

Not that I was intending to.

Fabien sits up a bit, bending his legs at the knees. He then takes my hand and pulls me to him. I tense for a moment, and then I realise that, *yes, I do want this*. He pulls me in the nest between his legs, a hand to my waist, my back flush to his chest. I huddle as close as I can, surrounded by his heat.

Strange, how the most familiar person to me right now is a man I met a few days ago. But it feels good, to be cradled like this.

Safe.

He deposes a soft kiss on my hair and I can't stifle my sigh.

'Tell me, Mihi,' he says, his voice low, 'what is it in the Red Kingdom that you fear so much? That keeps you from going back?'

I try to turn in his arms. But his grip is firm. 'I'm not afraid of anything,' I say, wiggling.

He chuckles, low and wicked. 'You're such a terrible liar. Of course you're afraid. You have no real reason not to go to Lafala. You have nowhere else to go. Yet still you refuse.'

'I have no real reason *to go* to Lafala, you mean.'

'Liar. You have every reason now. You can't hide here for the rest of your life.'

'Have you been speaking to my grandparents?' I say.

'I have been known to speak. Though I don't enjoy it even half as much as Hugo.'

I giggle and shift again. The evidence of what exactly my squirming is doing to him is poking my backside. I bite my lip, unsettled and heated. He winds both his arms around me, tugging me close. Stilling me.

I'm too tired for lies, even to myself. And Fabien would have none of it, anyway.

'There's no place for someone like me there,' I admit.

'Then you carve a place for yourself. It's not as if you're banished or something.'

'Or something,' I mumble, mimicking his low voice. 'How can one woman change the ways of an entire kingdom?'

'Maybe that woman should look in the mirror. Maybe then she'll see what I see.'

I turn around, slowly, and this time he allows me to. In the firelight, I see myself through his eyes again. That wilful, wild creature, her braid dishevelled, her burning eyes. The anger, the fear, the stubbornness.

That—

That woman could do it.

That woman could go to Lafala and face her fears.

'There's the small matter of my father banishing me, as a child,' I say.

'Ah,' he says. 'Is your refusal to go his punishment, then?'

I'm terrified of being rejected, indeed. But if this is a form of punishment, who would it be dished out to? My father has made no attempts whatsoever to retrieve me.

But Celine did.

'Family can often be disappointing,' says Fabien. 'But

sometimes, you must allow them to surprise you. And maybe do something as outrageous as accept a helping hand.'

I laugh, again.

Look at me, sitting here in Fabien's arms, laughing. Wondering at how he can see all these things. 'You don't know me at all,' I say, tucking away every corner of vulnerability. 'I'm a stickler for rules. I never change them.'

'I think that how we see ourselves and how the others see us are, sometimes, two very different things.'

I stare into Fabien's eyes, taking in everything. Watching the way he sees me is an addictive feeling in itself. A man I could never look away from, who understands me. The touch of recklessness. And the courage. So much courage.

I'm not thinking that he's a seigneur's third son. My sister's captain of the guards. I'm not thinking about future complications when I close the distance between us and kiss him.

I need this tonight. I want it. And by the way he responds, I can feel how much he wants it, too.

It's a volcano, unleashing, rocking me to my core. It's molten lava, flowing through my veins.

I want, I want so much, and tonight, buoyed by Fabien's own courage, I take. And how I burn with it. Fabien pulls me tight into his lap, every arching motion rocking my sensitive nub against his hardness. Against its entire length, and Mothers of the Forest, there is lots of it. My fingers are pulling at the laces of his shirt, restless hands rubbing against scorching skin.

More. I need more. Our tongues tangle in the same game

from earlier, giving and taking, but I already know kissing isn't all we're going to do tonight.

And I welcome it.

He sets me on fire like no one ever before. I'm alight with desire, glowing with it. His hands rove up and down my back, but it's not enough. I wind my hands around his neck, shift closer.

'Lower,' I whisper onto his lips. 'Lower.'

His lips curl in a smile against my mouth. One of his large, rough hands shifts on my thigh, squeezing and caressing, moving upwards. I arch my back, exposing my neck for him. 'That's it.'

His fingers slip underneath the hem of my sleeping shift and he deposits a trail of burning kisses on my neck. I moan, completely lost to this. And then, he touches me just there, dragging his fingers tortuously slow.

I grab onto his lush hair, rocking onto his hand. Willing him to go deeper. To give me more.

He teases my pleasure nub and I whimper. He swallows the sounds I make with his mouth, covering mine, while one of his fingers plunges into the core of me.

This.

Mothers of the Forest, this.

And how it feels. Sparks of pleasure travelling everywhere, darting to my spine, melting in my limbs.

Fire, he's all fire.

He suddenly breaks the kiss to ask me, 'Stickler, are there any rules I should be aware of?'

'Arrogant lout,' I say, and bite his lip.

He responds by tightening his grip around my waist – and slipping another finger inside of me. The stretch, the pleasure, the slight burn. He chuckles and kisses me again, but I'm already feral.

All of this.

The deadly woods at night, the responding howl of a dangerous creature in the distance. The slight breeze that blows over my overheated body. The way his fingers move inside of me, the way I move with his hand, the pleasure that bolts and bolts and bolts through me.

I teeter on the edge. But, this time, I welcome what he has to give. And when I'm so coiled up that I can't even breathe anymore, I suddenly shatter into smithereens. I flutter around his still-moving fingers, pleasure breaking every dam, making my heart race. His kisses are soft as I ride out the crest, still soft when I crumble on his chest. His hands draw wide circles on my thighs.

I catch my breath, holding him close. Unable to stop touching him. 'You're beautiful, did you know that?' I say. My throat feels raw. 'That's what I thought the moment you came into my study. That you're the most gorgeous man I ever saw.'

'I was pining after you before I even met you,' he says. 'Though you exceeded every expectation I ever had.'

'Flatterer,' I say.

I'm curled into him, my head on his shoulder, his hand loosely around my back. I'm drawing lines down his chest, his belly, up and down his thighs, learning the shape of him. So much strength. Such beauty.

And, unavoidably, I'm drawn to *that*. The hard bar in his breeches. When I slip my hand over it, he groans.

Then, 'Mihi.'

'I want to.' To learn the shape of him. To see. To feel for myself. I unwrap the laces of his breeches – slowly, I'm not up for feverish moves right now – and release his hardness. I can't stop, won't stop touching him.

Not when he throws his head back, not when his hips arch as I begin sliding my hand up and down his length, when his eyes close with pleasure. I revel in this, letting my hand glide over his hardness. Faster. Harder. Fabien's eyes fly open and his hips jolt. 'Mihi,' he calls in a strangled voice.

I giggle, thrilled.

'Minx,' he says, narrowing his eyes at me.

'No one has ever called me that,' I say.

No one has ever made me feel like this. Am I finally falling apart, or is this because of him?

It doesn't even matter.

I grip him harder, move my hand in long strokes, circling my wrist. Fabien's hands claw at the ground before settling on my hips, digging into my flesh. Yes. I need him closer again. I lean forward, and kiss him, gentle and thorough. His hands are on my neck, on my back, on my hips. Learning me just as I'm learning him.

How fast he likes it, how hard. What brings Fabien to his release. The dazed look in his eyes afterwards. The way he looks at me – that woman I see reflected in his eyes – so much more than earlier today.

And as far as I'm concerned, there could be no tomorrow. Not as long as we have tonight. Not as long as we have *this*.

* * *

Morning comes, though, and finds me in the narrow bed that my grandmother assigned to me. Fabien is wrapped around me, surrounding me with his heat.

I needed a long time to fall asleep. I teased away the loose ringlets of hair on his forehead, watched him scrunch his nose in his slumber.

And I thought, long and hard, about everything I had to do.

All of them are right.

I can't stay here. I need to leave. I need to face whatever fears I have and go to Lafala. I can't be a coward. I'll never forgive myself if I am.

I stand up gently, trying not to disturb the great lout, stretch a crick in my neck.

Fabien shifts in his sleep.

Mothers of the Forest, this bed is narrow. And he's a giant. And I—

There's a soft knock. I pad on bare feet and open the door. My grandfather is standing in the corridor. 'Badgerling, you two need to get dressed. There's something in the woods, coming closer. I don't like it.'

I don't even have time to face the mortification that my grandfather found me sharing my bedchambers with a man. I hurry to Fabien's side and nudge him. He lifts his head quickly, his eyes still swollen with sleep. He moves to wrap an arm around me, but I'm already stepping back. I pick up his discarded cloak from the floor and toss it at him. 'Gwenhael says we need to go. Someone's coming.'

He sits up, rubbing his eyes, shifting his shoulders. 'Lucius's Flaming Finger.'

My grandfather says from the other side of the door, 'I've saddled and tied your horses on the other side of the clearing. Mathilde is already out, scouting.'

'I'll go fetch our weapons,' says Fabien, his voice still thick with sleep. He rubs his nape and I stare at the line of his powerful shoulders before scrambling to pick up my clothes from the chair I tossed them on the night before.

The peace I'd found last night is dissolving quickly, and my heart hammers in my chest. I hate this, I hate this so much, being thrown on another path again.

Hugo is stoking the small fire when I finally come out, fastening my cloak, and my grandfather is pouring something into a cauldron.

Fabien is inspecting his blades.

'I wrapped a little something for you to eat,' says Hugo, no trace of his usual mocking smile. 'You should go. I have a suspicion about who might come trampling after the two of you.'

A rush of uneasiness makes me shudder. The who, indeed. I'm not brave enough to speak out loud the name of the High Inquisitor. I look to my grandfather. 'I'll be gone in a moment, too,' he says. 'Don't you worry about me. They'll never be able to find me in these woods.' He turns towards Fabien. 'You look after her.'

He nods. 'Of course I will.'

There's the clop of hooves, and both and Fabien and I are up on our feet, drawing our weapons, while my grandfather makes calming gestures with his hands. 'Easy.'

It's my grandmother who emerges out of the woods, on horseback, stopping just short of running us over. Her braid is disarrayed and she's breathing hard. 'Paladins, half a dozen of them.'

'Is the High Inquisitor with them?' says Fabien.

'I think he is.'

Hugo tucks his silver medallion underneath his shirt. 'You all go on your way,' he says. 'I can handle them.'

I'm doubtful, but Mathilde and Fabien say in unison, 'He can.'

I'm preparing to protest when Fabien waves me towards our horses, and Gwenhael jumps in the saddle, behind Mathilde. The hounds are clustering around them. 'We'll ride north,' says my grandfather. 'Send me a signal when they've left.'

Hugo nods.

This is absurd. If Hugo still has a Gift – which I assume he has – he can only hope to survive an encounter with the High Inquisitor. He must see something on my face, because he says, 'Don't you worry about me. Off you go.' And then he proceeds to pour himself ... stew? Into a wooden bowl.

'Come, Mihi,' says Fabien.

No one seems in the least worried about Hugo, so I allow Fabien to help me mount my horse. I give my grandparents a lingering look.

'Take care, Anne-Mihielle,' says Mathilde.

Gwenahel says, 'Come and see us when you can, eh?'

I swallow a rush of tears. Gwenhael takes the reins, swings the mount around, and disappears into the trees to the north.

Fabien nudges me with his elbow. 'Where to?'

'Greenport, I believe. And from there, Lafala.'

Fabien whips his head away quickly. Probably so that I wouldn't see his smile. 'Lead the way, *Erste Jägerin*,' he says.

I sigh. And then steer our mounts west.

Mothers of the Forest. This buggering day hasn't started in any way better than the one before. And I wonder where we'll be, by the end of it.

WHIRL

CELINE

*I*t's uncanny how well Philippe manages to avoid me, how little time we spend together, even if we're both at the Royal Palace. Slipping out of our bed early in the morning, slipping into it late at night.

I know these ways of his. It's nothing different from the way he behaves at Fort Cantor. But by the fourth day, I'm beyond tired of it. Of not knowing what is wrong with him. With *us*.

I'm blending in with the shadows, in a corner of the sitting area, when Philippe comes to our bedchamber. He pries off his boots at the door, approaching on silent steps. The slouch of his shoulders tells me he's tired, and still he flinches when he realises that the bed is empty.

'How does it feel not to find me where you thought I'd be, Husband?' I say.

The bewildered expression in his eyes as he finally sees me is unmistakable.

'Celine?' he says, coming closer to the armchair I'm splayed in.

I hug my knees. 'Sit down, Philippe. We need to have a conversation.'

He ruffles his lovely, dark hair. 'I'm tired, Celine.'

'And so am I.' I wave at the armchair across from me. 'Sit down. Please.' The last word comes out a little choked, and I think it's the plea in it that makes my husband take my request seriously.

'What is this about?' he says.

'I think, Husband, that's what you should tell me.' His hands grasp the gilded armrests of his seat. He's irritated. 'You don't like games? Well, nor do I.'

'What is it that you want, Celine?'

No more skirting around what's truly plaguing me. 'I want you to tell me why you're avoiding me. Why we hardly spend the night together. I love you, Philippe.'

Two years ago, I chose him. Not the duchy. *Him.* And I would choose him over anyone else, every single day of my life. But I suspect the same isn't true for my husband. And how that hurts.

'This is tearing me apart. What is wrong with us? What happened?'

Philippe grinds his jaw. I wait for a long time, but he says nothing.

I have plenty to say for both of us. It's time to bring things out in the open.

I can't go on living like this.

'You hate me a bit, don't you?' I say, fighting tears. 'Ever since you banished your mother and step-brother from the Red Kingdom. When you took the duchy from them. You hate me for what I asked you to do then.'

This must be his twisted idea of making amends. He can't forgive easily. When it comes to us – him and me – he probably can't forgive himself for loving me, in spite of what I've done. And the only way he can accept this is to punish us both, by depriving me of what I crave most in this world: his kind words, his embrace, the feel of his body wrapped around mine.

Philippe lets his head hang, rubbing his hands all over his face. It hurts to do this. But we must.

I have to know, I have to.

'Philippe?' I say. 'Please. I need you to tell me. I need to hear it.'

When he lifts his head, his eyes are red-raw. 'It's not that, Celine. Though the Mothers of the Forest know I feel guilty enough. I don't hate you for what I did. I hate myself. I never wanted any of this. The power, the duchy.'

This, I know.

'Then?' I say. 'What is it?'

Philippe bites his lip. Takes a deep breath, before he says, 'I don't wish the same upon my child. I can't do this to them.'

'What do you mean?'

I think I know what he means; I think I understand, but I don't want to believe it. Not this.

Philippe says, 'I don't want my child to become King.

Langly is enough work. Any boy we'd have would have to inherit it. I'm aware of this. But forcing him to become King, I... It would feel like I'm cursing him. I can't... I can't do that.'

My mind races through all the possibilities, all the possible explanations. 'Is this why you won't bed me?' The question may be crude, but there is no more room for uncertainties.

Philippe says nothing. He can't even look at me.

It feels as if the inside of my chest is folding together, collapsing upon itself. And so is my entire life.

I want children. I want them so much. And more than anything, I want children with *him*.

'So, what were you planning to do, Philippe?' My voice doesn't sound like my own. It's rage and impotence and the sum of all broken things.

'Wait until the situation ... takes care of itself?'

'Which means?'

Philippe puffs his cheeks.

'You're no fool, Philippe. What were you waiting for?'

His words are strangled. 'For Maël to take the crown.'

There are so many meanings to this simple sentence. And a sentence – for me – it is. Philippe wanted to wait for my father to die, first. And then, for Maël to return and take the throne. All of that, before he was intending to ... engage in intimacies with me again.

That could take years. Years of waiting. Of me pining for him.

And he hadn't said a thing. While making choices for me.

'It is unimaginable,' I hiss, 'that you could do such a thing to me. Determine the course of my life. Take away my choices from me. I'm not a puppet.'

'Am I puppet, then? Isn't that what you also did, Celine? Two years ago?' His voice drops, but I can't mistake the determination in it. 'When the choices you made forced me to become the Duke of Langly?'

'You said nothing of this. You simply avoided me. How could you? How could you lie to me like this? What changed?'

Philippe stiffens. 'When we married, were you completely honest with me, then? You never told me I was expected to breed the next Red King. That your brother was never expected to live past childhood. And how could I have known? It was the best kept secret in the Red Kingdom.'

My thoughts are a maelstrom. He lied; he betrayed; he kept me in the shadows about this. He decided for me; he didn't ask; he didn't care how I'd feel.

I'm broken. We're both broken. Everything is broken, and there is no way out. I wrap my arms tight around myself.

I'm so alone. So, so alone.

Philippe reaches out his hand, as if to comfort me, but the look in my eyes must say everything I feel in this moment. He tightens his fingers into a fist. 'I'll sleep somewhere else tonight,' he says.

'Isn't that convenient for your plans?' Rage washes through me and, beyond the terrace, the sea answers with an agitated swish of waves. My Gift stirs in my blood. 'This isn't the end of it,' I say, though it isn't as much of a threat as it is hope.

Philippe rises to his feet. 'Of course it isn't, Celine. I love you more than anything. You have no idea how hard it is for me to stay away from you.' He studies the back of his hands. 'But we must be our own people, Celine. With our own wishes. Not simply vessels to accomplish someone else's dynastic dreams. Maybe, one day, you'll understand. That we have to carve our own way for ourselves, so we can be happy.'

'I don't think I can ever forgive this.'

Philippe opens and closes his mouth. And then, he says, 'Rest, Celine. This isn't the end. It isn't. You'll see.'

CAUGHT

MIHI

*I*t's been a day and a night since we ran from my grandparents' house. A day and a night of doubts. Of wondering if I'm doing the right thing by returning to the Red Kingdom.

As he shows me around my sleeping quarters on *L'Espoir*, the cog that will bring us to Lafala, I noticed how exhausted Fabien is as well. He's been much too quiet. As if what we're about to do is gnawing at him, too. The end destination.

It will be different for us, no doubt, once we're at the Royal Palace. He's no more than the third son of a seigneur – and I'm a princess. An illegitimate one, but still.

I like him so much that it scrambles my wits. I barely take in the interior of the small room. There isn't much to it. Two hammocks hanging one above the other, a small table pushed against the walls. Or nailed to them. I don't know, I'm not one much for ships.

Never would I have thought, even last week, that I'd find myself here. Something inside of me curls tight upon itself. I don't like changes, as a rule. And things are changing much too fast for my liking. My entire life is a lost ship sailing through a storm.

And I feel *this close* to drowning.

'I hope this isn't too shabby for you, Princess,' he says.

I bristle at what he calls me. At the implications. At the cage snapping shut around me, even before I have stepped a single foot inside the Red Kingdom. Dallying with Fabien, as we did in the Hallowed Forest, would be an unforgivable trespass at the Red Court.

And I already hate Lafala for taking my choices away from me.

I'm looking at the two hammocks when I say, 'Are you sharing quarters with me?'

His broad shoulders stiffen. I can't quite read his expression. 'There are more sleeping quarters on this ship.'

My stomach roils and we haven't even set sail yet. So much for 'exceeding every expectation he ever had'.

'I'll bring in your luggage,' he says.

I scoff. What luggage? We ran with the clothes on our back, the weapons on our belts, and the saddlebags tied to horses we stole from Paladins. We didn't have any extra 'luggage' when we ran from the Hallowed Forest, either.

Fabien moves to leave the room, but the space is tight, and

his arm brushes against mine. I close my eyes, inhaling his scent. Steel and wooden spice. His heat. I swear, the man is a furnace.

Before I can catch myself, I grab him by the elbow, before he makes his escape. 'Fabien.'

He squeezes his eyes shut. 'You shouldn't,' he says.

'I hate this,' I say.

'You have no idea.' He untangles himself from my touch. Much more gingerly that I would have ever thought possible for a man of his size. 'But we started this dance, and now we have no choice but to finish it.'

His voice is low, swirling down through my chest, shooting to my belly.

I'm not sure which of us moves, but suddenly we're standing so close to each other. A whisper away. I feel his breath rustling the hairs on the top of my head, and yearning fills me. I can't help but lay a hand on his chest. Feel the thunderous beats of his heart.

I look up – and what I see in his eyes steals my breath.

It's anguish, wrenching need, the same that pulls at every fibre of my body.

'Why?' I mouth.

Then there's the clank of boots on wooden boards approaching, and he flinches and quickly moves two steps away from me. A tall, lean man stands in the corridor. He's maybe the same age as Fabien, with shorter-cropped hair and dark brown eyes. Which he now swivels knowingly between the two of us.

He was the one who greeted us when we arrived on the ship, before Fabien quickly whisked me off to the sleeping quarters. The man says, 'They're lifting the anchor. And you must be starving. How about dinner?'

Fabien mumbles something about luggage and making arrangements and escapes from the chamber as if his breeches are on fire.

Is this how it's going to be? I'm staring after him, when the lean man asks, 'Did I interrupt something?'

I puff my cheeks. 'Do you know what? I don't think you did.' Then, I scold myself for blabbering to someone I don't even know. And I don't like the assessing and slightly pitying glance he's throwing at me.

I grab on to the door like a shield. 'How about you see about that meal?' I say, closing the door between us.

Once it's firmly shut, I lean my head against the wood, listing the reasons why I need to keep it all together.

* * *

I wash my face; I rinse my mouth. Fabien finds a clean shirt for me somewhere, which he deposits wordlessly along with my saddlebag.

Nausea twists my stomach, and I'm not sure that it's just the roiling of the ship.

What could I have done differently, so that I wouldn't end up in here? And, more importantly, should I even consider turning back time, to make things right again? But I'd need to jump back more than a week. Back to before I confronted the High Inquisitor, when we rescued that Water-Twirler.

Such a hop would mean that I'd have to take away so much from another mage's Gift. It would necessitate a tremendous amount of power.

And I don't think I could ever be that selfish. To do that to someone else.

All is not lost, I try to tell myself again. What did Fabien tell me about moving forward?

I don't think there's any way back. And, in the end, good things might be waiting for me in Lafala.

Somehow, though, I don't buggering believe it. And the more days that go by, the harder this reality will become to undo. But where would I find a mage on the deck of a trading cog? Even if I could be selfish and take away their Gift.

Well, I wouldn't have any remorse about taking Gifts from someone like the High Inquisitor, but that would never buggering happen.

I suppose I'm stuck.

Remy, I think. What has come of him? Did the Mage-Hunters whisk him away to safety, while the Paladins were busy chasing us? I hope they did.

And then, it strikes me. Had Ullar known that I made a mistake? Was that why he told me to leave, when we spoke in his study?

Maybe I should have done as he said and left there and then.

But it's unlike Ullar to spare my feelings and not tell me plainly what he thought.

Was he sending me away, then, because I'd failed as a *Erste Jägerin*? Pain knots in my chest, makes me bend over.

* * *

By the time I stride into the quarters that Fabien and the man who came to my room earlier seem to share, I'm able to hold my head high again.

I survey the two of them, sitting next to a table pinned to a wall, their heads bowed and close. 'You said something about food,' I say.

'Look who's up and about,' says the tall, lean man with a grin.

'Of course she is. She knows this is not the end,' says Fabien. His low voice feels like vintage wine. Smooth, it travels to my belly, warming it, and then to my limbs, making them tingle.

It's not the tenuous promise of pleasure that brought me here.

It's the refusal to declare myself defeated.

She knows this is not the end.

How did *he* know? I came here with a plan. After I'm done with eating, I'll withdraw to my rooms, and sing a Call-song for Ullar. It hasn't been long since we left, and he'd be able to come see me for a short while; we must still be in the waters of the Green Kingdom, and not beyond the magical shields.

I'll ask my questions then. If Remy and the other Mage-Hunters are all right, first and foremost. And, if I'm brave –

and I must be – I'll ask why it was, exactly, that he wanted to send me away.

As for Lafala … I'll see what I have to face once I get there. I don't like the idea of going there any more than I did a week ago, but since I was forced then to do what I buggering didn't want to do – run – I won't run from what I'm afraid of now.

I'm Anne-Mihielle. And this is who I am.

Fabien says, '*Erste Jägerin* or not, Mihi knows who she is. A title doesn't make her, or unmake her.'

He's a bit rueful as he says this, and the bottom of my stomach drops out. How did he know? How? Simply by looking at me? And even if I've been trying very hard not to think of me and him, and all the complications, I can't help but wonder. Was he offering just fleeting comfort, that night we spent in the Hallowed Forest? Or does he want more?

I stare at the tips of my boots, making my way to the only free seat at the small table.

The foundations of my life have been shaking. I'm still walking on shifting sands, and the last thing I want is romantic complications.

All well and good, if it weren't for the fact that I *want*.

By Lucius's Flaming Finger, how I want.

'Isn't it so, Mihi?' says Fabien. 'Your worth is much more than the one that other people, or a name, attach to you.' He uncorks the demijohn on the table and fills the tin goblets. There are also cold cuts of meat and cheeses laid out for us. 'It doesn't change who you are. You're just the same as you were three days ago.'

Am I?

I don't know. I truly don't. It's all happening too fast, and my grip on everything is slipping.

'Aren't you so buggering wise when it comes to someone else?' says the lean man, in a dry tone. 'What if you applied some of that wisdom to yourself? It would be fitting, don't you think?'

I pick up the goblet and sip from the wine. It's rich on my tongue, the flavours reminding me of blueberries and a mountain breeze.

'Arnauld wine,' Fabien says, ignoring his friend.

How ironic, I think. It wasn't long ago that I had Arnauld wine, in such different circumstances. I take a deeper swig. There's a sweet aftertaste I don't remember. It's not entirely pleasant.

Nothing of all this is entirely pleasant. It's like trying to swim in a storm at sea, every move bringing me just a step closer to drowning.

But even if my grip is slipping…

I'm still who I think I am. I do not hide, I do not whimper, I'm not a pawn in somebody else's games. I won't just stand by and allow myself to sink. I take in the lean man, from the tip of his hair to the line of his shoulders. 'I don't think you've had the pleasure of introducing yourself. You seem to know plenty about me – and you clearly have plenty of opinions about me, too – so how about awarding me the same privilege?'

His smile is wide, but his eyes are assessing. 'I'm sorry, Demoiselle, if I ever gave you that impression. I assure you I have no opinions whatsoever about your behaviour. Or your conundrums. My opinions are limited to … my friend's behaviour.'

Friends, then. As I suspected. Not just two people who are accomplishing the same mission together.

Fabien says, 'I suggest you keep the opinions to yourself. I for, one, don't care to hear them. I suspect Mihi does not either.'

Our fingers brush when we reach for the same loaf of bread and the touch sends sparks up my arm. Our gazes meet, and there's something in his eyes that keeps me riveted. Things I don't understand, things I can't see beyond, things that pull me closer to him.

There's the uncertainty of what awaits the moment I lay foot in the Red Kingdom, and I long more than ever for the settled rhythms of my life as it used to be just days ago.

Move forward, he told me, didn't he? I look away from Fabien and to the lean man. 'Your name, please. You know precisely who I am and what I'm doing here, and that seems a bit unfair, all things considered. I would like to know who I'm breaking bread with.'

He chuckles at this. 'Fair enough. My name is F— Frederic.'

'Like the second Duke of Langly?'

'And the fourth, too, depending how you count,' says Frederic.

I'm close enough to Fabien to feel his leg jerking. Yes, Langly has a complicated history, with the duchy having passed back and forth a few times between the twins, the first duke's heirs. Until the duchy settled on Maël, and then, my sister.

'And he has a poor taste in jokes, as you can see,' says Fabien scowling. 'Sometimes, I wonder why I tolerate the idiot.'

Frederic shrugs and I puzzle a bit at the strange exchange, while nibbling on the cold cuts. I wash them down with wine. For a while, no one says anything.

'Don't forget to breathe between bites,' says Frederic.

Oh, but I can take a bit of ribbing. I did grow up with the Mage-Hunters, and their manners can't be described as 'courtly'.

'And what did you say that you do for my sister?' I empty my cup to the last drop. Fabien has poured himself a second one, I notice.

'More wine?' Frederic offers, topping our goblets, though his is nearly untouched. 'This is a vintage from the cellars of the Duke of Langly himself. It's twelve years old.'

'Did my sister send it with the letter that Fabien delivered?' I ask, raising my eyebrows.

I also know a thing or two about dodging questions – which this man clearly is. He's wearing a leather jerkin on top of thin chainmail. Breeches made of fine wool. A white cloak with the pouncing lioness of Langly hangs on the back of his chair.

A soldier, then? An employed one? 'Are you Celine's pantler, perhaps?' I try to goad him. No soldier would like to be compared to a servant in charge of the pantry. 'Did my sister renounce your services for a while, for my own comforts?'

Frederic guffaws, but the sound is muffled. The ship sways,

and I wonder if we've struck a particularly high wave. I grab the edge of the table to steady myself, and the swaying stops, only to start again with a vengeance.

Fabien, unperturbed, butters a corner of his bread.

I blink.

'We work together,' says Fabien.

'As my sister's guards?' My head swims in dark waters even as I ask the question.

'We have the same employer,' says Fabien, maybe a tad too carefully. Am I this exhausted?

I want nothing more than lay my head on the table and sleep. For days, maybe.

Yes, days will do.

Frederic pushes the wine goblet towards me. 'Still thirsty?'

My tongue feels as if it's glued to the roof of my mouth.

Next to me, Fabien rubs his face, hard. He blinks then, as if trying to bring the plate before him into focus.

'Tired, eh?' says Frederic. 'I wager it was an exhausting day. A bit of rest would be just the thing.'

Rest, yes.

Rest sounds so good.

I clear the surface in front of me with a lazy movement of my hands. Plates and goblets clatter to the floor. I lay my head on the table, on the side. From here, I can see the overturned goblets, the dark stains of wine on the wooden floorboards.

Blood. Everything looks so much like blood right now.

* * *

When I wake up, my head is pounding, every single bone in my body is aching, and there's an odd weight around my wrists. I try to snap myself up in a sitting position, alert at the wrongness of everything.

I blink in the half-darkness. I'm in some kind of sleeping quarters, in a corner. An empty hammock swings above me.

Have I fallen?

I try to get up on soft legs, and there's a clink as I lay a hand on the floor to push myself up.

Chains.

Manacles, around my wrists.

Lucius's Flaming Finger.

I pull hard at the chains, to where they're anchored in the wooden walls.

Bugger, bugger, bugger.

It feels as if I'm emerging from a haze. I hadn't drunk that much wine, but then, I was tired. Not so tired, though, not to have noticed that someone carried me into another room. And bound me in chains.

By Sabya's Darkblades. This isn't an accident. I push myself up to my knees, frantic. I need to get up and get free and get out, but where, if I'm on a ship in the middle of the sea?

They'll pay for this.

He will.

The door opens with a soft creak and a tall silhouette stands in the threshold. I can't make out his features – he's holding a candle, the light too bright, too much for me – but I can tell it's not Fabien. I know so well the way he stands, the way he moves, the way my stomach flips when I look at him.

But this is not *him*. It must be the other one.

'Ah, you're up,' Frederic says in a smooth voice. He advances further into the room, stopping a good distance from me.

I take in the length of the chains tying me to the wall, make quick calculations.

'Don't bother. They're not long enough. And they're solid.' He throws something that lands with a plop at my feet. 'It's just water, don't be afraid. I'll have a chamber pot brought to you. Though coming close enough to emptying it will be a challenge. That is, if you won't throw it at my face.' He shrugs. 'It is how it is.'

I fight my way through the mists still surrounding my thoughts. 'You poisoned me.'

Frederic takes a few steps closer, crouches, still a good distance away from me. 'I'm sorry. You're not a prisoner. The chains are for your safety, as much as for ours.'

The realisation hits me like a punch in the gut, knocking the air out of my lungs. Fabien did this to me. I trusted him. I liked him. And he used this against me.

'I'm sorry it had to be this way,' Frederic says. His voice is softer than I've ever heard him, not that I know him at all. But that edge of sharp humour is gone. 'We're taking you to meet someone.'

'Why?' I ask.

He shakes his head. 'It's better this way. He made a botch of things, somehow, and you wouldn't have accepted what we had to do. You're a fighter through and through, eh?'

I claw at the ground. I'm furious. Beyond furious. There are no words for this.

But they have no idea what they've started. If they think I won't retaliate, they don't know me.

Frederic gets to his feet. 'He'll explain everything when he wakes up.' He walks back towards the door. 'He had a bit more of that wine than you. If it makes it any easier for you, please know that he won't agree with what I did.' He points at the chains. 'I think, Anne-Mihielle, that his judgement is some-what impaired when it comes to you.'

CELINE

'Angry' does not even deign to describe the way I feel. I'm far and beyond it. With 'angry,' I can't even begin.

The day after Philippe and I had our conversation that turned everything I ever thought about our marriage inside out, the coward found something to do in Langly, and fled to Fort Cantor.

That, I understand. Mothers of the Forest, I should know that there's always something to do in the duchy.

Philippe was never raised to move amongst the high nobility. He was raised to manage nothing larger than a modest farm – and now, he has taken on much more than he ever thought to do.

That, I understand, too.

But lying to his own wife, for almost an entire year –

because I've deduced that was the point when he realised what my brother's frail health meant for us and for him – *that* I will never understand.

I am not my father's lapdog. If he had any concerns about what our unborn child might or might not have been compelled to do, he should have opened his mouth and *said* something to me. Not deprive me of said child. Not push me away as if I had nothing to say in this marriage.

Doesn't he know me at all? Doesn't he trust me?

I seethe as I wander through one of the many inner gardens of the Royal Palace, and take a seat – alone, yet again – on a wrought-iron bench in front of the statue of my mother.

She's depicted as the doyenne of the Golden Pavilion, the marble taking a grey hue on this cloudy morning. The rich cloak, the uniform of the magic school, falls in frozen folds around her legs, hiding how tiny her silhouette was, in truth.

The name she bore, as the doyenne, was Madame Faucon. There's an impossibly small falcon-shaped pin that keeps that entire heavy cloak together, and I think—

What a load of pish.

She has been celebrated all around the kingdom, because she gave her life to birth my brother. She died moments after he came into this world, delivering a child she should never have been allowed to have. The physicians had been adamant once she gave birth to me that I was to be her last.

What did she do instead? She tried to please my father, save the kingdom, and all that humbug.

In our kingdom, is a woman's value no higher than what

her womb can bring forth? The answer is probably yes, according to my father.

But then, I wonder if my mother spared a thought for me when she decided to give my father another child. Did she think of what her death would do to me, how alone I'd be?

My marriage has crumbled, and I have no one, not a soul, to tell about this.

'A lovely statue.' I shiver at the sound of that voice – mountain springs in high summer. A few paces from me stands the priestess of the Mothers of the Forest. Gelda. A name that is easy to remember.

'That's my mother,' I tell her.

'I know,' she says. 'I knew her.'

I take in her delicate frame, the slim wrists. She doesn't look a day above my own age. 'You seem a bit young to have known her well.' I gesture for her to take a seat at my side.

She smiles, and it's full of the warmth of a late summer day. 'She hasn't been gone for such a long time, has she?' She ruffles her green, fluffed cloak as she sits down.

'Seven years,' I say. The first five were very long. The last two rushed by, as in a dream. So much to do. So much hope. And if there were times when I wasn't exactly happy, I had a certainty that, soon, I would be.

With a shudder, I realise that hope was crushed when Philippe told me why he keeps his distance. Alongside every improbable thing I believed about the two of us.

'You seem upset,' says the priestess.

I take in her open, sweet countenance, but I'm not

desperate enough to start pouring my woes out to the first person who crosses my path and is willing to listen.

I clear my throat and scour my mind for whatever I do know about her. Which isn't much, except that she came here with Philippe. There is a mad split moment when I wonder. Philippe is always gone for terribly long. And he did bring her in his tow to Lafala. No man's urges would ever resist the schedule of imposed abstinence that Philippe has forced on us. What if the abstinence has been forced only on me?

It tastes bitter, the surge of jealousy, but I can't help myself and ask, 'Are you from Langly, then?'

'No. We, the Mothers, are of all the Three Kingdoms and of none. The lands and the people are equal in our eyes. And we owe them our care and nurture. We want the good of our people, more than anything.'

In our kingdom, we revere Sabya most among the gods. The warrior who founded Lafala and the Golden Pavilion. We honour her by learning to wield our magic. But since magic is something that mostly only the aristocrats possess, her worship is often limited to the upper classes.

The people honour – covertly or not – the Mothers of the Forest. The entities that, presumably, can channel the blessings of the land towards them.

'Do you belong to a certain temple, then?' I say.

She gives me her beatific smile again. 'We have no temples, except the small ones the people build at crossroads, so they could ask for our blessings, and give us their offerings. We never ask for much. The Mothers only want to give.'

This doesn't sit quite right with me today. I remembered

all the talk about my mother's 'sacrifice' and how she was praised for it. How it was *expected* of her.

'In a wider sense, our temples are the woods and the fields and the mountain pastures,' says Gelda blithely. 'But the Mothers themselves are separated into covenants.'

I have a thousand questions I want to ask her. About what kind of gifts the people bring to the small temples, and what they expect to receive in exchange. I'm not completely ignorant: I did see, during my travels through the kingdom, puppets made of strings and burnt-down tallow candles and tiny animals made of rags, piled up at certain crossroads.

But I know next to nothing about worshiping the Mothers. It was never a part of my upbringing. Nothing that a noble young lady should have known about, though I wager that Philippe would know if I asked him. No sooner does the thought cross my mind than I feel a pang in my chest.

For all the ways in which he enriched my life. For what we could have been.

'I had a friend, once, who joined the priestesses of the Mothers,' I say, a bit absently. Not quite a friend. She was maybe fifteen years older than me. I saw her at the Red Court the few times when she was allowed to visit – a priestess among the rank of the seigneurs was quite a scandal. 'Veliara. She was a third daughter of one of the lesser Valmons branches. Do you know her?'

'Ah,' she says. 'There are many priestesses, scattered throughout the Three Kingdoms. And we always travel so much to serve the people. Often, many of our paths never cross.'

But my scattered thoughts are coming together. 'You said you knew my mother?' A doyenne of the Golden Pavilion, before she was Queen? And a priestess of the Mothers claims acquaintance with her? 'What did you have to do with each other?'

'A few dealings.' She sniffs. 'On a few occasions. As I've said, our lives intersect with many. We are connected to the land, Your Highness. To the fields, to the trees, to the birds and animals. And sometimes, when we honour them, they give us Gifts. Like knowledge.'

I'm not sure I'm meant to respond in any way to this. I've dealt long enough in polite society to realise that the priestess is trying to tell me something. To educate me in the ways of the Mothers … or something else.

'Yes?' I say. 'How do they impart knowledge?'

She shrugs those tiny, delicate shoulders. 'Sometimes it's about the great circles of life. Sometimes it's more specific knowledge. Like an event they witnessed.'

I frown.

Gelda sets her luminous sky-blue eyes on me. 'A bird came to me from the Green Kingdom. Flew straight and true as an arrow to Lafala this morning.' She leans forward, dropping her voice. 'Your sister. The *Erste Jägerin*. She was making her way to you, answering your call. And then, she fell prey to the machinations of the Fallen Court.'

I dig my hands in the ample fabric of my gown, to prevent myself from reacting in an unseemly way. What she says seems like nonsense. I don't want to believe a word of it.

But—

How would she know that I'd written to my sister? I've told no one, except Isabella and Fabien. How would this priestess know, if a bird hadn't whispered this to her?

I swallow, try to collect my roaring thoughts. 'How so?'

'We are friends of the land, and its creatures are our friends, in exchange. The gulls, the ospreys. They have eyes to see. And we have ears to hear what they tell us.'

My heart is racing by now. I smooth obsessively a non-existent crease in my dress. 'What— Is there anything—'

Gelda tilts her head. 'The birds tell me your sister is a prisoner. Racing on a ship towards the Blue Kingdom. But they are bound to pass through these waters. The land gives us the knowledge, Your Highness.' She arranges the hem of her fluffed cloak, lowering her eyes. 'But it is for us to make the choices. Especially the more difficult ones.'

Choices.

My sister – a prisoner. Of the Fallen Court.

My father has alluded to them a few times and made it clear that I should be weary of them. I'd thought they were just stories meant to frighten children. But I realise now he never said much about what they do, or who they are.

Of course. I'm just a girl. Not meant to worry about such things.

And now … they have my sister. I have no reason to believe that Gelda is lying.

She seems to know so much.

'The ship travels under the banners of the Blue Kingdom,' says Gelda. 'Make of that what you will.'

Contrary to what my father believes, I'm not stupid. Nor

am I unaware of diplomatic complications. I couldn't just arrest the ship without creating an incident.

Alone, I'm so alone. As always.

What do I even do?

Gelda pats my knee lightly. 'I see that I've given you much to consider. Apologies, I did not wish to ruin your morning.'

'No,' I say. 'No. Thank you. Telling me was the right thing to do.'

But what is the right thing *I* should do?

Gelda rises to her feet, then drops to a small curtsey. 'If you wish me to, Your Highness … I could let you know when the ship reaches the waters of Lafala.'

Yes. Yes. But then, what am I to do about it? What *can* I do?

I stare at the priestess, a bit overwhelmed. Knowing already that I can't simply sit around and leave my sister as prey to these people.

A prisoner, Gelda called her.

Lucius's Flaming Finger. And what about Fabien?

'Do you happen to know what happened to my captain of the guards?'

'I'm afraid I do not,' she says.

My gaze brushes from the priestess to the statue of my mother. I'm not to be put to only one use, as my father thinks. And I know, already, that I won't leave my sister feeling as alone as I do.

I won't.

And then, I start to piece things together. 'They're heading for the Blue Kingdom?'

Gelda nods.

Mothers of the Forest. Queen Valerie has been harbouring our enemies, Maël and Hugo, for two years. What do they intend to do with Anne-Mihielle? Why would they have taken her?

I won't stand for this. I won't.

What a boon it is that the priestess has spoken to me. 'Thank you so much,' I say. 'You have no idea what sort of favour you have done to me.'

Gelda smiles. 'Of course, Your Highness. That is our purpose. The Mothers only wish to serve our people.'

MIHI

If thoughts of violence could break chains, the ones tied around my wrists would be blown to smithereens.

I hate them. Both Fabien and Frederic, who have done this to me. Especially Fabien.

I trusted him. I—

I squirm when I come to think what I've done with him. How close I allowed him to me. And for him to—

I could roar in anger. All I want to do is break free, slice him into little bits, and then hang him by his balls.

Or maybe the other way around.

But this will do me no good.

So I make myself as comfortable as I can be, try to calm my sawing breaths and think. My limbs are stiff, and my head feels as if it's filled with wool, but they haven't harmed me otherwise. There isn't even a tear in my clothing, not a scratch on my skin.

And I am not helpless.

I've not been raised to be helpless. I've been raised to be able to come out of a sticky situation.

Hopping through time is just one side of my Gift. I have also a bit of Cantor side to it. The Spell-Sundering.

My chains aren't made of spells, but nonetheless, my abilities allow me to muster the light and weave it with the help of songs. There isn't much light in the chamber, except for that coming from a tallow candle.

And I can't use light to slice through my chains. Perhaps more skilled Cantors could, but whereas I can wield plenty of raw power, there's a certain finesse that I've always lacked. I might throw the light blithely using a song and carve a huge hole in the hull of the ship.

No, that won't do.

But something else might.

One of the first Lightsongs that Ullar taught me was a Callsong that I could use wherever I was to call him to my aid. Ullar is immensely powerful and has a rare skill, which allows him to transport his entire person wherever he wants, or wherever the Callsong sounds.

I'm not sure how long I've been asleep, though. I'd been meaning to Call to Ullar before Frederic slipped that sleeping poison into my wine. Have we left the waters of the Green Kingdom? Are we beyond the shields?

Because he won't be able to come if we are.

But this is the best chance I have.

The words of the Callsong are tremulous. My limbs are shaking with fury. I can face everything and everyone, but not if my hands are literally tied. I close my eyes and sing my way through the song.

Nine-year-old children learn nursery rhymes.

I learned Lightsongs.

I reach the final notes, drawing them out, drawing out the light from the candle. It flickers and sputters, and I send it right out, through the nearly invisible cracks between the planks that the ship is built of.

Shadows lengthen and recoil, and I wait, praying, watching. It shouldn't take long, if we're not beyond the shields and he can come, for the Lightsong to reach Ullar. The light of the candle dances, still weak. The shadows tighten and unspool, like tar, flowing slowly. I crouch, my eyes darting into all corners, full of hope.

'Ullar?' I whisper. 'Are you here? Help me.' I dangle my chains. 'Look what they've done to me.'

My eyes swim with tears. Yes, I learned long ago how to get out of a fix, but I still want to know that there's someone who would come to help me, no matter what. Someone I can rely on. Someone who would gather me in their arms and tell me that it will all turn out just fine.

But there's nothing, just silence. This is why Ullar taught me to always rely on myself. To be prepared for no one to be there to help me.

I've been training my entire life for this, and yet a lone tear still falls down my cheek. I hurry to wipe it with my sleeve. Warm metal brushes my skin. 'Ullar?'

There's nothing.

Nothing, no one, just silence.

'By Sabya's Darkblades,' I almost scream, 'where are you?'

Endless moments of silence pass – half an eternity? It certainly feels like that.

Then, the door opens with a screech and Fabien steps inside. His hair is ruffled; his shirt hangs askew, and his eyes are swollen with sleep. He stops a few paces away from me. 'Mihi,' he breathes.

He drops into a crouch, rubbing his face, hard. His eyes are bloodshot. 'I'm so sorry.'

The knot of feeling in my chest bursts. I swipe blindly with my manacled hand, even if I can't reach him. I'd like to land a kick of my foot in his belly, into the soft parts, where it hurts. 'Don't even. Don't you dare.'

'He poisoned me, too. He knew I'd never agree. I never wanted this. I never…'

I can't even think clearly. I'm alone and chained and the one person I trusted to get me out of a fix led me here.

Bloody bastard. Bugger him and all his family. When I get out of these chains, I will throttle him.

'Let me go, then.'

He takes me in, so much emotion welling in his eyes. I can feel that he's warring with himself. I decide to be clever instead of vengeful.

There will be plenty of time for 'vengeful' later.

'Please,' I say, softly. 'I thought that we were close. Friends. Even more than that.'

He sighs. 'Oh, Mihi. You are so much more than I ever

expected. And I never expected any of the things that happened between us.' He leans forward. Closer.

Good.

I want him close. As close as he'll dare.

He stretches his hand forward, but then catches himself at the last moment. 'I wanted to tell you the truth. But I wasn't sure you'd come with me, if I did. And then, we were much deeper in it than I'd have ever thought, and it was selfish, but I wanted more, and I didn't want you to hate me. I know you'll end up hating me anyway, but I was foolish and weak and couldn't stay away.'

My heart is hammering in my chest. And I want … I don't know… And I hate him, I hate him, I hate him, and I need … so much.

And worst of all, I want to believe him.

I steel myself with everything in me, calling back Ullar's words. I can't trust anyone. I can't rely on anyone, and I'm more the fool for already having made that mistake. He won't catch me doing it again.

'Then release me,' I say, trying hard to keep at bay the too-much that I feel.

Oh, how I hate him.

And myself, for being so gullible.

'I can't do that,' Fabien says. 'It's too late now for … every-thing. It's done. He forced my hand when he poisoned us both. He did what I didn't want to. And honestly, I'm afraid of what you'll do if we release you. Do you think I can't see that you hate me now? You're not as good a performer as you think.' His tone is flinty. 'No, he's right, we can't release you. Not now. You'll be a hazard to us and to yourself, at sea. It's too late now. Too buggering late.'

He's right about that. As soon as he releases me, I'll twist his neck. Somehow. In spite of his huge size. He rubs at his face and drops into a sitting position, propping his elbows on his knees.

Bloody twisted bastard. And fool that I am, for trusting him.

For *kissing* him.

I was running from chains, only to end up in chains. On a ship in the middle of the sea. Had I stayed in Xante, at least the Mage-Hunters would have known where I was.

No one knows where I am now. I couldn't even reach Ullar.

'What do you want?' I say, and I realise how defeated I sound. 'Forgiveness? You can forget it. You can scurry out of here, if that's what you're seeking.'

He clears his throat. 'It will be worth remembering, Mihi, when I say what I need to say, that I have only told you two lies since I've met you. I'm not a liar. Usually. I may be many things, but not that.'

I rattle my chains again and snort. 'It sure seems like it.'

He dips his head lower. 'I am not. Two lies, that was all. The rest, every word I've told you... I meant everything.'

Hot shivers cross my spine, spread through my limbs. How do I even begin sifting the truth from lies? Because when we were in the Hallowed Forest, and even before, it had seemed to me that he could see right through me. Like when he asked me what I'm afraid of in the Red Kingdom.

Even before, with that pretty speech of his about moving forward. And I hung on to those words, and took them to heart, and I let them affect the decisions I made.

Were they no more than manipulations?

It seems that even I am not immune to a pretty face and to the right sort of flattery. Flattery that I was more than happy to swallow.

How did he know? How could he have *known* me so well, from the very beginning?

Who told him about me?

Make-believe, that was all it was.

But I don't know what to think, when he says, 'You're remarkable, did you know that? I never met anyone like you. I wish things didn't have to be this way. But then, we'd never have met, would we?' He stares at his hands. 'And what a loss that would have been.'

I hate you, I want to scream. I wish he wouldn't say these things. I can't listen. I can't. 'Shut up,' I say, finally. 'Mothers of the Forest, you like to hear yourself talk. Do you have anything of worth to say to me or not?'

It's unwise to rile him, I know. Considering the position I'm in. But I can't listen to another word. I don't want to be tempted to believe him. My heart, my mind, all of me screams, *Why? Why did you do this to me?*

But saying as much would betray weakness.

'My name is Maël,' he blurts out, almost in spite of himself. 'Not Fabien de Goderic. That was the first lie I told. This is half of it.'

This strikes me like a blow to the head, mashing my

thoughts together. Every memory of every moment that we spent in one another's company. Every single thing that he said to me.

This makes no sense, and yet, it makes all the sense in the world. 'Maël de Langly.'

'Yes,' he says. He shifts, as if this bit of truth makes him uncomfortable as well.

Mothers of the Forest.

Buggering Mothers of the buggering Forest.

I allowed the man who was ousted by my own sister and her husband from his ducal seat to touch me. I held myself tight to his shoulders; I kissed him as if my entire life depended on it.

Bugger, bugger, bugger.

How could I have possibly been so stupid? How could I have been so blind to all the signs?

My head positively spins now. What he said to me about knowing how I feel. About losing everything and finding his way again. The way he avoided me once we boarded the ship, and the way he said that I *don't know*, that I *have no idea*.

The man who marched into my receiving chambers, carrying my sister's letter, was Maël de Langly. The man who I ran away with from Xante was Maël de Langly. The man I brought to my grandparents' home was Maël de Langly.

The man who bloody conferred with bloody Hugo de Langly, and who hadn't been in the least surprised to find the latter alive and well, was Maël de Langly.

The man who told me that I knew who I was, even if I wasn't the *Erste Jägerin* anymore, was Maël de Langly.

'Why would you do this to me, then?' I ask. 'If the same happened to you? Why would you inflict… Was it because of my sister, then? Was it revenge?'

He stiffens. 'This has nothing to do with your sister. Nothing.'

'You had her letter,' I say. 'I'd say it has everything to do with my sister. After all, that was how you took me away from Xante, wasn't it?' My thoughts spin and twirl. I want to retch. I want to scream.

'There was no place for you in the Green Kingdom, anyway,' he says. 'There was—'

'Did you have something to do with that? With what the High Inquisitor did?' With what happened to Remy, with what he wanted to do to me.

'No,' he says. 'But interestingly, your Court Astrologist told me to be in the Hunters' House very early that morning.'

Ullar? No.

'Why should I believe you?'

He shrugs. 'What reason would I have to lie to you now? This is where we stand. Just look at us.'

Me in chains, and him … trying to explain himself?

More lies, but why? Why would he need to?

He sighs again, as if the weight of the world is resting upon his shoulders. 'The second lie I told you was that I was taking you to Lafala.'

I snort. 'I gathered as much.'

He ignores my jab. 'We're heading for Crane Harbour.'

Of course. It makes sense, now that he says it. Because

that's where he's been hiding for the past two years. The Blue Kingdom.

How odd, how cruel and twisted is fate, sending me where Ullar wanted to send me, too, just a few days ago.

Except that I don't think I'm going where our honoured Court Astrologist wanted me to be.

'Why?' I say, even though it's useless, even though I know I should, probably, expect a lie.

But nothing could have prepared me for what he says to me. 'I'm taking you to meet the Marchionessa of the Fallen Court. She thinks the two of you need to have a chat.'

KNOT

CELINE

I'm wrenched by insecurities, unsure what to do about my sister, and the threat surrounding her. But I will do something about it, there is no doubt about that.

I don't care what my father thinks I *should* be. In my heart, I know I fight for those I care about. And I'm not weak and defenceless, as everyone makes me out to be.

I'm much more capable than everyone seems to think.

I'm sifting through the possibilities, when Isabella drifts into my chambers. 'You seem worried,' she says, tucking her hands in her sleeves. Even if the magic school has been closed for years, she still wears the teal cloak of the Golden Pavilion.

Isabella used to be the doyenne. Just like my mother, before her.

I take in her stiff posture. Her manners might be quite

bleak sometimes, but hasn't she supported me through my hardest times, when I was trying to find my grip on Langly?

The decision to tell her about what's plaguing me is easy. 'I am worried,' I say. 'I heard something about my sister.'

She cocks an eyebrow. 'Your sister? Anne-Mihielle?'

I take a deep breath. 'It seems she's a prisoner of the Fallen Court. On a ship rushing towards Crane Harbour. A ship bearing the Blue Kingdom's banners.'

My words fall on frozen silence, so thick that I could cut it with a knife.

Nothing moves on Isabella's face, and I wonder if she heard me. 'The source seems to be believable,' I forge on.

'And who would this source be?' says Isabella, pulling at her sleeves from the inside.

'A priestess of the Mothers of the Forest, named Gelda. She came here with Philippe.'

'Gelda,' says Isabella slowly, as if there might be something wrong with her hearing. 'Gelda. And what does this Gelda look like?'

I shrug. 'She's slender and delicate of build. Perhaps my age. Hair the colour of wheat and eyes the colour of the sky.'

If Isabella wasn't blinking, I'd think she wasn't breathing at all. A statue, or the like.

'She claimed she knew my mother,' I forge on.

'Oh, she would have,' says Isabella.

I want to ask for clarifications, but Isabella says, 'Where is she now?'

'I— Is that relevant? I don't know. I assume somewhere

around the Royal Palace, where she's been for the past few days.'

If I hadn't known any better, I'd think that Isabella just swore through her teeth.

'Gelda doesn't matter,' I say, and Isabella's glare pins me with disbelief. But I will not be cowered, and I will stick to the point. I am more than everyone else believes me to be.

I tell myself the words of the Golden Pavilion, the one we repeated ourselves again and again during our training: *I am the master of my own power.*

Perhaps I should have never allowed myself to forget this.

That I have power in and of my own right. That I'm more than duchess and wife. And what a mockery my marriage has been. Perhaps I should have reminded myself long ago that I am more than this. That, as warped and changed as it is, I still have a Gift. And that I can wield it.

I start, 'We need to do something about my sister.'

Isabella pauses for a long time before she says, 'You have something in mind.'

'This cannot stand.' The power of my Gift froths within my blood. And instead of ignoring it, this time I reach out for it. I embrace it. 'The Blue Kingdom has been fostering Hugo and Maël. If they have my sister, that can only mean a single thing.'

'Which is?'

'They intend to harm her. Or use her as a trading coin, so Maël and Hugo can return.'

'That is', Isabella says slowly, 'quite a leap.'

'It is not,' I say. 'Don't make the same mistake as everyone else and think I understand nothing of politics.'

'Perhaps it's a matter that does concern diplomatic relations between Bluefort and Lafala,' Isabella concedes. 'So why not ask your father to intervene?'

It's the same as always.

Leave the politics to the men.

Don't worry your pretty head with it.

'You know that I can't,' I say. 'He wouldn't care. I was the one to write to her. I was the one to ask her to come.'

I even sent Fabien after her, only to lose her to the Fallen Court. Did he even reach her?

He would have had time enough.

Did the Fallen Court find her first?

The alternative would have been her refusing me, so she could go to the Blue Kingdom. But Gelda said she was 'a prisoner', and I have no reason not to believe her.

I finger the medallion at my neck, the one made of the remnants of the Crystal of Power. My Gift thrums and there's a spray of water from the sea.

An answer.

The key is in the sea. I've thought long and hard about this.

I am the master of my own power.

'There is no other way,' I say. 'We must make sure that the ship never reaches Crane Harbour. We must stop it when it reaches Lafala.'

'Celine,' Isabella says, 'that would amount to a declaration of war.'

'Of course,' I say. 'If our warships are sent to seize it.'

Isabella watches my every move, every gesture.

I breathe out, 'But not if a storm forces it to dock in Lafala's harbours.'

'A storm?' she says.

'A mighty and terrible storm,' I say. 'Dragging it to our port.'

Isabella blinks, as if she can't believe what I say. But it would be thoroughly possible.

Just outside the terrace, the waves are rising.

Between Isabella's Storm-Calling and my Water-Twirling, with the enhancers that we have, we could do this.

If Isabella agrees to help me.

And this is the crux of it.

I take in her stony expression. 'Please, Isabella. Please. I've lost so much these past few days. And I could never live with myself if I stood aside and did nothing.'

'If we're ever found out,' she says, 'it could be cause for war. You don't even know if that woman is lying to you for her own purposes. You don't know this.'

What I don't know is why she would do such a thing. Gelda didn't have to help me.

But she did.

'Please,' I say again. 'My sister— She's the only family I still have.'

Isabella's gaze is knowing. I want nothing to do with my father, and he doesn't truly care about me. And my husband...

I don't want to stick my hand – or my heart – into that nest of wasps. Not now, when I have a purpose.

'She's my sister,' I whisper. 'We can't let them take her away from me.'

Isabella sighs. 'In spite of what many people might be tempted to think, I have a heart. I shall have to think about it, Celine. What you are asking, it is no small thing.'

BLANCHE

When the High Steward of the Fallen Court calls for me, I have no choice but to answer. And when her Call sounds rather desperate, that reply comes immediately.

I ghostwalk into Isabella's quarters at the Royal Palace. 'What happened?' I ask.

'Hello, Mother,' she says, without even the hint of a smile. She seems even more preoccupied than usual. And Isabella has always been thoughtful, even as a child.

The eldest, through and through.

My heart weeps to think again of the enormity of the responsibility that was bestowed on her at eighteen when her father vanished. It was eight years after I'd gone to live in the heart of the Opal Mountain. At eighteen, Isabella should have been a careless young lady, taking her time over the choice of a husband. But she was never inclined to find a man on whose shoulders she could dump the weight of her responsibilities.

I'm not even sure she likes men *that* way.

But at eighteen, she had a duchy to manage, and an inheritance matter to settle. I curse Robert again for leaving them. For all his secrets and lies that forced my daughter to rise to responsibilities beyond her own age.

Though, having done so, little scares Isabella. And now she's frightened – something that scares *me*. I yearn more than anything to be able to wrap her in my arms. Even to do as little as to squeeze her shoulder. But I've been torn from my physical self – when it comes to dealing with my family – for decades. I'm made of thin air, almost an illusion of a presence in their lives.

I remember, though. What it feels like to hold my children in my arms. To catch them when they stumble and they're about to fall.

And by Sabya's Darkblades, I'll do at least this. Try to catch her before she falls.

'What can I do for you, Isabella?' I say.

'Celine knows about Anne-Mihielle,' she says breathlessly. 'And she wants to draw the ship into the ports of Lafala.'

My thoughts turning to Maël first, I say, 'No.' And then, 'How?'

Not even I am aware that his mission has been successful. I can't ghostwalk into the Green Kingdom – Sabya's shields see to that. My mind races. So, Fabien has been able to persuade the *Erste Jägerin* to come, after all? Did he have to enlist her grandparents' help?

So many questions.

Isabella tucks her hands in her wide sleeves. She says simply, 'Gelda.'

I feel like I've been punched in the stomach. Oh, I'd known Gelda was free, but I had no idea she would move that fast. I shouldn't even be surprised. 'Where?'

My daughter's hazel eyes meet mine unwaveringly. 'At the

Royal Palace, until today, at least. And before that, in Langly. The Goderic lands, to be more specific.'

'By Lucius's Flaming Finger and seven of Sabya's Dark-blades. She doesn't waste a moment, does she?'

Petty schemer that she is.

'I'll speak to Mihiel about her,' she says.

'Leave that to me,' I reply. It's the least I can do for my daughter. Spare her Mihiel's unpleasantness.

'Gelda has managed to convince Celine and Philippe that she only wants to be kind and helpful.'

I could roar in frustration. That's what she does. An art developed to perfection. That's how she managed to come so close to me, fifty years ago. Pretending to offer support. To develop my Gift again into something else, to help me topple my brother's reign.

That's how she fooled me. My son, Kylian, too. Even Hugo – over and over and over again. Can I blame him completely for who he has become, with a mother like that?

'Celine can't command our warships to seize *L'Espoir*, so she intends to use the sea and a storm to draw the ship in the port.' Isabella is almost serene as she says this.

'Maël,' I say. 'The curse. We don't know what would happen to him.' Fear tightens my chest, rushes my words. 'That can't be allowed.'

Isabella shrugs. 'I don't see how it could be stopped. If Celine puts her mind to anything... And she has set her mind on rescuing her sister from the Fallen Court.'

Another string of curses makes their way out of my mouth.

'That girl. She causes so much trouble. Little catastrophes, no matter what she starts.'

Isabella has a small, wistful smile. 'She's well-meaning, you know. But also a bit of a blunderer. Can't quite explain it.'

'She's childish and rushed,' I say. 'Perhaps the captain of *L'Espoir* can be convinced to avoid the waters too close to Lafala. Not to come within range of the city.'

'It's October, Mother. I doubt that he could be persuaded. You know how perilous these voyages can be with the autumn storms. It is fanciful of you to think the captain will avoid Lafala just because you wish it so.'

'You are suggesting something,' I say.

Isabella nods. 'I'll play the part that Celine asks of me. We can't afford to lose her trust – not now.'

My mind rears against this, but Isabella is right. The Fallen Court has a tense enough relationship with the Red Crown. We can't afford to lose the support of the princess. Though she doesn't know what Isabella is to me. But a precious source of information, that she is. How would I have ever found out about Petit-Mihiel? And the steps I needed to take to secure the safety of my family?

But.

'Unnecessary,' I say. 'I'll speak to Maël. I'll tell him to avoid Lafala at all costs. And if the ship never appears, it will make Gelda seem like a fool.'

Isabella cocks an eyebrow. 'Until it is known that Anne-Mihielle is kept at Bluefort.'

'It will not be. Known, that is.'

Isabella harrumphs in disbelief. 'You speak to Maël, then.

And in case the worst happens, and *L'Espoir* does come to Lafala, I'll play my part in Celine's scheme.' I'm preparing to argue, but Isabella ploughs sternly on. 'Just to ensure it is done safely for Maël and whoever else might be on that ship. To make sure that nothing goes wrong – and all according to the Fallen Court's wishes.'

I ponder. 'How is it, Isabella, that you make it seem that you agree with me, and yet, you defy me?'

Isabella grins reluctantly. 'When will you learn that most of our family is as wilful as you and Papa? Stubbornness runs in the family.'

Mothers of the Forest, how right she is. How much safer my family would be if they simply complied with my wishes.

'Good luck with Maël,' says Isabella. 'You'll have need of it.'

* * *

I first see Mihiel, though, not Maël. I walk straight into his bedchamber, with not a thought to spare about the state I'll find him in.

This is Gelda: always pushing me to the edge of reason. And pushing me to be afraid. She's been the bane of my family for decades.

Luckily, Mihiel should know to be guarded against her. He loathes her as much as I do, for all the trouble she brought to Langly two decades ago. The King is in his night clothes, with a silken, corded gown thrown on top.

A servant is rubbing his swollen legs. He catches my eye above the man's shoulder and waves him away. I shimmer out of view behind the curtains, until I hear the door closing behind him.

The King purses his mouth in displeasure, but I cut him short before he can say something galling. 'Gelda's here. On the Palace grounds, as we speak.'

Mihiel mutters something under his breath that sounds like cursing. 'How can it be?'

'She insinuated herself into Philippe's retinue, when he returned from Langly.'

There is little that could make the King's jaw drop, and this counts among one of those few things. 'Can I trust you to handle this?' I ask.

The reach of the Fallen Court doesn't extend so far as to have bearing on what happens on the Palace grounds. Not as it once did.

But Mihiel responds without hesitation, his jaw clenching. 'I want her out of my house as much as you do. Rely on me to do as I say.'

I take in my long-time opponent, his determination to see the priestess out of the palace. And I think about how some battles are bound to go on forever. How we can be locked in them, even if they wring every last drop of lifeforce from us, and we still go on.

Because there are some battles – like the ones to keep my grandchildren alive – that I'll fight until my dying breath. I wonder when will I stop worrying about them. And what I'd do with myself if that ever came to be.

THE HIDDEN ACOLYTES

MIHI

*W*e make arrangements about the way that I see to my needs, about the way that they feed me, that are embarrassing. Not a moment goes by when I don't think what a monumental fool I am. The chains are a constant reminder of that.

I should be scared out of my wits, I tell myself, and not blithely go on, trusting that Maël won't harm me. He doesn't deserve my trust. He deserves my blade. Through his heart.

This should serve as a reminder whenever I'll be inclined to trust feelings. Ullar *had* warned me. Over and over again, as I grew up.

I could say it was the most outstanding pillar of my entire education. *Trust no one. And emotions, less than anything.*

Maël comes the next day, throwing in my corner a bundle in a piece of cloth. I unwrap it, my eyes pinned on him. He stands a few paces away from me, waiting for something. 'Breakfast,' he says.

It's bread and cheese. 'Some honey would be nice,' I say.

Maël's brows furrows. 'Was that a joke, Mihi?'

Honestly, I don't know. This is so absurd. He hasn't explained anything, except that I'm supposed to see the Marchionessa. And even if Ullar wanted me to do as much, I don't want to see her while I'm a prisoner.

And on the other hand, can I blame them for keeping me in chains now? I'd definitely wring their necks if they let me go. Being the middle of the sea or not.

Frederic strides in. I don't care for him. For the affected carelessness, for the sly smile. 'So she's calmer now,' he says.

'You have no idea,' I deadpan.

And there it is. That sly smile that I want to wipe out with my fist.

Maël doesn't care about it, either, judging by the savage snarl he throws his … friend? Companion? They work for the same employer, they said.

The Fallen Court?

'Who are you, really?' I say.

That smile spreads. And then he gives me an exaggeratedly courteous bow. 'Fabien de Goderic, Princess. At your service.'

The air whooshes out of my lungs. I look between the man who I though was Fabien – and who is, in fact, Langly's duke-in-exile – and the man who says he truly is Fabien. 'And do you work for my sister or not?'

So many things suddenly make sense. Fabien was famously Maël de Langly's good friend. It wouldn't be a stretch to think that he betrayed Celine for his old acquaintance.

I don't care at all for the assessing glare that the real Fabien throws me. I notice a purple spot – a fresh bruise – along the side of his jaw. It looks like it's been caused by someone's fist. I can imagine how he might have come by it. I don't allow my thoughts to drift further than that. As to why that might have been.

'The letter was real, Mihi,' says Maël. 'Your sister truly wants you to return to Lafala. But—'

'Maël,' says Fabien, and his voice is full of reproach.

'Don't,' says Maël. 'Leave us.'

Fabien plants his feet wider, crossing his arms.

'You've done enough harm as it is,' says Maël.

'All I've done,' says Fabien slowly, 'is prevent you from doing something stupid.'

'You're not wanted here,' says Maël, drifting closer to his friend. Puffing out his chest.

Well, this is interesting, to say the least.

The two exchange a long look before Fabien finally retreats, shaking his head. 'Buggering fool.'

Maël shuts the door behind him and returns to crouch, as close as he dares. Which isn't close at all. 'I owe you a few more explanations, I think.'

I sit back, leaning my head against hard wood.

Maël reaches into his pocket, pulling out a coin and tossing it into the air. It glints red.

I've seen it before.

'So, he doesn't work for my sister, either,' I say.

'Your sister and her husband do think he works for them. And I believe his loyalties are much more torn than he likes to claim. I believe he cares about Celine. And I believe he knows very well that you'll tear into her when you reach Lafala. She wronged you. And Mothers of the Forest, you can be magnificent and feral at the same time, Mihi. I suspect he thinks he's protecting her. Like he thought he was protecting me by making you hate me. But there's no kindness in trying to protect one from oneself, don't you think?'

'I think I don't know where to start with all you've said,' I reply.

Maël throws me a piercing look. 'And I think you do.'

I think he's trying very hard to make me not hate him again. And I desperately don't want him to succeed.

Is this where Maël's need for revenge plays against Fabien's supposed loyalty to Celine? 'Is he in love with her?' I ask.

Maël shakes his head. 'Maybe he cares for her, but Fabien was never drawn to women.'

'And yet, he handed you Celine's letter. The one you brought to me,' I say.

'He didn't have much of a choice. As I don't have one, now.'

'The famous Fallen Court?' I say.

'Yes. You see, as in many things about this conundrum we find ourselves in, it's a matter of loyalties. The Fallen Court gave me a home when I lost my own. More than a place to stay.' Maël settles into sitting with one knee on the floor and one hand thrown on top of his other knee, which is bent. 'You see, I think this arrangement can be mutually beneficial for us. I think you'll like the Marchionessa. And I think you could settle just fine at Bluefort. There is so much that someone like you could do. You're so valuable, Mihi.'

What a mountain of horseshit. If Maël thinks he can sweet-talk himself out of this, he's out of his bloody mind.

But I say none of this. He seems inclined to talk, so I let him. Listening for weaknesses I can exploit. Soft places I can stab into.

Later.

'The Marchionessa is very single-minded, just like you,' Maël goes on. 'Some might even say she's difficult. She just doesn't take any turd from anyone, but don't tell her I told you that. She might take it as a compliment. And she can be a real pain in the arse.'

In my head, I try to summarise every single thing I know about the Fallen Court. They started in the Red Kingdom, as far as I know from Ullar, as a sort of secret society of women, working in the shadows. Over the years, this became a union of powerful leaders, mostly from the Blue and Red Kingdoms, tied by more than the relationships between the seigneurs and their subjects.

From what I could gather, they lost most of their influence in the Red Kingdom, though, when the first Marchionessa – Blanche de Langly, Maël's grandmother – simply vanished. And their main foothold is the Blue Kingdom now. Bluefort.

As far as I remember, just like us, Ullar was unsure if the Fallen Court was working for the Dark Mother or against her. I suppose it depends on where the Marchionessa's interests lie. And who she is.

Ullar seemed to believe that Blanche de Langly crawled

out from under a rock – where she's been hiding for decades? I thought it was absurd, but who knows.

'Who is she?' I ask. 'This Marchionessa? Is she Blanche de Langly?'

Maël swishes his head towards me, and the coin he was playing with drops to the floor with a clank. 'How do you know? Did Mathilde say anything? I don't think she was supposed to.'

'What?' My fingers are numb, and it isn't just because of my manacles. 'What does my grandmother have to do with all of it?'

Maël cocks his head. 'Come to think of is, maybe she *should* have told you something.'

'We're not very close,' I mumble, which is short for, *My grandmother gave me up to a mage she barely knew, so she could roam the woods freely with her undead* ... husband? I'm not sure if they ever married.

I'm quite sure, though, that she was pregnant with my mother before Gwenhael was killed in the Year of the Red Maiden, at the battle of Lafala, but honestly, I didn't even want to ask.

'I think you can tell where I stand with my grandparents,' I say, even if I'm not entirely sure of it myself. They received me much more warmly than I had expected. And then, they hid this from me. It's all so confusing. 'They knew you were lying to me, then?'

Maël shakes his head. 'They only knew I was in the Green Kingdom because of a contract. And that I was looking out for you. And they thought I was Fabien – unless Hugo told them otherwise. After we left.'

'They didn't know who you were?' My head aches.

'Why would they?' he says. 'They'd heard about me, but they've never left the Hallowed Forest. Not in decades. They'd never laid eyes on me before.'

I'm not sure if he thinks that this will make me feel any better.

Maël pushes the coin towards me with his foot. It spins on the floor, halting to a stop a few inches from me. 'Take a look at this.'

I pick it up. It's not a coin. It's twice as large and made of solid silver. On the one side, the goddess of hunt is depicted, her bow strung, two dogs at her heels. Her gaze is set on an invisible target.

On the other side, a cloaked woman is engraved, her hair and clothes melding together. The figure is studded with small, red rubies.

'What is this?'

'That, Anne-Mihielle, is a mark of the Fallen Court. If you accept the mark, you accept the contract.'

The Fallen Court. Long has Ullar been suspicious of them, and their dealings.

And now I know they are real. With their contracts, and their missions, and their underlings.

And their plotting and scheming.

I almost ask what this contract was about, but I think I know. I toss the coin back and he catches it with a swing of his hand.

'And why are you showing me this?'

'I am showing you this, wolfling—'

'Don't call me that,' I hiss.

'Because this is what I showed to Gwenhael when we first arrived at your grandmother's house. Why they trusted me implicitly.'

Does this mean that my own grandparents are not to be trusted? But Gwenhael did try to say something, while Maël and Hugo were 'gathering wood'. We spoke of Lafala, in the end.

By Sabya's Darkblades.

If only I had listened.

If only—

Lucius's Flaming Finger, I will not blame myself for this. I will not.

And curse Maël for trying to win my good graces. For trying to pull me to his side again. From the devastated looks he throws me, to all the coddling and persuading and—

Bugger him. He hasn't said a word, in fact, about why the Marchionessa wants me.

'Bucket,' is all I say. 'I need to throw up.'

He rises to his feet, a bit alarmed, grabbing the bucket. All fluid motions and restrained strength. His sleeves are rolled up, and I can't look away from those thick wrists, the corded muscle of his forearms.

His shoulder is still bandaged where he took a blow for me, on the day we ran from Xante. And every time I look into his eyes, I see not only the sadness, but myself: the glorious, bright Mihi, a woman who not even chains can keep restrained.

He's right, at least, about that.

What's with this sudden interest in Maël of Langly? Would you care for me to arrange a meeting? he'd said when I met him at the inn. Did he laugh at me, on the inside? Because I was naïve enough to believe him?

Bugger him. If he thinks I'll play to his tune, he's delusional. He stops a few feet from me, as if remembering that he shouldn't get too close, then sends the bucket rolling on the floor.

I lurch to my feet, as best as I can with the chains and manage to grab the metal bucket.

I throw it back at him, with all the force I can muster, fuelled by every single thing I think of him.

He parries it with his arm, just barely, hissing and cursing low. Rubbing at his elbow. 'I think I deserved that. Though something tells me you're not angry with *me* right now.'

'Bugger you,' I say. 'Bugger you and your entire family, to the tenth generation.'

'I have nothing against you buggering me, in principle, but I think in the current situation, it wouldn't be advisable.'

That is *it*.

He is driving me insane. Trying to soften me up, as if I don't know what he's doing, as if I'm stupid enough to be his stupid puppet again.

Maël and his lies. I've had enough of it.

'Get out! What are you even doing in here, with me? It's not as if I can go anywhere.'

He lifts his hands to pacify me, taking a few steps towards the door. It almost feels like a dance, my pushing, him trying to find his way back to me. 'I know how you feel. I know exactly how you feel. Caged. Caught. At the mercy of someone else.'

'And if you know how horrible this is, then what kind of a bastard do you have to be to inflict this on me?'

It's unwise to provoke him. I don't even know what Blanche wants from me. If I play the nice, pliant prisoner, maybe I can persuade him to drop me off in Lafala, in my sister's lap, instead of forging on to Bluefort. He certainly behaves as if he's ridden by guilt. As if he's torn. But—

It would mean that I believe he feels something for me, something that I could exploit. And I'll never again make the mistake of trusting his feelings for me, nor my own emotions.

The rage pounds and roars in my blood, making my thoughts swirl. On top it all, the boat tips and swings, as if it has caught a giant wave.

'The kind of bastard,' he says, 'who will make sure that nothing bad happens to you, Mihi. I promise you that. I think you should talk to Blanche. That's all. But I will not allow any harm to come to you. On my honour.'

'What honour?'

He flinches. 'Fine,' he says. 'You'll see.'

Yes, we'll see. We'll see, as soon as I'm out of these chains.

But for now, all I want is for this arse to leave me alone.

I've had enough.

Enough.

'Get. Out!' I roar.

This time, he takes the hint. He gives me a long, sorrowful look, but at least he has the decency to disappear through that door.

BLANCHE

It's a wonder I find the ship in the middle of the sea, but I'd taken precautions to see *L'Espoir* for myself while it was anchored in Lafala.

I can never ghostwalk somewhere I've never been, or seen depicted in a drawing or painting. It is another of the limitations of my Gift.

Speaking, fortunately, is not one of them.

It's not Maël I find in the quarters that belong to him on *L'Espoir*, but Fabien. 'So you've been successful and retrieved her,' I say.

'Oh, I think Maël will have plenty to say about retrieving.'

'Go find my grandson,' I tell him.

Before he complies, he says, 'Take care. He's smitten. As hard to believe as it may seem.'

I try to pry, but he waves me away. 'You'll see.'

I wonder at the off-hand comments, when the door opens, nearly sweeping Fabien off his feet, and Maël comes in. He's a tight ball of fury. The power of his Gift crackles in the air, and the small chamber heats. I thought he'd spend a nice few days in Greenport, 'seeing what it had to offer', as he'd put it in his own words.

He seems far from having just revelled.

'Grandmother,' he says with a curt nod.

Fabien leaves us, slamming the door shut behind him.

'Why didn't you tell me about the High Inquisitor? Was this another one of your games?' Maël's rage makes the air shimmer.

'Tell you what?' That he's on the hunt for mages? I thought that much was obvious.

What has my grandson truly been up to? 'Did you clash with him? With the High Inquisitor?'

I told him to stay away. I told him. What have I risked by sending him from Bluefort?

'Don't play coy with me.' His voice nearly trembles with fury.

I have no idea what he's talking about – nor do I have time for this. Oh, I wish I hadn't given him the contract, if I'd waited for just a few more days... Now I have to do my best to prevent him from sailing headlong into trouble.

'I won't play coy, then,' I tell him, hoping that he'll allow me to get to the point. 'But this isn't what I came to say. You must avoid sailing too close to Lafala, at all costs. Unspeakable danger will await you if you do. You must speak to the captain.'

Maël cocks an eyebrow in disbelief.

The motion makes him look just like his grandfather, and the sight disquiets me beyond words.

'Why would I do such a thing?'

'Is my word not enough?'

A muscle in Maël's jaw ticks. He looks rough – dishevelled

hair, the heavy shadow of stubble, rumpled clothing. 'Not a day ago, I was on the receiving end of the rage of a very powerful, very old mage. And I think I was this close to one of us completely obliterating the other. So no, I will not take your word for it.'

I still. 'What mage? Anne-Mihielle?'

He rubs the stubble on his chin. 'Not just her. Her mentor, too.'

'What do you— A day ago?' Considering they're already at sea, and I could ghostwalk here, they're already beyond the magical shields of the Green Kingdom... 'Is he here, with you?'

'No,' he says. 'He can Nimble. Anne-Mihielle Called to him. And he didn't jump back to Xante until I promised I'll guard her with my life. Odd, considering what he *did*.'

Nimbling. That is a Gift that pertains to the most ancient of gods. A rare and powerful skill – to be able to transport oneself from one place to another entirely. Not ghostwalking, as I do. Nimbling is physical, too. 'Who is he?'

'The Court Astrologist of Xante. The man who trains the Mage-Hunters.'

I don't like this. Not a single moment. 'What did he want?'

Maël crosses his arms. 'He was ... enraged at the conditions in which we're keeping Anne-Mihielle. The chains, to be specific. He came here. He looked at her from the shadows.'

'Chains?'

'I didn't want it to come to this. It's all Fabien's fault.' His voice rises, and the air almost sparks with contained fire. 'He forced my hand and ruined everything. We have no alternative now but to keep her in chains until we reach Bluefort. Not after what Fabien did.' He shakes his head. 'Never mind. I'll handle Fabien. What I don't understand is why the Court Astrologist served Mihi to us on a platter. He came to me the day after I … after … the letter was delivered to Anne-Mihielle. And I suspect he orchestrated a buggering incident with the High Inquisitor purely so that she'd be forced to leave. He told me to be at the Hunters' House when it happened.'

I reel, barely able to put things together. And then … rage. Heaps of it. 'You went to Xante. Even though I told you expressly not to. You—'

Rage, yes. Also from Maël's side. 'Are you even listening to me? He betrayed her. He raised her, and trained her, and then landed her into our hands. The Fallen Court's. He knew precisely what he was about. I think Mathilde and Gwenhael had been talking to him. He knew a lot about us. And he delivered her to *us*. Callously.'

'You think it's a ruse, then? He tries to infiltrate the Court – through her?'

He laughs his bitter laugh. 'Trust me. She doesn't want to infiltrate anything. I don't know how you'll get anything out of her. Fabien and I made a true botch of this.'

My head is pounding. 'I told you not to go to Xante. It was unnecessary. It was—'

'You're not listening,' he roars. 'She doesn't deserve this. She doesn't deserve to be betrayed like this. She has no one. No. One. You must promise. Once you get your answers, you'll see that she's delivered to Lafala. She needs to go there. She deserves more than this.'

He waves his hands about and I'm still reeling. I've never seen Maël so agitated. 'What— What is even— What difference does it make to you?'

Maël sets his jaw. 'Promise me, Blanche.'

I think about complications. Answers. An attempt to kidnap the Blue Heiress. 'I can't promise anything,' I say. 'But I'll see what I can do.'

Maël stands tall and unmoving, and somehow, I find this more frightening than his rage.

I say, 'Keep course for Bluefort. Avoid Lafala at all costs. Celine plans to unleash a storm, so she can reel your ship in. To "save" her sister. This could be dangerous for you, Maël. Speak to the captain. Make sure she never lays eyes on your ship.'

Maël crosses his arms. 'Fine, Blanche. I'll see what I can do.'

We face each other. I plea. But I don't get another single word out of him.

By the time I return to the cave, I have a sinking feeling that I have no idea what I have unleashed.

Hugo is nowhere to be found. Oh, there are sightings – alleged – in Crane Harbour. But not one of the Fallen Court contacts can truly say that he's been seen in a week.

I seethe. How did I allow myself to be tricked into this?

His mother's child, to his very bones.

Sabya's armour creaks. There's slight movement in the golden throne to my right. 'You worry, Ghostwalker,' she says. 'Speak.'

I take in the surface of the amber boulder. The dark, spidery cracks, that have been expanding in the past year. The current disarray in the Blue Kingdom, with the Heiress who was almost stolen, the problem that the succession on the Red Throne will present. The uproar with the High Inquisitor in Xante.

We are not ready for this. For her. For the Dark Mother to re-emerge.

'Who troubles you?' Sabya insists.

'Gelda,' I say.

Sabya frowns. 'Your daughter-in-law? The one who granted the Gift of Necromancy to Mathilde?'

'The very one,' I say. 'She returned to the Red Kingdom again, and she's causing mischief.'

'She *returned*. Where from?'

'The Green Kingdom, I suppose.'

Sabya nods sagely. 'You must look into this.'

I narrow my eyes. 'I am. Why did you think I'm fetching Anne-Mihielle?'

'And you think she might tell you enough about the deal-ings of the Green Mothers?' Sabya taps her gauntleted fingers on the golden armrest of the throne. It results in a clank, that's far more melodious that I'd have thought.

But Sabya is a Light-Cantor, like me.

'Who else might?' I say. 'And why the Mothers?'

'You said Gelda granted a Gift. This makes her a Mother, and not a priestess. And you say that there are many of the Mothers – and their priestesses – who hide in the Hallowed Forest.'

I nod.

That much I know from Mathilde. They prefer to keep away from the dealings of the Mothers of the Forest, away from Court, but there are a few things even she can't ignore.

'Mindwalker, I don't know you to be foolish. You think that Gelda hides in the Green Kingdom and no Mothers know about it? No Mothers and priestesses honour her?'

'I thought—'

That I preferred not to think.

That I had much else to think about, and so I relegated Gelda to a lost corner of my mind. Because, until recently, I hadn't even known she could return to the Red Kingdom and start her manipulations. Perhaps she's been manipulating all this time, and I knew none of it.

'What are you trying to tell me?' I say.

'That if she was in the Green Kingdom, if things are as centuries ago – probably not – then Gelda wouldn't have floated about. She would have been part of one of the two covenants of the Mothers of the Forest.'

Lucius's Flaming Finger. I should have thought more about this.

'Enlighten me,' I say.

'There is the Golden Covenant,' she says. 'Their symbol is a golden fir tree. Do you know there is a golden fir tree, carved of stone, in front of the Valmons Palace?'

I shake my head. 'It's not gold anymore. It hasn't been since the last Valmons Queen was replaced with my ancestors. It has begun to grow dark, a different colour.'

It is midnight-blue, like moonstone, without the glimmer.

'What does this have to do with everything?'

Sabya does have a tendency to go off tangents, and if I don't shepherd her back to our conversation, we might forget altogether what we were speaking about.

'Light-Cantor, have I mentioned that you can be quite impatient?'

'Several times.'

'The Mindwalkers of old showed more respect to their goddess.'

The Mindwalkers of old didn't have to spend decades in a room with their goddess and see what she was all about. Her occasional ramblings, for instance. And how she's often a lot of bark, but no bite.

Sabya sighs. 'There was the Golden Covenant on one side, and the corrupted Mothers on the other. The Dark Covenant. Not what they called themselves, but Darg and I did.' There's a passing grimace on her face, as there always is, when she mentions her former lover. 'Their symbol is a dark fir tree. Encased in amber. You can imagine—'

I gasp.

The dark fir tree.

Why didn't I even think to ask Sabya about it? Perhaps I

thought she'd be as forthcoming as she usually is with information.

Which is hardly.

I remember the medallion that Maël plucked from the priestesses' charred bodies. I sent him to fetch Anne-Mihielle, and all this time Gelda has been under our noses.

Sabya goes on. 'But bestowing Necromancy? The Gift of Life, as they call it? There would have been few capable of it in my time. Perhaps none, aside from the Dark Mother. The ability to channel the powers of the land would have been unimaginable.'

That is the difference between the mages and the Mothers. They channel from the land, while our Gift is in our blood. Somehow, the Dark Mother could do both.

'Unfortunately, Gelda is a very common name among priestesses,' she says.

'It is,' I say reflexively. Could there have been a different Gelda who spoke to Celine? But Isabella seemed quite sure.

Had Isabella seen Gelda herself? So many questions I should have asked.

And yet … the dark fir tree. The Dark Covenant.

Gelda. She seduced my son and pretended to be a simple girl of the people. She and Kylian were already married and Hugo was on his way when she saw again the other people who already knew her from the Year of the Red Maiden – like Madame Faucon, Celine's mother. Queen Amelie, still alive then. My good friend.

'How accurate is your information about the covenants of the Hallowed Forest?'

Sabya purses her lips. 'Before you, the last Mindwalker was born during the days of the last Valmons King. Since you know little about the Green Kingdom, I think my "information" is at least one hundred and fifty years old.'

I take her reproach in stride. She's right. I should have looked more to our neighbours.

And I've not looked to my family at all.

PORTENTS

CELINE

For three days, I don't know what to believe about Gelda's words. If I've been listening to the ravings of a lunatic, or if *I'm* the lunatic for hoping what she said was true. I plan and hope and try to discard my feelings.

My sister... I could have my sister back soon. And how sorely do I need one in my life.

I tell myself – and Isabella tells me, too – that my plan is madness. Yet at the dawn of the third day, I'm ready.

An osprey drifts through the open terrace doors into my chambers.

It drops a piece of cloth at my feet, a few words written on it.

The ship. L'Espoir. *Noon.*

I crumble it in my hand, watching the bird take off again. My mind whirrs with thoughts. I'll send small ships in recognition; they will signal to me when *L'Espoir* reaches Lafala. They could withdraw from sight afterwards, so we could cause the storm that will pull the ship my sister is on into port. Everything carefully thought of, every detail accounted for.

And then, the hand of fate.

I can't help thinking. They have a saying in the Red King-dom, that a bird coming indoors is a sign.

It is an omen.

Of death.

MIHI

This blasted nausea doesn't get a single bit better for every hour that I spend on this blasted ship.

If anything, it's getting worse, like the rocking and shaking of this bloody ship is getting worse. I need to get away from these chains, from this room. From this cog.

But where? How could I run away, if I'm in the middle of the sea?

I can't swim for dozens of miles. I'll be running to my death.

Except, of course—

I could run back into the past. I could turn back time, to a moment before all of this happened. I could handle Maël from the instant I first saw him, when he came into my study. But was it there where it all went wrong? Maybe it was when we rescued that Water-Twirler in the village near Xante.

Yet, if I were to make a time-hop of that magnitude, stretching for weeks, I'd need a tremendous amount of power.

Fabien has none, as a Goderic. Nor does the sailing crew. But Maël—

The duke-in-exile did have a Gift once, but two years ago it was taken from him, along with his duchy. Or so the story went. How much truth is there to that claim? I never thought to send a questioning surge through the blood of the man I'd thought of as Fabien.

But if Maël comes close enough this time, I could try to see if there is something of his Gift left.

I'm chewing on these thoughts when the very man I'm thinking of comes in. Today, he seems cheerful. What does he have to smile about? The loathing I feel for him reaches yet unknown heights.

He crouches in front of me, as usual. 'Change of plans, wolfling. I'm taking these off. No need for you to bother to do it yourself. Maybe you've noticed the storm coming our way.'

'Excuse me if I didn't. Being chained below deck and all that.'

He pats his pocket, and then extracts a small, rusted key. 'I have good news for you, Mihi.'

'You don't say.'

His grin becomes wider. 'My grandmother came to warn me two days ago not to come too close to Lafala. Because your sister was brewing a storm to rescue you.'

'A storm?' For a moment, I think I haven't heard him correctly.

He nods. 'We're approaching Lafala now. And the storm is brewing. Pulling us in, just like Blanche said it would. I convinced the captain – and it didn't take much convincing – to sail close to shore.'

I stare at him, dumbstruck.

'I'm taking you home, Mihi,' he says, and his smile seems a bit frozen. 'I couldn't do so directly. There would have been too much uproar with Fabien and I wouldn't put anything past him, but then this opportunity presented itself.'

I don't know what to say. I don't know what to think. This man is confusing and confounding and I loathe him, because he keeps pulling the rug from underneath me. With him, I'm always searching for my footing.

'You lie,' I say.

He shakes his head. 'Let me release you from these chains, and you'll see for yourself. But only if you promise to play nicely.' His voice is low when he says, 'You can go home now. All will be right.'

'And the Marchionessa?' I reply, unwilling to believe him.

'She'll be able to find you in Lafala. Promise me you *will* speak to her. I think times are coming when you'll need each other's strength.'

How about you? I want to say, but bite my tongue.

He'll probably return to Bluefort. And that will be the last I'll see of him, and that would be right.

I never, ever want to lay eyes on him again.

If what he says is true.

'I'm truly sorry for how things turned out,' he says. 'I've made mistakes. Sometimes, I just wish I could do it all again.'

He stares at me and I'm not sure what he means. If he wants me to give him the opportunity to do so. Does he realise that I can turn back time? Was I foolish enough to tell him? Taking a leap back in time is not something to be taken lightly. There are rules; there are ripples and disturbances that can skew the natural course of events.

'I thought you were releasing me,' I say.

'First things first.' He toys with the key. 'I need a promise from you. There's no point in you using your magical tricks, is there? You're going to Lafala. It's what you wanted.'

I watch him, turning his words on all sides. Trying to find the cracks, the lies.

This is far, far too convenient for me.

That he would let me go without a fight, after the trouble he went through to fetch me.

'How about your contract?'

His eyes are glassy when he says, 'There are more important things in life.'

I shift, uncomfortable. My chains jingle. 'What do you want in exchange? Not to say a word to my sister about Fabien's involvement in these plans, for instance?'

Or the fact that her captain of the guards is a part of the Fallen Court. That would be a blow to her, surely. And to the Court itself.

'That would be a nice boon,' he says. 'Though I'm not sure Fabien has done anything to deserve it. No, all I ask is for you to tell Celine to stop the storm once you've reached her. We'll be on our way to Crane Harbour, then.'

'And Fabien?'

'Leave it up to him to decide what sort of lies he'll tell your sister, when the time comes. I don't care.'

His tone tells me that he means everything he's said. But I can't trust him.

What he says sounds too good.

He sighs. 'I see that you don't believe me, though, of course, you have no reason to. This is … problematic for me. Because if you don't trust me, I can't trust that you won't do anything foolish. So I can't let you go, can I?'

I smile sweetly. 'But of course you can. Have you ever given me a single reason not to trust you?'

He laughs. 'If you promise me you'll behave, you can go up on the deck, like the rest of us.'

This is far too easy. 'I promise.'

'Not so fast,' he says. 'You'll try to put a dagger through my throat, or simply toss me over the rails, at your earliest convenience. And I don't like that. Not in this storm.'

Honestly. This man.

Arrogant, conniving bastard.

He says, 'You'll need to spell a promise on your Gift. And don't try to trick me, I know the words.'

This is a rare thing, that a true mage almost never gives. A promise bound to and by the Gift.

If I break my promise, my own Gift will turn against me, hurting me in all possible ways. Maybe, in the end, when it's done, the Gift could leave me altogether.

And where am I without my Gift?

But the fact that Maël wants to exact such a promise from me does tell me that he is genuine when he says he means to release me. And that he doesn't want the trouble that will surely come with breaking my chains.

Maël says, 'If you don't mean me any harm, how hard would it be for you to make a promise? It's just words. You'll just have to add to the binding, *I promise I won't do anything to harm Maël or Fabien on this ship.* That's all. Quite reasonable, isn't it? It doesn't prevent you from doing any harm to me, in the future. You can try to take all the revenge you want. At some point.'

Uncanny, how he doesn't fool himself that I'll ever be able to forgive him for what he did.

He leans towards me, so close that I could almost touch him. But I'm frozen as he says, 'You and me, Mihi, we're cut from the same cloth. I wouldn't forgive you, either, if you did to me what I have done to you. I'd definitely take revenge. Later. Because for the moment, we're clever enough to put our own interests first, aren't we? And it's in your best interest to get out of these chains. But we don't forget, either.'

Lucius's Flaming Finger.

This. Man.

But he's right. As much as it galls me to admit it, he's absolutely right. I'm clever enough to know that I'd rather be up there on the deck, than down here. That I'd rather see if he's telling the truth, and if we're within reach of Lafala.

'Isn't it a bit foolish to go on the deck in a storm, instead of staying in the cabin?' I say.

He chuckles. 'Of course it's foolish. But this isn't a usual storm. I think that if Celine sees you, she might calm down. And there's the matter of actually reaching Lafala. That is her goal ... but I'm not sure how well she can truly control a storm, and the sea.'

My decision isn't a decision at all. It's not as if Maël has much of a choice, either. According to him, this ship is going to Lafala either way.

I stretch my manacled wrists. 'Fine, then. I'll come. You can take these off now.'

He clacks his tongue. 'The promise.'

I stare at him. Despite the half-smile on his lips, his gaze is unflinching.

Against my will, I find this awfully compelling. The determination. The wit.

For me, he's sheer poison.

I hate him so much that my breath hitches.

I stare at my chains – I can't even look at him anymore – and start reciting the words. 'I promise by the Gift in my blood, this child of leaves, of winds, of creeks. By the seed that blooms, by the stem that breaks out of the earth. I, Anne-Mihielle of the Hallowed Forest, promise not to harm you, Maël de Langly, and not to harm Fabien de Goderic, for as long as we are on this ship.'

There's a thrum in my blood, a clench in my muscles. My Gift froths and sizzles, and every patch of my skin hurts. I grit my teeth against the sensation, breathing hard. Maël seems concerned.

Because I'm a Spell-Sunderer, my spells and Lightsongs are

a tad more effective than the ones spoken by mages who have other Gifts.

It feels as if my own blood is burning me from the inside. Sweat beads at my nape and I close my eyes. *It will go away*, I tell myself. And, surely enough, within a few moments, it does.

When I open my eyes again, Maël expression has changed from a frown to a wolfish grin. 'You're resourceful, I have to say. And stubborn. Is this why Gwenahel calls you *badgerling*? Didn't I tell you that I know the words? You forgot the part about the sea. And considering that we're at sea, that was clever of you.'

I'm on the brink of throwing a tantrum. It is true – my sister did mention in one of her letters that she bound Maël's Gift and the curses tied to him by the power of water. Isn't he afraid, I wonder, to be in the waters of the Red Kingdom? What would the curse do?

I'd ask, if I believed for a single moment that he'd give me an honest answer.

'Do it again,' he says. His gaze rakes me from top to bottom. There's something about his eyes that makes my cheeks flush. 'A fighter, to the end, aren't you?'

But as if to reinforce his words, the ship sways harder than before. It throws both of us completely off balance. But instead of pulling back, Maël swings forward to catch me. I don't need to be caught. Yet I'm able to think quickly enough, and the moment his arm wraps around my waist, I lay my hands on his thighs and send a thread of questioning power through his blood.

He must feel the zing of it, because he lets me go quickly. But I already have my answer. That thrum in his blood, the reply to my question. The presence of his Gift, and its restlessness.

The way back for me, should I need it, once I'm up on that deck.

Not just the way back, but the way out, by taking his Gift.

It would be appropriate, as revenges go, I think, taking in the deep crease between his brows. 'That wasn't very nice,' he says, flexing his fingers. 'The promise.' His tone is colder now.

Distrusting.

As it should be.

But the storm is decidedly worse and it's stifling to be cooped up here. I need to be up *there*. To be able to see.

I say, 'I promise by the Gift in my blood, this child of leaves, of winds, of creeks. By the restless sea, by the heat of fire. By the seed that blooms, by the stem that breaks out of the earth. I, Anne-Mihielle of the Hallowed Forest, promise not to harm you, Maël de Langly, and not to harm Fabien de Goderic, for as long as we are on this ship.'

This time, the response in my Gift makes me feel as if my blood vessels have filled with fire, pulsing from my chest and into my limbs, setting me ablaze with raw pain. The onslaught of sensations makes me buckle, makes my stomach clench, knocks the breath out of my chest. Maël eyes widen when I fall to my fours. And he's instantly there, one arm wrapped around my back, fingers brushing my hair out of my face. And to my eternal shame, I lean into his steadying strength.

'Breathe,' he whispers. 'You're fine. You're just fine. Breathe.'

The pain is blinding. My entire body is trembling. If I break my promise, it would be ten times worse than this. And yet, I still feel the rasp of his calluses on my skin. The tenderness behind his gestures. And I tell myself I'm too out of breath to push him away. That it's nothing more.

We stand like this for a long time, before I untangle myself.

He releases me slowly, then proceeds to unlock my manacles, and jumps to his feet, his hand outstretched.

'Now,' he says. 'Are you ready to see Lafala, for the first time in fourteen years?'

BLANCHE

A Callsong reaches me, but it's muted. I'm tired, so, so tired.

It drains me to come out of the cave. Sometimes, the Lightsongs that we have to weave around the Dark Mother exhaust me so much that I could weep.

Callsong. Open your eyes.

There's a creak of armour. Steps, coming closer.

My eyelids flutter to no avail. 'Was that a Callsong?' I say.

Sabya's voice is unusually soothing. 'Sleep, Mindwalker. Rest for now. Sleep.'

THE PULL OF THE SEA

MIHI

*T*he sea churns and churns, tossing us around, as if we were on a toy ship in a boiling cauldron. I'm on the deck, between Maël and Fabien, holding tight to the ship's railing as if my life was depending on it. Maybe because it is.

Between the waves that rise as high as the ship's mast, trying to wash us away, I can barely glimpse the silhouette of the Royal Palace on the shore. It's a symphony of gorgeous buildings of different heights, built in marble. Golden roofs on top of them all, glinting in the sun. Behind it is the splay of the huge city, and even further back, the mountains, embracing it.

It feels as if my sister is trying to pull us directly to the palace. Can a ship this size even find harbour there?

Salty spray soaks me from top to bottom. My skin stings as

273

if I've been slapped. Does she plan for the ship to even survive this battering?

'We're being pulled to shore,' Fabien shouts. 'What is this?'

Maël shrugs. 'Probably Celine.'

'What does Celine have to do with all this?' Fabien throws Maël a savage look.

Oh.

He doesn't even know.

'She wants her sister back,' Maël says.

'You knew about this.' It isn't even a question, the way Fabien says it. His face flushes red, and I don't think it's the relentless slap of the waves. 'This is why you brought Anne-Mihielle up on deck. Are you insane? The ship won't survive this. As soon as it reaches the shallows—'

All around us, the crew are losing their heads.

'I agree. We have to do something about this, if we don't want to lose the entire crew,' Maël says. 'Maybe put Mihi on a boat, and let her go? I wager Celine would leave *L'Espoir* alone then.'

I try hard to keep my eyes open. Was this what he'd wanted from the beginning, when he released me from the chains? Were his sweet words more lies? Did he realise that if he wants to save his skin, he'll have to let me go?

'Not yet, though,' says Maël. 'Celine won't even be able to see her from here. We'll have to hold on tight for a bit.'

Fabien opens and closes his mouth, as if words fail him. 'You lied to me.'

'Truth wouldn't have gotten us very far, old friend,' says Maël.

A huge wave rises next to the ship, like the claw of a sea monster, and before I even have time to shout, Maël covers me with his body, one arm clenched tight around my waist. He grunts as the wave clashes with us, his body taking most of the battering. I feel his muscles stiffening around me, holding tight. Water splashes me in the face and, for a moment, I can't breathe.

I have no idea how we might survive this.

In the aftermath, I'm still clinging to him. He is solid and warm, like a blanket made half of sheer muscle, half of stubbornness and ill-will.

'Get below deck! Get below deck,' bellows the captain.

I can't move. There's a lull, and the air clears for a moment. The gorgeous silhouette of the Royal Palace beckons in the distance. It could be a world away, for all I know. There's a pit in my belly and I'm terrified, and not just because of the storm. The Palace used to be home, and then it wasn't. And that's where I'm going, if I live to reach it.

Maël lets me go slowly. 'We'll need to lower a boat. And hope for the best. And I'll go with her.'

'What?' says Fabien.

'What?' I echo.

I stare at the churning sea beneath, at the sway and foam of the currents. I have no idea how we're meant to survive it. He's unhinged. Why would he come with me?

Fabien says, 'Blanche will strangle you. If you're not dead before that. And then, she'll strangle me for letting you go.'

'Are you mad?' I tell him. 'The curse, binding you *out* of the kingdom? Is there any truth to that?' I break away from him, watching a deep frown etch itself into his face.

'I'm not letting you go; I'm not watching from a distance to see if you sink or not. I made a promise to take care of you. To your Court Astrologist, and to myself most of all. I dragged you in this storm of turd; I'll help you find your way out.'

Ullar? What does he have to do with all this. 'I—'

Maël lifts his hand. 'Not a word. Not a single word. I'm coming, and that's the end of it. Besides, I can't expect you to row your way back to Lafala, if the storm abates. Who do you think I am?'

A liar, basically.

'I'll have none of this,' says Fabien, his hands gripping the railing.

'I don't care,' says Maël. 'Just try to stop me. And we'll see what happens.'

'You can't go,' says Fabien.

'I won't bring the entire ship down for this,' says Maël. 'It's enough.'

'Call for Blanche,' says Fabien. 'Make her tell Isabella to stop Celine. This is madness.'

Maël simply turns his back on him, barking orders that have to do with a boat that needs to be lowered.

'Just whatever you do, don't get into the water,' Fabien yells.

Maël steps away.

I turn to Fabien. 'Will it kill him?' I ask. 'The sea, the curse?'

Fabien's gaze could make my blood freeze. If I were impressionable in general, and if I weren't out of my wits because of the storm, already. 'We don't know. It will most likely spit him out of the kingdom, like it did two years ago. Send him away.'

I nod, though I feel like a fool. But Maël is the bigger fool between the two of us.

'Could it be that the storm is much worse because Maël is on board?' I ask. 'Because of the curse?'

'I wouldn't dismiss that,' Fabien says reluctantly. 'But if he thought that the curse was making the storm worse, and he's going into that boat with you to spare the crew – and me – I'd say that's rather unhinged and staggeringly noble of him. There you go, that's Maël for you.'

'But where does that leave me?' With him, in the boat. And the curse.

'I never claimed that it made sense. Maybe it does. To him.'

I could toss him into the water, I reflect. After all, the promise I made was bound to the fact that we'd be *on the ship*. As soon as we're off the ship, he's fair game.

I'm wondering if that makes any difference to what I'm about to do.

* * *

If Maël and I thought for a single moment that going into the boat was a good idea, I'm endlessly disappointed and not at all surprised to realise that it was not.

The little boat is tossing and turning in the water, no more than a leaf in the wind, and there's no chance that we could do any sort of steering, let alone rowing. I would have retched my guts if I hadn't emptied every last bit of the contents of my stomach already.

'Maël, you blasted bastard, I'm going to kill you with my own hands at some point, if we ever get out of this alive.'

Because, even if we agreed that we should get the boat down, he's the reason why we were caught in the eye of the storm. The reason why there was a storm, to begin with.

If Maël had brought me to Lafala in the first place and hadn't chained me and tried to drag me to Crane Harbour, we wouldn't be standing here. Maybe Fabien is to blame for some of it, after all? If he hadn't poisoned us, where would have Maël taken me? What would he have done?

Does it matter, even?

'Just you wait, Mihi,' he says. And then the unhinged arse does something even more unhinged.

He gets up on his feet, waving his arms towards the Royal Palace. As if they could see anything from there, in this churning of waves, this whipping wind, the grey swirling around us.

Behind us, on the ship, Fabien is gripping the rails, leaning so far forward that he might fall any moment now.

He's not happy about this.

Maël still stands, defying the storm, defying fate.

Sabya's Lightsong guide us all.

What had I been thinking?

And then the wind quietens. I take the first deep breath in ages, it seems to me, until behind me, the *L'Espoir* begins to spin.

CELINE

Isabella and I are on the terrace of my chambers, the medallion with the broken pieces of the Crystal of Power at my neck. I channel my Gift into the waters of the sea, modulating its movements in fits and starts. I channel my fear, I channel my anger, into the distance.

The scouting ships I sent earlier today indicated to me which was *L'Espoir* – the heavy cog with the blue-and-silver banners.

I beg Sabya and the Mothers of the Forest for forgiveness, should anyone else be hurt. But I have failed my sister for such a long time, for so many years, that I can't fail her again.

I must save her from the Fallen Court's clutches.

Next to me, Isabella is making elegant moves with her hands, directing the storm above, while I make the sea boil beneath the ship. Her lips are pursed and there's a deep frown on her face. 'Celine, whatever you're doing, pull back a bit. It's too wild. I'm only trying to steer the ship towards us using the winds. The water is churning too much.'

I feel for the thread of power going from me into the sea. I tug at it, try to feel its strength. Try to rein it in. But the problem is…

The sea, unlike the waters of a brook, unlike the waters of a stream, tugs back. Hard.

For the past two years, since my Gift changed when I used it to bind Hugo's and Maël's, I have not had much time to practise by the sea. I spent much of the time inland, in Langly, trying to save the duchy and trying to save a marriage that my husband did not want to be saved. He didn't even try.

Blind fury boils in my blood, and my Gift dances and leaps, feeling the roaring fire. The sea whooshes and rages in response.

This is *not* a good moment to think about Philippe.

The sea has its own power, its own wild whims and currents. And beneath the surface, ancient magic drums and thrums. I can feel it through my Gift.

'Isabella,' I say, 'I'm not sure I was prepared for this.'

'I know,' she says flatly. 'That is why I'm here. Just try not to sink the ship entirely.'

I'm feeling for the currents to tug the ship towards me, but it doesn't feel like a rope, rather as if I was trying to build one out of foam and froth. There's a strong whoosh in my blood, and a giant wave washes over the cog.

'Isabella,' I say, breathlessly, 'This wasn't me. I didn't do that.'

She breaks her concentration for a moment to look at me, and the wind becomes gentler. Too gentle, because the sea is roaring and pulling, and the ship is sucked into a spin.

Isabella stiffens and begins steering again with her Gift. She's a Storm-Caller, and what an accomplished one. I'm staring at her in wonder, when she says, 'Celine.' She moves her hands swiftly, making the wind push the ship away from a forming whirlpool threatening to suck it into the deep. 'We need to stop, unless we want them to land at the bottom of the sea.'

Stop.

If we stop…

They'll get away from here.

They will take my sister.

Far, far away from me, to a place where I may never be able to reach her.

'I can't stop, Isabella. We're so close.'

She prepares to say something, but then—

'What is that?' I ask. 'Is that a … boat?'

'Stop,' calls Isabella. 'Stop right now, Celine. That's a rowing boat. And only two people are on it. Who do you think they might be?'

I sprint down to the small docking area under my terrace, squinting into the distance. The sea is still roaring its anger, and I will my Gift to quiet the waves. On the boat, there's a man, unusually tall, standing and waving his arms.

And at his feet, bent over, there's a small silhouette, her neck craned up towards him.

I think she's shouting something at him.

Her dark hair, almost entirely loose, whips in the wind.

And in the deepest parts of me, I know. I just know that it's my sister.

My Gift rises to meet her, rises to meet them both, making the boat shake even more violently. The man teeters, on the edge of falling. She throws a hand out, grabbing him by his thighs, or by his breeches. Steadying him. But the toss around the boat is so violent, that it nearly throws them both over the edge.

Inside of me, everything goes quiet.

Who braved the storms, to join my sister? Is that Fabien? What has happened to him?

Have I done anything else, but endanger her?

Maybe not.

I stop. Completely and entirely, terrified of what I almost did. The blanket of silence engulfs my Gift so violently, that the churning around the boat stops with a vicious tug. Around them, the sea laps, quietly withdrawing into itself.

Next to me, Isabella lets out a long, shaky breath. 'Yes, Celine, yes. That must be them.'

EYE OF THE STORM

MIHI

This monumental fool is about to get himself thrown off the boat. He wobbles dangerously close to the edge, leaving me no choice but to stop time for a moment before I can steady him and prevent him from falling in the deadly stir of the sea. When I end the time-freeze, I yell at him to stand down and stop the nonsense.

Oddly, he listens. The sudden movement almost sends us both toppling forward and straight towards that whoosh below, when, by some sort of wonder, the storm suddenly ceases. Where waters were foaming around us, they peter out to an unnatural calm, rocking the boat slowly. Maël sits down, sighing.

'I think they finally saw us,' he says.

I'm about to say something very nasty to him when a wave

of nausea hits me hard, leaving me no choice but to bend over the side of the boat and retch.

He leans forward, catching with his fingers the many strands of hair that have strayed out of my braid. 'I think we'll be just fine now.'

I haven't quite regained my ability to speak, but I throw him a look that I hope conveys what I feel. It should be a withering stare.

He chuckles while I rinse my mouth with seawater.

There's a tug underneath that boat, so violent that it makes my teeth clatter, and we're pulled forward, as though we were on a string, towards the Royal Palace. We pass the sharp edges of Lucius's Cliff in a hurry. Maël turns back to watch the cog – the waters around it also coming to a still, finally – before he lets out a shaky breath.

He then narrows his eyes, looking in the opposite direction, and my gaze follows his. On the shore, next to the small docks of the Royal Palace, two women are standing next to an empty boat. 'That would be your sister there, I think.'

'They were behind the storm, you said?'

I don't care what their intentions were. I don't care that they've stopped now.

They should get ready for a verbal lashing for what they've done.

The biggest arse in all Three Kingdoms throws me a look that I can't quite decipher, then touches my forearm. Tentatively, as if he's half-afraid of how I might react. I wish I could say my impulse is to draw away or to hiss, but I can't.

I don't do any of those things, not after I've been tossed

and thrown about today. It doesn't justify the fact that I let him touch me, that I don't slap him for this, but there it is.

We were both on this boat, inches from sure drowning, and we survived.

And *he* was here because he thought it might save an entire ship and the people on it.

I don't want it to count for something, but it does.

'I suppose this is the last I'll ever see of you,' he says.

I think about debts that have to be paid; I think about promises I made. I could shove him out of this boat. I could stop time and throttle him. But the storm has drained the anger out me.

I'm wrung out. 'For now,' I concede.

His fingers clench on my forearm, as if he's trying to hold on for a bit longer. I know what comes next; he doesn't need to tell me.

He'll throw himself into the water and swim back. It should be fine. He should be fine, considering there's no more frothing around the boat. The curse should drive him away from the Red Kingdom and towards the ship.

It wasn't the spells and bindings around Maël that rocked us; it was *them*. Those women on the shore.

Maël looks at me as if he's expecting me to say something. A final revelation. A final curse, parting from my lips.

'What are you wating for?' I tell him. 'For me to shove you out?'

He chuckles at this, and it's low and raw after all the shouting in the storm. It makes something rattle within my chest. He is drenched, and his hair is plastered to his face, and he still manages to look something close to charming.

Bloody bastard. 'Perhaps, Mihi, in another time, in different circumstances, we might have had a great time together. Perhaps we still might.'

'Well, I wouldn't wager on it, if I were you,' I say dryly.

'I wish you would have come with me.'

'I thought I did,' I say. 'And look what happened.'

He smirks. 'I just wish we could have known each other better.' He plunges into the water without even a last word of goodbye, without even having the decency to give me a moment to reply.

Better echoes in the air around the boat as he sinks underneath the surface.

'*Bon voyage* to you, too,' I shout at no one.

Typical of him.

He always has to have the upper hand and the last word. I turn to watch the women on the shore, now approaching fast. One is taller, wearing a wide cloak – I have no idea who she is. The other one is small and plump, with dark hair. My sister, probably.

My stomach is in knots, and I'm sure it's not just because of the storm. Fourteen years since I last stepped a foot in Lafala. Fourteen years since I last saw my family, and many years since I stopped thinking of them altogether as 'my family'. Since they became some distant, half remembered faces that hadn't even tried to hold on to me.

Who had let me go.

I loathe the thought that I'm here looking for shelter.

For a moment, I wish that Maël had carried me on to the Blue Kingdom as he'd planned. I'm sure I could have handled the famed Blanche of Langly, the Marchionessa, better than I can handle whatever is coming for me here.

Ullar seemed to have thought that I could do well in Bluefort.

Maël himself said that she only wanted to talk to me, but he might have been lying. It wouldn't be the first time.

Maël.

I turn around, watching for signs of him, but there are none. None at all. He could have resurfaced and dived down again. It might have been wiser to do so, to hide himself from sight. So they wouldn't see him, and drag him back.

I count, watching the expanse of water between the ship and the boat. It's nothing that he couldn't brave, if he's a strong enough swimmer.

I suppose he knew what he was doing.

I'm counting, counting, counting, but there's still no sign of him.

That thread of power pulls the rowboat hard and fast towards the palace, but there's something else in the water, stirring. A lick of magic, struggling beneath the surface. There's a blaze of light, not far ahead of me, gone in the blink of an eye.

And there's a disturbance, a ripple of magic that stings. Something that unsettles the Spell-Sundering side of my Gift. Something that makes me unable to stay still.

I take off my boots. Then my drenched cape.

A hiss of steam swirls above the surface.

Lucius's Flaming Finger.

'Maël?'

Without thinking twice about it, I jump.

* * *

Once I'm underneath the water, the cold tightens my muscles, darkens my vision. No time, I have no time as I catch a flash of movement, the ripple of a bare arm, the edge of fawn leather breeches.

I whisper a word to the sea, making it open the eyes of my Gifts, as I swim towards that flash of movement.

Slow, too slow, and not enough air. So I stop time, and push myself forward. I see him, deep underneath the water, his limbs at strange angles around him.

He's a fool, but he'd still know better than throwing himself into the sea, if he didn't know how to swim.

No.

I push myself to the surface, unfreezing time, grabbing greedy gulps of air, before shooting back down.

Shooting for him.

Blasted fool, he *will* be the death of me.

CELINE

I can do nothing now other than to stand on the narrow beach, closing as much of the distance between us as I can.

Can do nothing but wait as a quiet hum of my Gift pulls her boat to shore.

That must be her, that *must* be her. My sister.

The man on the boat tilts sideways and throws himself into the water.

Not Fabien, then? Because why wouldn't he come to the Royal Palace?

Why wouldn't he *bring* her to me?

Anne-Mihielle is so close now that when she turns her head towards me, I can almost make out her features. The long nose, the pursed lips. I can't see her eyes though, not yet.

My heart starts fluttering as she comes closer and closer.

My sister is here; my *sister* is finally here.

Soon, I will see her.

Behind me, Isabella has become entirely still.

Not much longer, I think, as Anne-Mihielle turns around, looking over her shoulder.

A man on the *L'Espoir* raises both his hands in the air and splashes into the water, headfirst.

Is this a sign? Do they believe her to be in any sort of danger?

It's fine, I want to tell her. *It's just fine, I'm using only a thread of magic to draw you to the shore, to make sure you arrive safely.*

But she wouldn't hear me, and she doesn't, as she pulls off her cloak and then her boots and jumps into the water, setting her course back towards the ship, perhaps towards the man who is now swimming towards her.

'No,' I shout. 'Stay in the boat, it will bring you to me.' I turn to Isabella. Her face is pinched. 'Should I try and pull her through the water?' I ask her.

Isabella frowns, her breathing hitched. 'Something's wrong,' she tells me as I watch my sister disappear under the surface.

'What is she doing?' I breathe.

Isabella steps towards the small, white boat docked next to the shore. Its prow is sculpted in the shape of a swan's neck. 'Something is wrong,' she says, and her voice is breaking.

We both watch the empty boat racing towards the us, the stillness of water, underneath which my sister has disappeared. We can do nothing but watch, our thoughts circling.

'Where are they?' says Isabella. 'Where are they?'

'What?' I say.

The man from the ship is still swimming, strong strokes propelling him forward, cleaving through the water.

Mihi comes up for air, a small head bobbing shortly at the surface, before disappearing again beneath the waves.

Isabella steps on the swan-boat, gesturing for me to follow her. 'Come. We need to find them.' Her voice rises and there's no mistaking the tone of command.

The man, I think. The one who was with Mihi.

There's no sign of him, no clue at all.

Oh, no.

I lift my skirts and jump into the boat as fast as I can, while Isabella unties it with trembling fingers.

'Go, Celine, go,' she says. 'Take us to them.'

MIHI

As I dart back towards Maël, fighting my way through the water, I can tell he's struggling frantically against something. Something dark and vicious, pulling him down. Tugging at his limbs. I come closer and closer. His eyes are wide, and he writhes, and I don't think he can see me, not even if he's looking my way.

Bugger.

Oh, bugger.

Too late, I might be too late, I think, as his movements become twitches, become slower and slower.

Bugger.

I try to shout – I want to shout – but my voice is useless here, and he isn't even looking at me.

I push forward, my hands and legs burning with the cold, but I know I must push, push, push.

Late, I'm too late, I think again as I freeze time and do a mighty last shove, my fingers finally brushing the bare skin of Maël's arm.

I snatch him, but whatever it is around him recoils at my touch and sends me reeling back. Not by much – the water stops the backwards movement that makes my flesh snap around my very bones, and then he's slipping away from me, towards the great red sunken cliff. How far did we drift? How come we're next to Lucius's cliff?

But there's no time for musings.

He's slowly, so slowly, sliding towards the bottom, a downwards drift of a lifeless body, a feather scattered by the wind. This can't be the same man who told me just moments ago that he would have liked to know me better. It can't be that the light has gone out of his eyes; it can't be—

Oh, no. Not while I'm here.

Not while I'm watching.

If someone is going to make him pay, it will be me, and not a stupid curse placed by my sister.

I shove myself towards him, shove with every ounce of strength I have in my body, compelling my Gift to propel me. My fingers enclose around his shirt at the shoulder, and I try to pull him out, but that blasted *thing* tries to push me back again. I hold on with everything I can, clenching my teeth against the pain, against the force that tries to repel me, and that's when his body begins to jolt.

It's a shield of magic, a thread that courses through him. He'd be in horrible pain if he could feel anything, I realise, but I don't think he can. My eyes sting and I know, I just know, that this isn't how it ends.

I'd open my mouth to scream, but who is here to listen underneath the water? *Who listens, who listens*, I wonder, while my mind searches frantically for songs of unbinding.

Ullar's Spell-Lore, drip-fed to me since I was a child.

No, no, not *any* song of unbinding will do. I need a Water-song. A strong one. The most powerful that I know.

All of me is trembling when I begin to sing the 'Song of Melusine'. It's the brush of a tail underwater; it's the scrape of sharp teeth piercing skin. It's the glint of the shimmering colours of the rainbow, tainted green by the sea. It's the swirl of a clawed hand, tightening around the ties that bind Maël, ripping them apart.

I sing and sing and sing in my bubble of magic.

This is not the end, he told me, two days ago.

This is not the end.

There's a shiver in the water around us, and time is unfreezing. There's the sweep of an undercurrent, and then his body is thrown towards me. My lungs are burning, but I coil my fingers tighter around his shoulders, scraping the flesh. I try to pull him up, pull us both up. He's heavy, so heavy, such a bear of a man.

Too heavy, unnaturally heavy. The binds – the song hasn't cut through them.

But I know this: every one of the ancient songs, it has no ending.

It's the singer who writes the ending, a different one every single time.

There are shadows swirling in the water as we both begin to sink, nameless shades of deep green, and I know that I'll have to leave him, if I still want to save myself.

I send a questioning ripple of power, looking for traces of his Gift, anything that I could take so I could make a small jump in time.

That would allow me to save him.

Nothing.

There is nothing left in him.

No.

No.

There's a face peering from the shadows, glossy eyes and a

sharp nose, rows of deadly teeth. 'What do you want, Time-Hopper?' The swish of a tail. The sweep of green hair behind her. 'What do you want, Queen of the Edge?' She blinks towards Maël.

My mind is a murk. I think, *Melusine.*

The first of the Mervolk. Their ancient Queen.

Time is slowing and hurrying around me.

What I want, they will give me.

They will have to.

I will not die here, and nor will he. I send a ripple of power, again, but wide around me, feeling out for kernels of magic in the sea. Feeling out for traces of anything that could help us.

Melusine's face freezes in a cold grin. 'I see,' she whispers.

But I barely hear her as I reach into the depths of the sea and grab for its power, tearing at it, pulling it towards myself. I wrap it around my own magic, I wrap it around Maël, I wrap it around us, and shout the words into the water, the first words than come into my mind.

The first words, and the last of this song.

I free you by wind, I free you by water,
I free you by stone and fire,
I free you, I free you, I free you.
What has been done will be undone,
and it will return to where it came from.

The sea flinches around us, as if it's a great beast stabbed in its belly, resenting every ounce of power that I draw from it, resenting my commands.

I hate you, I tell the sea. *Let him go. Let* us *go.*

In the depths, there's a great uncoiling and a murmur, becoming thunder. The sea itself and the earth beneath it are shaking. Everything roars. Before us, the sunken cliff begins to spin, to rise at a staggering speed and I look down to see stone rushing towards us.

The sea seems to draw into itself, crushing Maël and I together, knocking my head to his chest, tangling my limbs with his. And then, there's a shudder, a great exhale, and we find ourselves flung towards the surface.

In the blink of an eye, I'm gulping air, Maël's head bobbing against my shoulder. I'm treading water, trying to keep us on the surface, when my legs strike hard, slippery ground underneath, when we find ourselves being pushed higher and higher.

All around us, the ground is rising from the sea. Within moments, there are feet of land between us and the edge of the water, and an island is still emerging. Not far from me, where just a cliff of red stone blinked out of the sea, now stands a tower. Its red, glinting surface is covered in seaweed and barnacles. An orange gemstone glows near its top, almost blinding in the sunlight. Irrational, considering the state of the rest of it.

My fingers clench around Maël tunic, as I think, *Lucius's Tower*? But there's no time for history lessons.

Whatever I did, it pulled this patch of land from the sea.

Whatever I did—

Maël's chest is completely still underneath my palm.

Oh, no.

Not while I'm here.

I lay him on the ground and begin shoving against his chest, hard, in manoeuvres I learned during my training as a Mage-Huntress, trying to push the water out of him. His body is hard and cold, unmoving. I bend down, touching my mouth to his, trying to push air into his lungs.

This is not the end.

'Breathe, you swine. Breathe,' I shout and I shout and I shout and try to give him the kiss of life. I bring my hands to his chest and pump them, trying to push out the water from his belly, from his lungs.

But no matter what I do, the only movement in his body is the one that comes from the way I shove against him. His head lolls from side to side, lifeless.

This is not the end.

He did *not* capture me just so he could bring me to where I was meant to go from the very beginning. He did not put me in chains just so he could die on this island that never was, that isn't even supposed to be here. The bastard has to *live*.

'Breathe,' I roar, my voice raw and cracking, pumping until my arms hurt.

This is stupid, such a stupid way to go, so fitting for such a fool.

My face is drenched and salty, rivulets of water clouding my gaze.

This is not happening.

No one can go that fast, nor that stupidly.

There's a clop and the sound of heavy breathing behind me. I turn my head in time to see Fabien dragging himself from the water, panting.

'Do something,' I shout at him, and he crawls towards us, rising slowly to his feet as he gains purchase on the slippery ground.

'What happened?' he says, watching me push into Maël's unmoving chest.

'The bindings,' I say. 'The water curse, I think. I was too late.'

There's a long pause, punctuated by Fabien's pants. I can't look at him. I can't. My eyes are fixed on Maël's lifeless body.

'I jumped from the ship as soon as I realised that something was wrong,' he says.

What does he want, for me to congratulate him?

I pump, pump, pump. Something cracks beneath my hands.

'You need to replace me,' I say, gasping for air. My lungs feel too tight, but my thoughts have settled. We have to keep doing this. 'You need to do what I'm doing.'

'What did you do, Mihi? What is this?'

'You need to replace me,' I shout. 'We can save him. I have seen it done by the Mage-Hunters; we can save him.'

I move out of the way, motioning for him to take my place. I watch him assuming his position, pressing down with his arms.

'Harder,' I say. 'With all your weight.'

'It killed him,' he pants. 'They killed him.' Fabien is

drenched and looks as exhausted as I feel. 'What did you do, Mihi?'

'I broke them,' I say. 'I broke the bindings.'

'You did more than that,' he says, flatly, and our eyes lock for the first time.

The tightening in my chest increases. 'I don't know what I did. I don't know what this is.'

'This is Lucius's Tower,' he says quietly. 'This, Mihi, is what the King of Kings sunk beneath the sea.'

The legend says that Sabya or Lucius sunk land into the water and brought the sea to Lafala.

But bugger Sabya and bugger the legends.

Where is she now?

'They're coming,' says Fabien, jerking his head towards Lafala.

I lift my gaze right in time to see a boat with the prow shaped like a swan's neck, stopping on the shore of the new island. Two silhouettes hop down, steadying each other. The small one must be my sister, taking halting steps towards me. The taller one, a red-haired, stout woman, trails her.

'Celine,' I say, while emotions change on her face faster than I can track them, her gaze shifting from me to Maël.

There's joy; there's dismay; there's a touch of fear. I would have recognised her anywhere, I think with a pang. Fourteen years is not too a long time to forget what one's sister looks like.

But it's long enough not to be able to make head or tail of someone's choices, their actions.

The unnecessary cruelty.

She seems to reach some sort of decision just as she starts racing towards me, but I turn to Fabien. 'Harder,' I say. 'Harder.'

I hear her stopping short of touching me, but I'm not looking, I can't look. My gaze is locked on Maël's huge, lifeless hand, his sprawled fingers. Moving slightly from side to side, edging closer to the belt to which his fearsome blades are strapped.

The pommel has a lion's open maw engraved on them.

That maw is full of teeth.

'I hope you're happy,' I say hoarsely. 'You did this.'

'Anne-Mihielle?' Celine says, her voice a whisper.

Fabien looks to the taller woman. 'Isabella, you need to Call for her. Maybe she can fix this.'

Isabella? Isabella de Langly? Here? To what end?

So many questions. So little time to make everything right.

Maybe something changes again on Celine's face, maybe it doesn't. Maybe her breath hitches. Maybe she's scared of what she did. Maybe she's just realising something.

I don't care.

I shout at Fabien, 'You're not doing it right,' and push him aside, even though my arms are aching.

Even though I can barely breathe.

'You need to Call for her,' repeats Fabien, and the tall woman – Isabella – begins to sing, and the surface of the sea flickers with golden light, and then in shades of darkness.

The song is a roar, a call, a plea.

'Mihi did this,' says Fabien. 'Mihi lifted the island from the sea; Mihi broke the bindings, but it was too late.'

I wish I could scream. I wish I could tear at something. But he needs me.

So I push, push, push.

BLANCHE

There's a sickening roar, coming from the very depths of the earth. A crack in the amber. There's the dim of a thousand horses marching, a prolonged wail cleaving through the stone.

Sabya jumps to her feet. 'Someone broke the bindings,' she says. 'Someone has weakened her prison.'

Sabya flinches and I hear it at the same time she does. It sounds like an avalanche of boulders rolling down a steep hill. 'The shields between the Kingdoms,' she says.

'Darg?' I say, my hair standing on end.

He has come for her. Finally. As Sabya always said he would.

'What do we do?' I say.

'Too soon,' says Sabya. 'It's too soon. You need to start warning the others. You need to tell them that something is coming for us from the Green Kingdom.'

I think, *Darg, indeed, then.*

I think, *My grandchildren.* I think, *Blue Kingdom.* I think, *First Valerie, to muster the troops, then Maël. Where in Sabya's name might Hugo be?*

I'm drifting through the halls of Bluefort when I hear the

Callsong. In the urgency of it, there's no mistaking. I must go to Lafala.

MIHI

Isabella touches my shoulder. 'Anne-Mihielle.'

They are arguing. Celine is shouting something about what this is, what is happening and Fabien explains in a low voice.

Bugger all of them.

The press around my shoulder is stronger. '*Erste Jägerin.*'

Then there's another red-haired woman, crouching beside Maël, and her appearance out of nowhere startles me enough to lift my hands and reach for a blade that I don't have. She extends her hand towards his cheek, and it doesn't touch Maël, yet seems to penetrate through the flesh.

'It was the bindings. And the water curse,' says Isabella, her hand firm on my shoulder, a command and a consolation. 'Anne-Mihielle broke them, but it was too late.'

The woman blinks up, as if looking from a dream, as if she's the one seeing the ghost. 'What did you do, Anne-Mihielle? What monsters did you awake from the deep?'

I punch at the solid ground of the cliff beneath me. 'I tried to save him.'

I'm ready to resume my work, when there's another hand on my shoulder. 'That's enough,' says Fabien. 'Mihi. It's over. Stop, Mihi, stop.' He pulls me gently away from Maël.

I stand at his side, blinking.

And then, there's a wail, piercing, like no wail I heard before, a wail that could shatter castles and flood a city and the pain in it could break a kingdom.

Isabella walks up to the ghostly woman's side. 'Mother,' she says. 'Mother.'

Blanche?

The look that the Marchionessa – presumably – gives Isabella is blazing arrows. 'What did you do?'

Isabella is her daughter. And Maël is Isabella's buggering nephew and she did this to him. 'They killed him,' I say before I catch myself. My tongue feels heavy in my mouth and my throat hurts. 'There was nothing I could do. I cut through everything, every spell, every binding, and it wasn't enough.'

'She lifted the island from the bottom of the sea,' says Isabella.

Blanche stares at me, something winking out of her eyes. 'Hop, Anne-Mihielle. You can save him.' She gets to her feet, rallying herself. 'You can time-hop, can't you? Save him. Please. It doesn't even have to be a long hop. Please.'

How does she even know about my Gift?

But there's no time to wonder. There's a flash of darkness at the foot of the tower. A swirl of shadows, thickening, moving towards us, until a man takes shape. A man who is neither tall, nor short, with a studded leather armour.

Ullar.

I could weep in relief at seeing a familiar face. Something deep within my chest unclenches. He'll know what to do. He'll know how to make this right.

'What did you do, Mihi? The shields between the kingdoms are down. All of them.' Ullar curses low through his teeth in his ancient tongue and Blanche shudders. My stomach sinks to the soles of my feet. 'Mihi, do you know what this is?'

I'm dreaming, I must have been dreaming; my body must be rolling towards the bottom of the sea, swept down by Maël's and this must be a mad nightmare—

Fabien and Isabella step aside and Ullar grips my hands and his touch is so solid, so grounding. I lean forward, let him catch me, sobbing into his shoulder.

I didn't even realise I wanted to cry. 'Mihi.'

Mihi, Mihi, Mihi, what the bugger did you do?

Ullar wanted to talk to Blanche, and they're all here now. How absurd this is.

I have no idea what I've done to bring down the shields from here to the Green Kingdom.

No buggering clue.

'I didn't do anything,' I say. 'I don't know what I did.'

'I heard you,' says Ullar. 'I followed you here.' He squeezes my arm. 'You've found them,' he whispers in my ear.

'What in Sabya's name are you talking about?'

I lift my gaze. Blanche is watching Ullar carefully, assessing. The contours of her ghostly shape are shivering.

Behind us, the tower rumbles, a metallic click.

Ullar says, 'Something's waking.'

Nothing makes sense. It's all a jumble, an assortment of people I've met or wanted to meet.

I must be hallucinating.

Blanche's mouth open and closes. 'I have seen you,' she whispers to Ullar. 'I know your face.'

'By the Mothers of the Forest and their gruesome ilk, what is happening?' The voice is like a clash of swords, metal whirring upon metal. The voice is the shiver of light into shadow. I hear her voice first, before she appears, too, next to Maël's corpse.

Golden armour, dark slick hair, tied in a long braid falling down her back.

She points her finger at Ullar, and a sword of light materialises as she lifts her hand. 'You spotty bastard, I knew you were behind this.'

Ullar's shock is a wave of darkness, enveloping us, knocking the breath from our lungs. It's the darkness where stars wink out of life. It's the last glimmer of existence, extinguishing.

'Sabya,' says Blanche.

By the time the Marchionessa says the goddesses' name, she has whirled towards Ullar with her weapons drawn and he has nimbled out of her reach by a few moments. The tip of her sword scratches my raised elbow. The cut is singeing.

'I promised you,' Sabya says. 'You will die by my hand, Darg. I will kill you.'

There's a whir of light and shadow, dancing too fast, a few paces to our left. We watch, transfixed, how the gods battle. It's more a matter of Sabya attacking and Ullar trying to repel her.

Darg?

Darg.

The word knocks into my head, a name I know so well.

Darg, who betrayed Sabya.

Darg, the Dark Mother's general.

My gaze moves to Blanche's just as she disappears out of sight.

And then, everything snaps into place. Ullar's age. His powers. The magical shields surrounding the Green Kingdom, the ones that I apparently destroyed.

Five hundred years ago, Sabya locked someone out, so that he could never come again into the Red Kingdom.

And I just set him free.

I watch Ullar – Darg?– avoiding a blow from Sabya, a sword aiming for his ribs, while a shield of darkness materialises in his hands. It's the darkness of the deepest night, of a hopelessly clouded sky.

Sabya roars and exchanges the sword of light in her hands with a set of double-bladed, double-edged swords. Her Darkblades.

A shiver goes through me. He told me we were to fight the Dark Mother. He told me that's what we were preparing for.

He told me this, over, and over, and over again as I grew up.

We are fighting the Dark Mother.

Are we?

Blanche snaps into view again, now standing right before me. Something wild is in her brown eyes now. 'Mihi, what did you do? The amber. It's broken.'

What, what, what.

What did I do?

'Mihi,' says Blanche, 'you nearly released her. The Dark Mother.'

Sabya lets out a frustrated scream as Darg winks out of existence again, appearing on her other side. 'Sabi,' he says. 'You need to listen. I didn't set anyone free. It was Mihi. And she didn't mean to. Sabi, you need to listen.'

'I didn't do this,' I plead. 'I didn't mean to release her. All I wanted was to save him.'

Blanche shakes her head. 'We're not ready, Mihi. If you're on our side – the right side – you'll hop. You'll undo this. All of it. Hop back where it started. Hop and find a way, find a way to—' Her words stumble. 'Save him. Save all of us.'

At the edge of the island, Darg and Sabya are locked in battle, blinking in and out of existence at the edge between light and shadow. Sabya roars, 'Die, spawn of darkness. The Dark Mother's lapdog.' And then a string of pretty much the same, but in their ancient language. Her small face is contorted in fury, while Ullar – Darg – seems close to desperate.

I have never, ever seen Ullar in my life lose his countenance over something. Over anything.

Celine drops to my feet, taking my hands. 'Anne-Mihielle. Anne-Mihielle. What is this? Why was Maël with you?'

I push her away. I can't bear to touch her. I can't bear to touch anyone.

And doesn't she see that our world is collapsing?

Mine has, under the weight of the lie that I've been told all my life.

What is up, what is down, I don't know anymore, as I watch them. The man who I called 'my father' in my mind.

Celine turns to Fabien. 'What happened? I trusted you.'

I want to shout, *Shut the bugger up, I can't hear my own thoughts.*

Who cares that you were foolish enough to trust him?

In the blink of an eye, nothing matters. 'Wake up, sister,' I tell her. 'It was what the Fallen Court wanted.'

Blanche levels her stare with mine. Her hands are trembling, I can tell, but when we're losing our heads, someone has to keep it. 'Anne-Mihielle, I don't care in the least how you do this, but you have to hop. The confluence, it's all wrong. Something's terribly wrong. This can't happen. Look at them.' She raises her voice. 'We've already lost. The Dark Mother can't be allowed to break free. And we'll all kill each other before she even starts.'

Fabien murmurs, 'I'm sorry.' Probably to Celine.

Who cares.

It's not as if it can change anything.

Yes, it can.

I can.

It's as if Blanche's words are finally piercing through to me.

I need to hop. I need to hop and confront Ullar and not-almost-release the Dark Mother and make this not-happen.

I have to time-hop and untangle the lies I've been told; pick a side, once I find it.

Blanche tells Fabien, 'Shut up, you harebrained, good-for-nothing…' Her words trail. 'You were meant to protect him. Rein him in.'

My head is pounding. Between us all, Maël lies motionless.

Did Ullar even know? Did he suspect, who he was sending me with? Did he know what he was doing, and what he wanted?

Across from us, Ullar dodges a dagger that is thrown his way. He and Sabya move so fast, that it's almost impossible for me to track their movements. Light and dark and the flash of golden armour and of leather gloves. An edge of movement.

I think, *Stop.*

I can stop this.

Just a pinch of my Gift and this moment freezes in time. I watch their faces. The agony, surprise, fear in them. Darg's sheer desperation. Sabya comes at him, keeps coming, hard and fast, until she will kill him.

He wanted to talk to Blanche, I realise. Just before Maël arrived in Xante, Ullar wanted to mend bonds. To send me to Bluefort.

'*The Dark Mother's lapdog*' Sabya called him.

He is still, and until further explanation, my father.

I nudge him out of the way of another of Sabya's short daggers, which she keeps switching in her hands for Darkblades. The advantage of not having to really draw a weapon, I suppose, just to be able to conjure them.

When time unfreezes, Sabya's face slackens for a moment, noticing me standing right next to them. She sniffs. 'Stand back. This is none of your business.'

Ullar calls, 'This is not your fight, Mihi,' right before he hurls a blunt shield of darkness to push me aside, right before Sabya raises a wall of swirling light and darkness between them. Shielding them from everyone else on this island.

Sparks of light and deeper, glistening shadows, glimmer through the swirling shield.

My knees buckle because, whether he lied to me or not, he's the closest thing I had to family in the absence of my blood relatives. Sabya's Gift tastes and feels his power, changes and shifts the very air around them. It draws on both the light and the shadow.

All the players in this game, save for the Dark Mother herself, are on this island.

Hop back in time... But merely a day or two won't fix it. I'll need to go farther back, though just how far back, there's no one here to advise me.

I'm only allowed to hop back twice in time to fix the same moment. Two times and it is over. The third path is set in stone.

Isabella slides onto her knees next to Maël, takes one of his hands into hers. Great tears roll from her cheeks to their joined hands.

Blanche moves partly in front of me, partly obscuring Maël's body, partly obscuring the mist of shadows. 'The Red Kingdom can't fight the Dark Mother without a king,' she says. 'Maël's death means that we've lost the war already.'

What is she saying? What is she even talking about?

As if she can read my thoughts, she says, 'Petit-Mihiel is dead. We all needed Maël in Lafala.'

But I can hear the unsaid reproach. *And yet, he went after you.*

Ullar emerges from the dissipating shadows. He takes a step towards me and then thuds to the ground, on one side. His breath is hard, laboured, and even if he might have lied to me, my instinct is to run to him.

I think, is this how a god dies? How can you even kill one?

A dagger made of darkness protrudes from his chest.

The legends did say that she stabbed him in the heart.

And before I can even open my mouth to scream, Sabya is right by me, her Darkblades poised above my head.

What did she hear? What did Darg tell her about me? She shoved me out of her way moments ago.

Stop.

I stop.

I stop time.

Sabya's face is contorted in rage, the Darkblades less than a foot from my head. Next to me, Fabien and Isabella are sitting next to Maël. Dejection, desperation, endless anguish. Preparing to jump towards me, there's Celine, her mouth frozen in the start of a scream. And next to me lies Ullar, drawing his last breaths.

Thousands of years of existence, to end in this. For nothing.

What a mess.

Were that it mattered.

The Marchionessa drifts closer to me and I don't even begin to question how she can move through frozen time. She gives Sabya a searching look. 'She's not always like this. She hasn't always been like this.' She turns those deep brown eyes to me. 'Are you my enemy? Is he our enemy?' she says, pointing at Ullar.

Darg.

I shake my head. 'I don't know.'

All that I know is that if I don't hop back from here, from this moment, Sabya will kill me. Or I will have to snatch one of Maël's blades, or Fabien's, and kill her.

How do you even kill an ancient goddess?

I wish I could tell Sabya that I'm not her enemy. Darg only spoke fondly of her.

But something certainly isn't as I was led to believe.

This is not the end.

I don't want to die.

I don't.

This is one huge, selfish reason to do a time-hop, but I probably would have done it for Darg – even if just to get some answers – and for Maël.

The Marchionessa would do anything for Maël, I can tell. And if I do the time-hop, we will need some clarity. We will need to speak, without me having to fear consequences from Sabya. My head is clear enough by now to realise that Ullar was right: Blanche knows plenty about Sabya. It was obvious when the goddess arrived.

If I want to redo the time sequence right, I'll have to know what I'm doing.

'We'll have to speak,' I tell Blanche. 'Once we're back in

time. Tell me how we'll do this, tell me how I can help you remember.'

No one ever remembers. When I jump back, no one ever knows what I did, except for me.

Blanche nods. Thank the Mothers of the Forest. But as I have nothing to thank them for right now, it's no more than a figure of speech.

Blanche says, 'Find me. Ask your grandmother for a mark of the Fallen Court – you do know about your grandmother?'

'Yes.' My grandparents. How they lied to me, too. When I came into the woods with Maël.

'Good. When you find me, tell me that Robert was born in the county of Anselmois, in a hamlet near Mora's Pass. Tell me that the first song he brought me was a bawdy song called 'The Heart and the Locket'. Tell me that not even Sabya knows what the 'Warsong for the Goddess' does. She had no idea when she wrote it; she still has no idea what it did to the Dark Mother.'

I close my eyes, take it all in. And then, I finally move out of the way of Sabya's Darkblades.

Blanche doesn't know; she doesn't need to know that I have accounts to settle with Maël. That will come later.

But she is right. If what they say is true, we have already lost. We're squabbling, and the Dark Mother is about to be set free.

And just like that, time begins to unwind again. The Darkblades begin to lower, little by little, and there's a great squeak from the iron door of the tower on the island.

No time, I have no more time to listen; Sabya is out to kill me.

I leap towards my sister, no pity in my heart.

'I'll see you soon,' I throw at Blanche.

Celine turns wild eyes to me as I grab her by the shoulders. This will hurt, and this will dent her Gift, even as I do the time-hop.

I will take from her, but she deserves this.

If it wasn't for her, none of this would have happened.

Where, I think. Where should I jump?

I don't have much time to make a decision.

I'll hop back, far back, when things still hung in the balance, when I'd have enough time to prevent these events. Before I boarded the ship, before I ran from the High Inquisitor, before they took Remy.

Far before that.

And the sheer magnitude of what I'll have to do already makes me sag a little. There's just one of me, and I'll have to fix all this. Finding out what went wrong in the past. Trying to save the Three Kingdoms.

As if I weren't an imposter, who knew one good trick.

As if I could do this.

But there's no one else, is there?

And time is, yet again, slipping away from me.

I close my eyes. Tight. I whisper to Celine, 'This is going to hurt. But you killed them.' I dig my nails deep in my sister's flesh, feel for the talons of my Gift, the hooks, the tethers, and sink them deep into Celine's essence, into her very blood.

My sister shrieks, a terrifying howl of pain, and tries to break free, but I'm holding her too fast, I've gone too deep, and she can't shake me off.

I take a deep breath and plunge into the past, taking my sister's Gift with me.

NEW BEGINNINGS

MIHI

There's a churning in my stomach, and the world is still spinning when I land back into my own skin with a thump that sends me reeling forward, and then back on my bottom. I blink, trying to bring my surroundings into focus.

I'm not on that strange island made of red stone, that I pulled from the sea without meaning to.

No, I am somewhere else.

A gravel path beneath my feet. Around me, hedges and bushes and thorns covering half-crumbling walls made of grey stone. Here and there, moonstones the size of a grown man. Above me, a glass ceiling, and beyond it, a spotless summer sky.

This is Xante. The Emerald Palace – the King's Garden, to be precise.

There's the crunch of boots on the gravel behind me, and I close my eyes against the sound. Not a good idea.

My head is still spinning behind closed eyelids and the nausea knots and knots and knots my stomach, and it's worse, much worse, because I have a sinking feeling that I've done it, and I know what day this is.

I turn around, only to collide face-first with a soft doublet covering a solid chest.

Then I make the mistake of looking up. Dark green eyes stare into mine, full of bewilderment. Light brown hair, carefully combed back. The delicate nose of the Heir of the Green Kingdom.

Bugger.

I've done it.

This is Claude.

And this is the day he proposes to me.

I stumble when I take a step back, but he catches me lightly by the shoulders. 'Mihi?' he says.

Yes, this is me.

Erste Jägerin, Mihi, still. Mihi, whom the Heir of the Green Kingdom wanted to meet on the Ides of August.

I'm the same and not the same, and this is a different situation than the one six weeks ago.

I'm Mihi who will have to make decisions that will change the course of history, Mihi who will have to be very careful not to destroy ancient shields that have been keeping the Three Kingdoms safe for centuries.

Mihi who buggering decided, apparently, that the course

of history depends on whether she accepts Claude on this day in August.

Mihi who didn't see both the mage who raised her, and the man she tried to save, lying dead on a small island made of red stone.

Not anymore, I tell myself. I erased that outcome from history.

I'm here and there, caught between a future that will never be, and a present that already was. Never have I done a hop as long as this. I'm reeling. I feel heavy as a millstone and as light as a dust mote.

On instinct, I open my arms, and wrap them around Claude's waist, using his body to steady myself, to enjoy the solidness of the past that has now become the present. He's not much taller than me, but he's here, and he's real, and I'm here, and not in that nightmare I was trapped in just moments ago.

Ullar lied, and Maël lied, and they all lied, and it was a buggering catastrophe.

Claude makes a strangled sound, but his arms tighten around me in a steadying grip. Six weeks ago— No, now, in this present, we are still together. He hasn't yet asked his question, and I haven't yet refused to become his Queen.

In my mounting panic, when I decided to make the time-hop, this was the only point I could think of, the only point where what I said or did could have made a difference to the way that my future would play out.

After today, nothing would be the same between us.

After I refuse him.

Not yet.

I bury my face into his chest, a silent prayer for him to anchor me into this moment, to keep the memories of the past few hours at bay.

But he can't. Nausea twists in my guts as I remember.

The splintered remains of the High Inquisitor's wooden likeness. Remy's bloodied face, his torn shirt. The sway of the boat in the storm. Maël's shock as he was dragged down into the depths by the curse put upon him by my own sister. His bloodless face on a red beach. A goddess with revenge in her eyes, and a golden armour, and her Darkblades.

The light going out of Ullar's eyes.

Darg.

The man who stated for as long as I've known him that we must do everything to stop the Dark Mother. Who made that goal into my life's mission. My mentor, the person who I've looked to as a father, the immortal Court Astrologist.

His name is Darg, I remind myself. And he was the Dark Mother's general. He was the one who betrayed Sabya when she needed his help most. The man who turned everything I knew about my life and my purpose into one giant lie.

Were we Mage-Hunters just tools to him?

The truth spins into a tangle of lies. Too much of an enormity to be looked in the face just yet.

Bugger.

Nausea creeps up again, making my stomach shudder. I let go of Claude, rushing past the moonstones, past the ancient trees and stop behind one of the giant ferns. My mouth opens on a silent scream. But it's not words that come out; it's the contents of what I had for breakfast on that – no, this – day in August.

My stomach heaves and heaves and heaves, and when it's done, I manage a few dizzy steps before I land on my bottom again. I look up. Light and warmth, filtered through the leaves of the trees above me, settle on my face.

Bloody Ullar and his lies that have lasted for centuries.

Claude shifts, and then walks hesitantly towards me. Today, he'll want an answer from me.

I close my eyes, taking deep breaths, grinding my feet into the gravel of the King's Garden. The grainy feel of it, the way the pebbles slip on top of each other. And yet, I still feel underwater.

I see dark hair, floating in tendrils, while the fight is extinguished from a pair of black eyes. A heavy body splayed on a beach that I conjured out of the sea, the crunch of his ribs under my arms, as I tried to pump life back into him. My head feels fuzzy and my arms still ache as though I'd just stepped aside, conceding to having lost that battle.

And a salty streak travels down my face.

Tender hands brush my cheeks. I open my eyes, willing myself into this moment.

This is my present, and there is no need to look into a future that will never come to pass. Not if I can help it.

That future will change, and it begins today.

Claude leans towards me, regal and kind and splendid in his green velvet doublet embroidered with golden thread, his silken cape trailing behind him. There's so much concern in his eyes. 'What's wrong?'

I crawl to standing and towards the closest moonstone. I sit down, rubbing my face hard, pushing shards of memories aside.

'Anne-Mihielle, what's wrong?' Claude touches my shoulder.

Everything is wrong. My past, my future.

Who I am, who I want to be.

Who do I want to be?

But even if things have always been spectacularly easy between me and Claude, and it always felt so natural to lean on him, he won't understand if I tell him.

He can't.

Not even I do.

I force a smile. 'Nothing. I'm a bit queasy today.'

Claude scrunches up his nose in that sweet way of his. There are so many details that snag my attention now. The way he brushes his mop of light brown hair to the side. The steady way he looks at everything, because Claude knows that if he wants anything, he simply has to reach out and grab it.

That is, until *I* happened. Until I refused him. There is yet time to give him a different answer.

That is why I'm here, is it not?

Bugger.

That sinking feeling in me feels more like falling now.

What was I thinking when I jumped back into this moment of all moments, when I made the most important decision of my life by refusing Claude? What kind of hare-brained idea was this? What made me think that I'm in any condition to make any kind of decision, as rattled as I am now?

Pink creeps onto Claude's neck, into his cheeks. 'Oh, does this mean...'

I gape, unsure, mostly convinced that I should bolt. 'What?' I say.

'Are you...' He gestures widely with his hands, pointing at my stomach. 'With child?'

Mothers of the Forest and Sabya's Darkblades. 'No!' I say. Perhaps a bit too loud. 'No, no, no.'

My stomach lurches, dangerously close to emptying itself again. I breathe in and out, through the mouth, before I manage to grit out, 'I'm fine. It must be something I ate.'

I don't mention that I was rattled to the marrow by a storm, not long ago, just off the coast of Lafala. Even to my own ears, it sounds mad.

Did I swallow too much saltwater? That must be it.

In spite of myself, I cock a half-smile. Lucius's Flaming Fingers, this is unhinged.

I'm unhinged, and Maël is the most unhinged person of us all.

I catch myself with a wince thinking of him. Alive, now, again? Probably.

I'm still unravelling. I almost want to laugh. I have a few moments to decide who I am, who Ullar has trained me to be, and make an informed decision about my future.

The buggering fear that makes my heart gallop is making me hysterical.

Yes, surely, that must be it.

In any case, I have no business being here, today. And once I decide that, I actually find a drop of peace.

In the previous time-hop, I made wrong decision after wrong decision after wrong decision. Trusting who I shouldn't have. Letting myself be carried away.

I take a deep breath.

No more.

Stop, Mihi, stop.

Stop and think.

There's so much to think about.

Step by step.

Firstly.

Claude has other plans. He gets ahead of me. He plants his feet into the gravel and says, gently, 'Because even if you were, I don't think I'd mind.'

'If I was what?' I blurt out.

The pink inflames his cheeks again. 'With child, I mean. I asked you to meet me here today because there is something I want to speak to you about.'

Mothers. Of. The. Forest.

No, no, no. Not yet. Not now.

I won't be rushed into anything.

No more mistakes. Not this time.

I don't have to make a decision unless a question is asked, and I won't let it come to that.

I take his hands in mine. His fine, smooth hands. The calluses on my fingers scrape against his unmarred skin. 'I have to go,' I tell him, and it's true.

I have to go now, before he asks and I have to give him an answer.

I have to go and sift through the lies that I've been told all of my life.

I have to go and prevent the worst that can happen, what has already happened in a future that is, as of a few moments ago, the past.

I squeeze Claude's hand and let his affection strengthen me. Sweet, confident, easy, Claude. This isn't goodbye, it's just a respite.

'I'll see you soon,' I say. 'I have work to do.'

It's not a lie. It's the truth, every single word of it.

* * *

There are many upsides to walking through moments in time that have already happened, including saving yourself the trouble of looking for people, when you already know where they will be.

The last time Claude asked for my hand – and I refused – the first thing I did was to look for Ullar, to tell him everything.

He was, in the end, the closest thing I had to a parent.

And what a poor substitute for a parent he has been, considering the recently uncovered set of earth-shattering lies.

I rush through the corridors of the Emerald Palace, heading for the training arena.

It's undoubtedly a terrible idea. In fact, I don't have two

ideas tied together about what I'm doing and I can't possibly imagine what I'd want with him. All I know is that going to see Ullar is a compulsion and I have to, even if I have no clue about possible outcomes.

How does one even confine an ancient god, if one doesn't have Sabya's power? Does one even confront him with the lies he's told all his life?

I try to pace myself, try not to rush into things, but I've never been particularly good at it. And I almost laugh again. How desperate I've been to hang on to the place I've carved for myself in Xante, and now—

Now, I have an inkling about what I have to do.

I stare at the walls of the corridors, that have grown around the roots that are snaking around the palace – or has the palace snaked around the remains of the sacred grove?

Dried branches are woven through the walls. Leaves and vines crawl downwards from the ceiling, creating intricate, woven designs, arching above my head.

And then, there's this. The massive open doors leading to the training arena.

The green sand on the floor. Palace guards, sparring under Ullar's intent gaze.

But my gaze is intent on *him*.

My fill-in father. Traitor, liar. Schemer.

He stands at the edge of the arena, his arms crossed, barking orders at the soldiers.

The set of his mouth is hard and shadows swirl in his eyes.

My feet carry me towards him, much faster than they

should. He gives me one good look and the shadows beckon and dance and reach out for me.

I'm transfixed. What has he been aiming for all these years since he's been training the Mage-Hunters? What sort of weapons have we been crafted into?

'Everyone, get out,' he says. The guards aren't even taken aback. They're used to his moods by now.

Ullar takes me in. He won't see anything unusual in the clothes that I wore that day – this day – at the Emerald Palace. My usual attire as a Mage-Huntress. The clean, yet well-worn green cloth trousers with their golden embroidery, the wrinkled shirt, a long braid sneaking down my back.

But as everyone else trickles out of the room, he could likely see the wisps of fading light trailing around me, the traces that a time-hop leaves. Of course he'd notice.

Trust him to see the evidence of the disturbances and the ripples that I've caused.

And again, fears trickle in. How can I ever dream of facing him, and winning? What possessed me to come here, with not a second's thought of fear?

'How far, Mihi?' he says in his low, raspy voice. Like the scrape of rocks.

How far did you jump back in time is what he means. After fourteen years at his side, in which he shaped me into whatever he wanted me to be, I have come to know him well enough that he doesn't even have to finish his sentences for me to understand.

I shiver.

I used to trust him. With my life. It's chilling to see him

through a new perspective. One word out of place, and he could obliterate me.

I can't do this alone.

I need to leave.

I need to find myself allies to face this.

To face *him*.

One good look, and I know.

Today is not the day when I'll be challenging him.

Not the day we'll talk about the lies and disappointment that pulled the rug from underneath my feet. Not the day when I'll have answers about what he wanted to achieve in the end.

Ullar shifts. 'Mihi. What's wrong? How far did you have to jump back? What happened?'

'I made mistakes,' I say softly, scrambling for lies that aren't lies.

Will he see through it?

One wrong word, and I'm done for.

No more turning back time for me.

And there's so much that I have left unfinished.

'I made a mistake,' I say. 'A few weeks from now, when we rescued a Water-Twirler.'

Stick to the truth.

Ullar seems to relax. 'Did you use their Gift?'

To make the jump, he means.

'A Water-Twirler's Gift, yes,' I say. Not a lie. Because in the end, that's what my sister is.

I push aside any thoughts of having to see my sister again, and what we both did.

No more mistakes, I tell myself again.

I can't say to Ullar, *Is the Dark Mother any particular friend of yours? Were we meant to assist her, too, in the end?*

'I'm a bit … frightened, Ullar,' I say. 'It made me think about what's truly important. I want to go to the Hallowed Forest and see my grandparents. I haven't visited them in a long time.'

Gwenhael did invite me to come again when we parted, though he won't remember it this time.

Never mind. I have to begin somewhere. I remember what Blanche said, before I turned back time to save her precious grandson. I feel sick thinking about Maël, but … but—

I can't tell up from down anymore, but I know this: if I want allies, I need to seek them at the Fallen Court. What I saw on the red cliff gave me this certainty: the Fallen Court is associated with Sabya.

And Sabya killed Darg. Ullar. The traitor, the liar. I saw it with my own eyes.

Stick to the truth.

But maybe not all of it.

The darkness begins to dance around him, choking the light from the entire hall. He wipes a hand down his face, and I can see the weariness that he's been carrying around with him for hundreds and hundreds of years.

The lies? Are they bearing down on him?

'What *did* happen, Mihi?' he says. 'Why was it worth a time-hop?'

The truth. At least, parts of it. 'Mage-Hunters were hurt,' I say. 'I couldn't let that stand, could I?'

'Tell me,' he says.

I give him a tremulous smile. 'I need to leave for a few days. I need to see my grandparents.' Not a lie. That's exactly where I'm going. I can't vanish – he won't stand for that. I have to tell him where I'm going. And make him believe it. 'I'll leave instructions with the Mage-Hunters, to make sure that the incidents aren't repeated. That everyone is safe.'

I'm a coward and I'm ready to bolt, and though I know I should face him, I can't.

This coward will yet live to see another day. That is, if I can get away from him.

I need to go. I need to find allies. I can't defeat him; I can't subdue him, not on my own.

I turn to leave, and he catches me by the wrist, forcing me to face him.

There's a sound like muffled thunder, which pounds in my ears and makes me feel like I'm underwater again. The light and darkness tremble and shiver in the air, as if they were oil and water, unable to mix.

I can't tell if it's my Gift or his, responding to our emotions.

I'm terrified – of him. Of what he might do. I can't untangle this if I'm dead.

'What happened to you, Mihi? Why won't you speak to me?' His voice is softer than I've ever heard it. 'Who did this?'

Tears sprout in my eyes. Unexpected. And a childish sob chokes me. 'I can't speak of it yet,' I say. 'Don't make me.'

His grip turns gentle. 'I wish you'd trust me, Mihi. There's nothing more dear to me than you. You know that, don't you? Whoever hurt you, I'll make them pay.'

Truth? Lies? Where were we on the scale between these two extremes? How much truth and how many lies?

I want to believe every word he says. It's more of a declaration of affection than any he's ever made before.

But how would it sound if I told him, 'If what you said is true, then go and kill yourself.'

Instead, I say, 'I'll tell you when I'm ready.'

He takes me in for a long moment. And then, he lets me go.

He lets me go.

Little does he know, I'm leaving so that I can bring the sky crushing down on top of his head.

AUTHOR'S NOTE

And here we are, dear reader, at the start of a new, exciting series. At least, exciting for me. I couldn't wait to properly introduce you to Anne-Mihielle.

Some of you might still remember fleeting mentions of her from *The Kingdom Is a Golden Cage*, the first book in the prequel series. Some of you have actually complained that those mentions led to nothing, in the end. I must ask you to be patient! I rarely mention something that I don't build up upon further along. As I wrote the books that take place in this world, I always kept in mind what was yet to happen, what I had yet to unveil.

If you've read *The Kingdom Is a Golden Cage* or *Rise of the Fallen Court*, you might have noticed that I have a penchant for Easter Eggs – hiding clues about events that are to come or hints that not everything is as it might seem. Or references to past events that our characters don't yet know about. There are heaps of them in both of the titles I mentioned, as there are hints in this book to reveals that are still to come. And every book is written in such a way that it's meant to be reread, especially after reading the next instalment in the series –this is the point where you might properly notice these Easter Eggs that I've hidden everywhere.

And as in my previous books, I have an absolute penchant for showing all the ways in which 'urban legends', time, and the propagation of stories have a tendency to change the fundamental truth about a person or certain events. Just as, in *The Kingdom Is a Golden Cage*, the stories that Celine and Magali believe about the first duke and duchess contradict what actually happens in *Rise of the Fallen Court*. It was all very much intentional and no oversight on my part. But this is the nature of legends and the way they distort the truth. Sometimes, unfortunately, my characters (and people, in general) act on the basis of common beliefs that are, in fact, lies that they've taken for granted all their lives.

For those of you who are new to this world, I'll tell you something about the sources that have inspired it. Basically, the Three Kingdoms are a pseudo-medieval, pseudo-Continental European world where magic exists. The history of the Romannhon Empire is inspired by the history of the Roman Empire, just as the Three Kingdoms are inspired by the areas of confluence between Celtic, Germanic, and Roman cultures that were at the base of the culture of medieval Germany and France.

Even the laws of inheritance that I repeatedly mention in the book are firmly rooted in history. The law that prevails in the Red Kingdom is what historians now call the semi-Salic law (the Salic Law was an ancient code of law of the Franks, a Germanic people that settled in present-day France). According to the inheritance law in this codex – in its semi-Salic variant – the inheritance could only pass to male heirs. The male heirs of male heirs had precedence, but in case there were none, the inheritance passed to the male heirs of the closest female relatives to the last holder of the title. This meant that women couldn't inherit crowns or fiefs in their own right. I've detailed this more in *The Kingdom Is a Golden Cage* (both the historical outset, as well as the reverberations for our characters).

Of course, the inheritance law is different in the Blue Kingdom (as you might have noticed), and I'll ask you to keep all of this in mind because there are more inheritance-related disputes to come (unsurprisingly, I think).

And may I tell you how absolutely thrilled I am to be able to show off the family trees of the main characters in the books? I feel this is the point where the two series converge, and if you think that the ruling families are a bit tightly knit, this is also inspired from medieval history. Families in power tended to forge marriage alliances to tighten their grip on crowns and fiefs. So, basically, everybody was related to everybody. It was a small and virtually inaccessible world that actually aimed to exclude others, and the family trees in my books reflect those underhanded practices.

Easter eggs, again! And I bet you'll be able to spot more in this book once you read the next instalment in the series. If it seems that a handful of things are non-sequiturs… Well! The resolution is still to come.

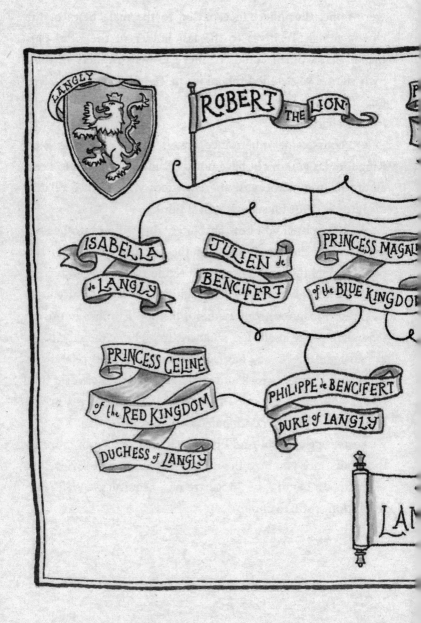

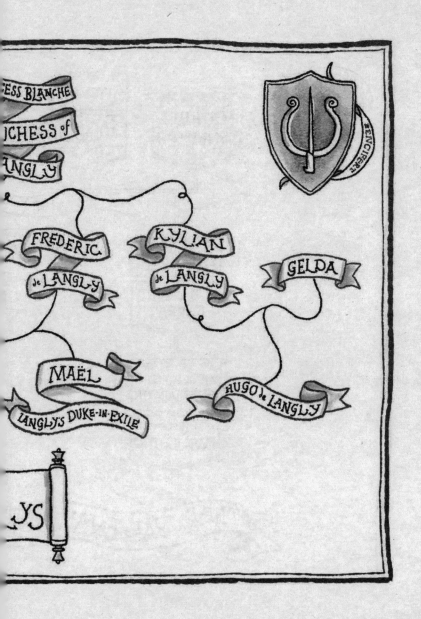

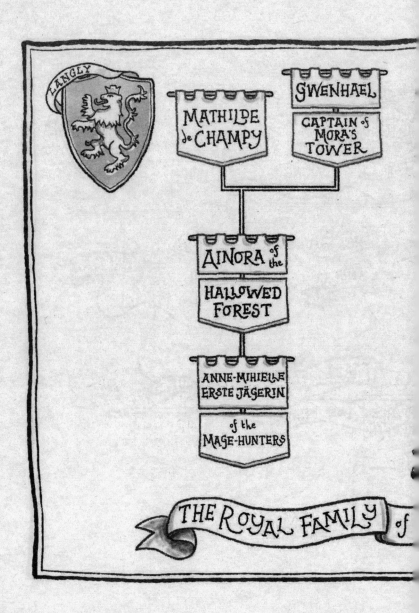

LANGLY

MATHILDE de CHAMPY

GWENHAEL
CAPTAIN of MORA'S TOWER

AINORA of the HALLOWED FOREST

ANNE-MIHIELLE ERSTE JÄGERIN
of the MAGE-HUNTERS

THE ROYAL FAMILY of

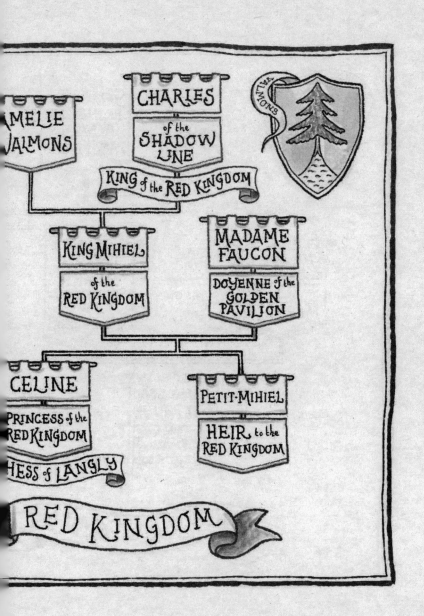

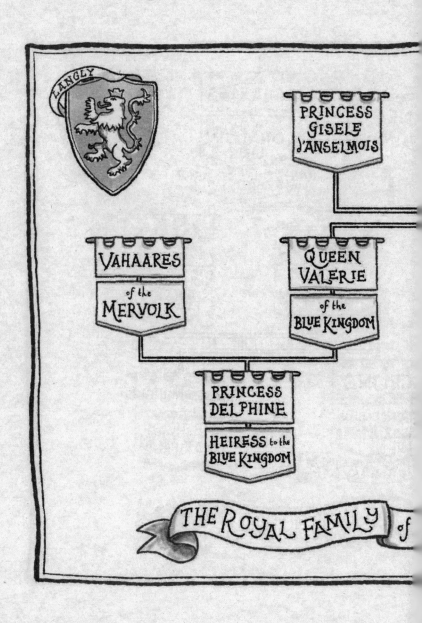

PRINCESS
GISELE
d'ANSELMOIS

VAHAARES
of the
MERVOLK

QUEEN
VALERIE
of the
BLUE KINGDOM

PRINCESS
DELPHINE
HEIRESS to the
BLUE KINGDOM

LANGLY

THE ROYAL FAMILY of

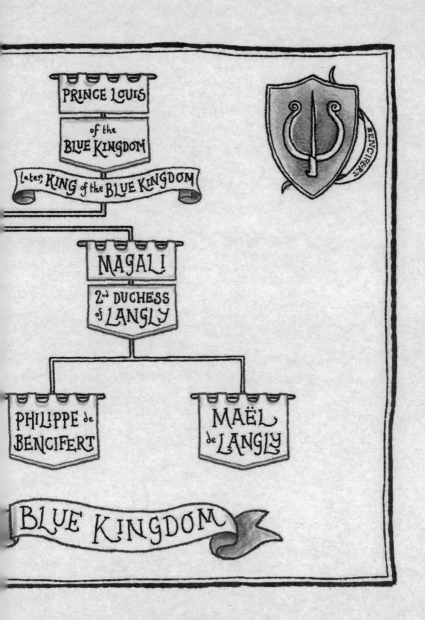

PRINCE LOUIS of the BLUE KINGDOM

later, KING of the BLUE KINGDOM

MAGALI

2nd DUCHESS of LANGLY

PHILIPPE de BENCIFERT

MAËL de LANGLY

BLUE KINGDOM

ACKNOWLEDGMENTS

I'd also like to use this opportunity to thank a few people who helped me (a lot) on my publishing journey.

First of all, my family, for all their support through the ups and downs. None of this would have been possible without you.

Huge thanks to my trusted beta-reader, shoulder to cry on, feedback-giver extraordinaire, clinical and character psychologist, Stephanie Carty. Stephanie is a gifted writer and her workshops have helped me immensely to pay more attention to the inner lives of my own characters (and what it says about them). Stephanie, you helped me so much through the lows in my publishing journey so far, and always encouraging me to keep moving forward. Stephanie, thank you, thank you, thank you.

Huge thanks to Charlotte Ledger, who, for mysterious reasons, has believed in me and my writing from the very beginning and has always been immensely supportive. Even when presented with the most bonkers ideas imaginable, you always said something in the lines of, 'Sure, I'd be thrilled to read that.' Our face-to-face meetings are always a joy and I think I could never run out of subjects to talk about with you.

And you're also an absolute genius in all-things-publishing. I feel so lucky to have you as an editor. Charlotte, thank you!

A very warm hug of a 'thank you' to Ajebowale Robert. Aje, you understood my vision for the series from the very beginning. It has been a pleasure chatting with you about the books and the future of the series, as has been working with you, and I can't wait for me to get all nerdy again as we'll talk about the next instalments and the characters. And all their entanglements.

Big thanks to Bonnie Macleod, who has been with me for a part of this journey. I'll never forget your no-nonsense approach, the swift responses and your thorough work. It has been such a pleasure working with you, Bonnie.

Many, many thanks to Laura McCallen and Lydia Mason, who have lent their keen editorial eye to this series and/or the one before. Your feedback has been priceless – how can a book ever get better if it doesn't have the benefit of fabulous feedback? It has been wonderful working with you both.

Also, huge thanks to the marketing team, Chloe Cummings and Emma Petfield, who make sure that my books are visible out there and bring them to the attention of readers. And many thanks to Arsalan Isa for the work 'behind the scenes'. Thank you all so much for everything!

Also, many thanks to all the people in charge of distribution and sales, who make sure that my books reach readers. And, not least, to the wonderful booksellers and reviewers who are bringing new readers into the Three Kingdoms.

I'm so grateful to all of you that I can keep doing the best job in the world – writing the books that I always wanted to write.

The author and One More Chapter would like to thank everyone who contributed to the publication of this story...

Analytics
James Brackin
Abigail Fryer

Audio
Fionnuala Barrett
Ciara Briggs

Contracts
Laura Amos
Laura Evans

Design
Lucy Bennett
Fiona Greenway
Liane Payne
Dean Russell

Digital Sales
Lydia Grainge
Hannah Lismore
Emily Scorer

Editorial
Kara Daniel
Charlotte Ledger
Federica Leonardis
Laura McCallen
Ajebowale Roberts
Jennie Rothwell
Emily Thomas

Harper360
Emily Gerbner
Jean Marie Kelly
emma sullivan
Sophia Wilhelm

International Sales
Peter Borcsok
Ruth Burrow
Colleen Simpson

Marketing & Publicity
Chloe Cummings
Emma Petfield

Operations
Melissa Okusanya
Hannah Stamp

Production
Denis Manson
Simon Moore
Francesca Tuzzeo

Rights
Helena Font Brillas
Ashton Mucha
Zoe Shine
Aisling Smythe

Trade Marketing
Ben Hurd
Eleanor Slater

The HarperCollins Distribution Team

The HarperCollins Finance & Royalties Team

The HarperCollins Legal Team

The HarperCollins Technology Team

UK Sales
Isabel Coburn
Jay Cochrane
Sabina Lewis
Holly Martin
Harriet Williams
Leah Woods

eCommerce
Laura Carpenter
Madeline ODonovan
Charlotte Stevens
Christina Storey
Jo Surman
Rachel Ward

And every other essential link in the chain from delivery drivers to booksellers to librarians and beyond!

Once upon a time there was a princess, locked in a tower, forced to bend to her father's will...

But Celine is no ordinary princess, and she has no intention of being a damsel in distress.

Celine has a lover, Hugo, whose cunning plan to rescue her is tied up in his own ambition to reclaim the lands and title that are his birthright. If only they can break the spell that binds him to the body of a cat, they will free the kingdom from the grasp of a cruel witch and live happily ever after...

This is a land of shapeshifters, magic, and illusion, where nothing is as it seems, even the truth.

Available in paperback, eBook and audio!

There hasn't been a Mindwalker in the Red Kingdom in centuries... until now.

But Blanche's ability is so rare, so valuable, that it must be kept secret.

Because Blanche isn't just a Mindwalker, she's also the sister of the king. And every night, at her brother's command, she faithfully wanders the minds of his enemies, searching for traitors, plots and secrets. But when she is tasked with seeking out the Condottiere, the leader of a band of mercenaries, she finds herself keeping secrets that will put her – and the competing factions vying for control – at risk.

When war breaks out, she is ready. But should she trust a man whose loyalty can be bought to fight by her side?

Available in paperback and eBook!

ONE MORE CHAPTER

One More Chapter is an
award-winning global
division of HarperCollins.

Subscribe to our newsletter to get our
latest eBook deals and stay up to date
with all our new releases!

[signup.harpercollins.co.uk/
join/signup-omc](signup.harpercollins.co.uk/join/signup-omc)

Meet the team at
www.onemorechapter.com

Follow us!
 @OneMoreChapter_
 @OneMoreChapter.
 @onemorechapterhc
 @onemorechapterhc

Do you write unputdownable fiction?
We love to hear from new voices.
Find out how to submit your novel at
www.onemorechapter.com/submissions